Hollownton Homicide

By

Gretchen S. B.

Acknowledgments

I want to start by thanking the *real* Tony Hollownton. I hope you find this fictitious version of you at least entertaining, even though it is about ten years later than expected.

I want to thank my Beta reader for making me give her pages every week and keeping me on track.

I want to thank Teri, the Editing Fairy, for making this story presentable for other people.

Thank you to Talina Perkins for giving this book such a beautiful cover.

As always, thank you to my friends and family who cheer me on as I work toward my dream of being an author.

Last of all, but not least, is "He who must not be tagged." Although he hates to be mentioned, he deserves credit for all his support.

Chapter 1

The rain pattered the dark window at the right of Detective Anthony Hollownton's desk. Being a native western Washingtonian, he managed to ignore the sound easily. The way Anthony saw it, rain was as much a part of life as work; it was just something you got used to, or you moved somewhere else. Under most circumstances, he loved the rain, and even considered the sound relaxing. Tonight, however, the sound seemed amplified, and he found it more than a little hard to ignore.

The blinds were partially drawn, so someone would have to deliberately bend down in order to see inside the precinct. The windows in the building were evenly spaced apart; and all the two-way desks against the wall sat between the windows.

Detective Hollownton shared his desk with his partner of two years, Rick Nelson. Presently, however, Anthony was the desk's only occupant. This particular rainy night, he was one of the few officers left in the rear section of the King County Police Department.

That did nothing to dampen the noise coming from the front of the large room. Cursing and yells of "I'm innocent" over the wall partitions continued to distract Tony and break his concentration. There was something different about tonight; the noise just seemed more disturbing than usual.

Anthony stood a few inches shy of six feet tall with thick, dark brown hair that, in his opinion, was long overdue for a trim. Not that he could find time to fix the problem. His small eyes were several shades lighter than his hair. He was "Washington tan," which most of the country would've considered pale. His very muscular build was the result of working out five times a week since high school. Less than a month away from thirty, Tony worked in the homicide division of the King County Police Department. He was a classic workaholic. The only other things he allowed himself to indulge in were going to the gym and using his season tickets to Mariners games, both of which he'd been neglecting lately.

The entire department was going nuts over the past few weeks. Everyone felt overloaded, including Hollownton and

Nelson. Something had to be very wrong for so many homicides to have occurred in such a short period of time. Or at least, that was what a local religious spokesman kept saying. Tony was not a religious man, but secretly, he agreed. The area had become a very different place from when he was growing up.

Anthony rubbed his scalp and looked at the tiny, digital clock on his desk. He moaned when he saw it was two in the morning; and realized his partner had gone home four hours ago.

"Get a grip on yourself, Tone, or your extra hours will have been a waste of time." After mildly chastising himself, he turned back to his computer screen.

He offered to finish up their paperwork so Rick could go home to his wife and their baby girl, something that didn't happen too often. Anthony's social life was nonexistent; and had been since he got into homicide two years ago. For him, it was no great sacrifice.

He ran his hands though his hair. He hated paperwork, although as soon as it was done, the department had one less case to worry about, and hopefully, one less psycho on the streets.

A scuffle broke out across the room between a suspect and the cop who brought him in. The suspect was a leather-clad thug, just looking for a fight. The guy was arrested outside the Showbox SoDo for fighting with pretty much anyone who exited the building.

The thug tackled the officer as he passed the chair where he sat. Luckily, the cuffs hindered the suspect's movement. The commotion knocked stuff off several desks around the two men. Tony moved to offer assistance, but before he could get up from his desk, the suspect was subdued by several officers in closer proximity.

Turning back to his computer, he groaned heavily. He couldn't get anything else done tonight. He clicked the *print* button and mentally scolded himself for taking so long and only getting as far as he did. The printer, on the other side of the large, table-filled room, started making noise. He pushed back his chair and stood when his desk phone rang; then Rick's phone began to ring a few seconds later. Several sets of eyes shifted over to him. He looked at them for a second before turning back to the phones, while deciding whether or not to ignore them.

Feeling guilty because if could be someone in trouble who dialed the wrong number, he picked up his phone.

"Hello, King County Police Department, Detective Hollownton speaking."

There was a long pause, and he was about to tell the caller to hold on so he could get Rick's phone, but it stopped ringing. Tony could hear the person breathing in shallow, ragged breaths. He realized he was holding his own breath. Something felt very wrong. Then the woman cackled at him, as only a pure lunatic could. That was followed by what almost sounded like a purr before she hung up. Hearing her laugh gave him a weird tingle.

Tony pulled the phone away from his ear and stared at it. "What the hell?" He put it back on the cradle and stared at it for a few more seconds, half expecting it to ring again.

The voice was creepy, and sounded like something from a nightmare, but there was also a weight to it, something almost touchable. It could have been a prank. But the woman sounded too old for that sort of thing. So much for one less psycho on the streets. *Why call the cops anyway?* Why his particular desk? Not that it mattered, since he would have picked it up from any desk.

His instincts made his body tense, but he mentally calmed himself. As one of his old high school friends used to say, "People are crazy, confusing, and should all be locked up." He silently nodded his agreement.

Tony stopped a few feet from the printer, and didn't even realize he started walking. What made him think of high school? He hadn't thought about it since he received an invitation to the ten-year reunion last year. The ten-year reunion that he made excuses not to attend.

Tony shook his head and continued walking. "I really need sleep."

There were several mumbles of agreement from the officers nearby. If he were regressing to high school, his brain most definitely was working on empty. He continued to think about the strange call until he got home and climbed into bed.

Anthony jolted awake in bed. What disturbed him? Did his alarm go off? There was a ringing noise. Turning to his left, he grabbed the phone next to his bed.

"Anthony Hollownton."

That was as polite as he could be for the middle of the night. If the caller had a problem with that, he or she would have to deal with it. He looked at his alarm clock: five am. That meant he'd gotten barely more than two hours of sleep. Why would someone call him at five am?

There was a pause on the other end.

"Hello?" he repeated, dread beginning to curl in the pit of his stomach.

He could hear talking on the other end, and silently pleaded that it wasn't the same woman from earlier. He was just frustrated enough to trace the call and chew her out. He heard a male voice on the other end. and exhaled, forcing his muscles to relax one-by-one. He had to get more sleep; he was jumping to ridiculous conclusions.

"Hey, Tony, sorry to call so early, man, but I gotta ask you a question." It was his partner. The tone in the man's voice sounded serious, and genuinely upset about whatever he was prepared to say.

Tony tensed again. *What if something happened to Amanda or the baby?*

"What is it, Rick?" Tony tried to sound neutral.

When he heard his partner sigh, Tony relaxed again, feeling more tired than before.

"Look, man, I don't believe it but Amanda asked me to, so I'm doing it."

Tony screamed with frustration in his head. He wanted to get back to sleep.

"Get to the point, Nelson. I want to go back to bed."

Using his last name showed Rick he meant business and urged him to get to the point.

"As you know, the land line is on Amanda's side of the bed, and she picked up three phone calls tonight since we went to bed. She says they were from a woman who laughs and hangs up. After the third time, Amanda called star-sixty-nine, and the number was yours, your land line, anyway. I wasn't sure at first, since you don't really use it. But when I double-checked in my cell, the numbers matched. I told her it was crazy, since you never have women over. I said that except for her and some other cops, you don't even know any women, no offense; but she insisted I call anyway to make sure."

Tony's jaw dropped. Now he was wide-awake. He must have been silent too long because his partner's voice came back on with a worried tone.

"Hey, Tony, you still there?"

Tony flicked on his bedroom light and scanned the room, finding it empty.

"Yeah, man, I'm here, just shocked. There's no one else here and I've been asleep. You know, it could be a prank caller who knows how to reroute numbers or something."

Tony debated telling his partner about the call at work, but quickly dismissed it. With a wife and four-month-old daughter, Rick had enough on his plate.

"Yeah, I figured as much. I was just calling to make sure. Sorry for waking you up, man. I hope you can get back to sleep."

Tony nodded. So did he. "Yeah, good night, Rick."

He heard his partner say something to his wife. "Good night, Tony. See you tomorrow, I mean, today."

As he hung up the phone, Tony looked closely at his room. There was nothing out of the ordinary. Against the wall, at the foot of his bed, was his forty-two-inch TV. To the left of the bed was the closet, which was still open from when he put away his work clothes, and no one was in there. To the right of the TV was the door leading out into the rest of the apartment, which was still closed. Everything on the nightstand was also right where he left it. Turning, he looked at the window above the bed, and found it still locked. He turned back, reaching into the top drawer of his nightstand and pulled out his gun before getting out of bed. If anyone was in his apartment, he intended to find them.

Chapter 2

Tony walked over to his desk, carrying two obscenely large coffees. After his partner's phone call the previous night, Tony searched his apartment, but found nothing. He went back to bed, but couldn't sleep, and instead, watched old TV shows until it was time to get up. As he set the coffees down, he looked around the room for his partner. As if summoned, Rick started walking over, with a huge grin on his face.

Rick Nelson was thirty-three. He often bragged about being older than Tony. Rick was also six-two, another bragging point. Rick had caramel-colored skin and darker eyes. He was in no way as strong as Tony, but wiry. Rick could outrun just about anyone, which came in handy more than once.

"Hey, Hollownton, didn't you get me any coffee?" Rick joked as he plopped down into his chair.

Tony grinned and pushed one of the cups over to his partner. "Now why would I do a thing like that? You prevented me from getting my beauty sleep last night."

Rick's grin faded. "Really? Oh, man, I'm sorry. I didn't want to…"

Tony held up his hand. "It's okay; I caught up on old TV shows."

Rick frowned and took a sip from the huge, white cup. As the liquid hit his tongue, his eyes widened. Gulping, he frowned.

"Coffee? Real, actual coffee? You hate coffee; are you sure you're okay?"

Tony just nodded and took a sip. It had been a while.

Rick was about to say something else when a tall, skinny, redheaded man came up to their desk. Both men went quiet as they turned to look at the newcomer. The young man just stood there a moment, as if unsure whether it was okay for him to approach.

"Yes, Will?" Rick asked.

Tony tried not to laugh. Will was an intern who idolized cops, which made it very hard to respect him. It didn't help that he had the appearance of a geeky, tech student. The bright red hair was relatively short, and there was nothing greasy or unkempt about him. He wore large, black-framed glasses over his pale green eyes. He was taller than either Rick or Tony, but he always slumped his shoulders. The clothes he wore were invariably on the baggy side.

Will took a deep breath. “Do you have any paperwork for the Hender’s case finished?”

Tony smiled and handed the young man the folder. “Here, Will.”

The young man hesitated before grabbing the folder. Nodding his thanks, he headed back across the room.

Rick shook his head and took a sip of coffee. “Poor kid.”

Tony nodded and hid his smile behind his cup. He had never been anything like Will, not even in his adolescence. Who could have been with friends like Christina? She was just too pessimistic for anyone to feel in such awe of the world. Tony’s grin diminished. There it was again: *why was he thinking about high school?* Shaking his head, he took a long drink of his coffee; he just needed more sleep.

When he put the cup down, he saw Rick watching him.

“Yes?” Tony asked, looking directly into his eyes.

Rick sighed and motioned to Tony’s coffee cup. “You sure you’re okay? I mean, coffee? You’re drinking coffee! You are the only thirty-year-old I know who admits you prefer hot chocolate over coffee. Which, let’s face it, is just sick, considering you’ve lived here all your life!” Rick took another sip.

Tony shook his head. “Look, man, everyone’s been stressed lately and working with very little sleep. So what if it caught up with me? And besides, it’s just too cold outside to buy pop.”

Tony reclined in his seat to crack his back, his way of dismissing the conversation. As he reached for the barely tolerable tasting liquid, he looked back at Rick. “How about those calls this morning?”

Rick put down his coffee with a frustrated sound. “That was so damn irritating. There was one more within minutes of hanging up with you. I hate prank callers.” Rick uttered irritated.

Tony put down his coffee.

Did that mean the woman meant to call him?

“I didn’t mention it earlier, but that woman called here this morning just as I was leaving.”

Rick moved forward in his seat. "What?"

Tony sighed and ran his hand through his hair as he relayed the call to Rick.

Once Tony finished, Rick leaned back and nodded. "That's exactly how Amanda described her. I wonder how many other cops have been called by this weirdo?"

Tony shrugged. It was good to know it wasn't just him. But knowing she called the same number more than once bothered him a little.

Tony rolled his chair closer to the desk. "Well, now that's behind us, so let's finish the last of this stuff up."

Rick smiled. "Lazy bum; what were you doing last night that you didn't get it done?"

A second later a Mariners stress ball smacked Rick in the chest.

"Hey now, that's abuse and I don't have to take it."

Tony rolled his eyes and put his hand out to get his ball back. Rick tossed it to him, but it rolled off the side of the desk.

Tony looked up at his partner, grinning. "You're kidding, right?"

Rick looked slightly embarrassed and tried to concentrate on the work in front of him. "Will you shut up please? I'm trying to work."

Tony laughed; Rick had very poor aim. Grabbing the ball off the floor, Tony turned his attention back to the paperwork on his desk.

The morning went by slowly. All Tony and Rick could do was trudge through the mountain of paperwork. This last case was simple. A wife called in to report she shot her husband of twenty years. By the time the paramedics arrived, the man was already dead, but had four bullets in his chest. It turned out the guy was abusive; something which both Tony and Rick found disgusting. Part of the situation bothered them. Why did she do it now? What made her snap? When they asked her, she said she really didn't know why.

It wouldn't have been so strange a reply if it hadn't been such a common answer. Many of the crimes committed in the last month were executed by people who just didn't know why they did them, or why they chose to commit them when they did. Even stranger, all the people confessed and seemed relatively calm about it.

Rick proposed they go down the street to a cop hangout, called the Dragon's Lair, and grab lunch after they filed the paperwork.

As they stood up, their captain walked over to their desk. Captain Binns was a short man in his fifties with gray hair that he always wore in a neat crew cut. He had a small beer gut and a bad temper.

"Nelson, Hollownton, Where do you think you're going?"

Tony heard Rick swearing under his breath.

The older man stopped inches away from the desk. He pointed back and forth between them. "You two have the lightest caseload in the department. So you get the newest case." He tossed a Post-It note on the desk and pointed at it. "That's the address of a fresh crime scene." He gave them a slightly disturbing smile. "Have fun." Then he returned to his office in the back of the room.

The two partners looked at each other.

"Well, so much for an early lunch," Tony said as he grabbed his trench coat.

Rick grabbed his coat as well.

As they walked out of the precinct, Rick spoke. "You realize there's something odd about this case."

Tony gave his partner a confused look. "Why?"

Rick shook his head. "Because he told us to have fun."

Both men went silent as they walked out of the building and got into Rick's dark blue Taurus.

After they drove for about fifteen minutes, Rick turned his head slightly, still looking at the road. "So, what do you think is wrong with this one?"

Tony smiled. He was thinking the same thing. Hearing Rick bring it up meant he was worried about what they might see. Rick couldn't stand gore, which was sometimes hard to avoid in a big, metropolitan area. Rick, without actually asking, sought a distraction from the daunting thoughts that were brewing in his head.

Tony turned in his seat. “It’s probably a dead mime or something.”

Rick smiled. “Who would kill a mime?”

Tony snorted. “Who wouldn’t?”

Rick laughed, and started to describe the scene in an invisible box when Tony got a bad, prickly feeling and stopped listening.

What was it? What was wrong? He scanned the windows of the residential area around him. It didn’t look special. Just an average, middle-class neighborhood like the one he grew up in. There wasn’t anyone out on the street, but Tony was willing to bet most of the neighbors were perched at their windows, hoping to catch a glimpse of whatever could bring so many cops. He abandoned his thought in time to hear Rick.

“Huh. No parking. All right; we’ll go down the street.”

As the two men got out of the car, Rick looked over at Tony. “Hey, man, you okay?”

Tony nodded.

Rick knew as well as Tony that was a lie, but he kept quiet and pointed toward the crime scene. The two men walked in stride silently, both with serious expressions. Then it hit him, Tony knew where the bad feeling was coming from and he picked up speed as they moved toward the house.

It was a big, earthy, purple house he recognized from his late adolescence. He hadn’t spent a great deal of time there, but enough to remember it. It was the childhood home of one of his closest high school friends, Christina Mirin. Anger and fear filled his body as he got closer to the house. If anyone hurt her or her family, the little parasite would die. He silently pled to anyone who could hear him, asking that Chris and her family were safe.

Then he sped up again; if they were safe, he wouldn’t be there. If they were okay, no one would have called homicide. He cursed, using the worst words he knew. If he had been a good friend, he would have kept in touch. He would have gone to the reunion last year. Perhaps he could have prevented this. Tony’s heart was drumming heavily in his ears. He reached the front porch at a run.

A hand grabbed his upper arm, using his momentum to yank him backwards. He tried again to get to the door, only to be jerked back. He turned, ready to yell at the person, and do anything necessary to help his friend. Rick's hands were on both of Tony's upper arms as he shook him. He was almost yelling at Tony, and his face was full of concern. Tony tried to concentrate on what Rick was saying. He had to get to his friend, but Tony could not understand a word that came out of his partner's mouth. His partner was speaking in a language Tony never heard before.

Tony's brain started to overload. All he could hear was almost a kind of chanting coming from his partner. The eerie words haunted Tony, making it hard for him to concentrate on getting into the house. The words almost became solid in the air around them, which seemed so thick, it was getting hard for him to breathe.

Then he heard a loud, popping noise and Rick spoke in English again.

"Tony, Tony! What's going on? What is it? Tony, get a hold of yourself!"

Tony spoke louder than he intended, and the anger was plain in his voice. "Stop shaking me. Do you know where we are?"

Tony followed his own arm into the house. He stopped and his jaw dropped. The house was green. It was green and looked nothing like it did a few seconds ago. It was much smaller and had a porch. His brain was screaming about what he saw and heard. Rick was dragging Tony away from the house and didn't stop until they were two houses down.

Tony shook himself and looked back at the house. Several uniformed officers came out the front door and stood on the lawn in a little cluster. *What was he thinking?* They were a good twenty minutes away from the city he grew up in. They weren't even in the county he grew up in. He continued to stare at the house.

No one but his partner had been outside to see Tony's display of insanity. *Was it insanity? Or from lack of sleep?* Why did he think it was Chris's house? Why was he thinking about high school at all? *No*, he told himself, *it wasn't high school; it was Christina.* She was the friend he thought of yesterday and it was her house he thought he saw. Was his subconscious trying to tell him something? Did he feel guilty about not keeping in touch? If so, why would it bother him now? Why would he pick one specific friend? Tony had too many questions; but he always trusted his gut, which was clearly pushing him towards Chris.

He turned to his partner, who dropped Tony's arms. He kept watching him as if he expected Tony to go nuts again. The words came out before Tony could stop them; and his voice was unnervingly normal.

"How many languages do you speak, Rick?"

Rick looked at him, somewhat startled. "One, same as you. What is it, Tony? You were running like a madman."

Tony combed his fingers through his hair and looked back at the house. "I think the lack of sleep is getting to me. I thought this house was a different one."

He looked closely at his partner. Rick's face showed he knew Tony was either lying or holding something back.

"Is it going to affect the job?" was all Rick asked.

Tony shook his head.

Rick nodded. "Okay, let's go."

That was all that mattered, and if Tony thought he could stay focused, Rick took him at his word. That was good, because if Tony couldn't explain what happened to himself, he definitely couldn't have explained to Rick. Both men turned and headed back toward the house.

As they reached the porch again, one of the uniforms noticed them and left the little group. He was an older gentleman, maybe fifty. His hair was completely gray and cropped very short. He was an inch taller than Tony, with a slight paunch, as if he no longer ran down the bad guys, but refused to let his body go soft.

As the officer got closer, Tony could see his face. The man's eyes were hard; he must've been a cop a long time. Seeing how disturbed this veteran cop was regarding the crime scene, Tony found himself dreading going inside more than he already did.

The older cop stopped about two feet away. "Homicide?"

Both men nodded as they pulled out their badges.

The uniform nodded back. "Had to make sure." He seemed like he was going to turn away, but looked solemnly at them. "Thought I'd warn you. It's pretty bad. If either of you is a religious man, start praying."

With that, the older uniform walked back to the group on the lawn, who by this time, all turned to watch the exchange.
In the corner of his eye, he saw Rick cross himself. Tony sighed; although he might not be religious, he knew Rick was a devout Catholic. Tony turned toward him.

After a few seconds with a bowed head, Rick looked back at him. "What do you think he meant?"

Tony shrugged. "Only one way to find out." He held the door as they both went inside.

Directly opposite the entry was a huge front room that appeared to be professionally decorated, and had no lived-in quality at all. As soon as he entered the house, Tony could smell the metallic scent of blood, and lots of it. He began to search the room for it.

There was a set of overstuffed white couches, several pieces of modern art, and a large glass table in the middle of the room. None of them had any bloodstains. The white walls and white carpet were still pristine.

What really stuck out were the half dozen cops muddling around. Tony groaned; there were always too many people at fresh crime scenes; and some almost always hung, getting in everyone else's way.

A short, stout man with receding black hair, and a matching black suit walked toward them.
Before the man could utter a single word, Rick flipped open his badge.

"Detective Nelson and Detective Hollownton from homicide."

The man nodded and waved for them to follow him. The men and women in the front room parted as the three of them walked by. Around the corner there was an archway that led into a living room/kitchen. Tony tried to keep his mind blank, so he failed to comprehend what was in front of him. He heard Rick curse and saw him cross himself again. There was a tech taking pictures and the only other person in the room was the victim.

Right off the bat, Tony could see why this scene might bother a religious person. The body was a nude male in his mid-thirties. He was hanging on the living room wall; and the only things holding him up were several very tight ropes about an inch thick. Both arms were held above shoulder height, and the man's wrists had been tied and stapled to the wall. Both wrists were sliced open and there were dark stains on the carpet, which, Tony was sure, would feel squishy if he stepped on them.

No, he told himself as he forced his eyes back to the body. He vaguely noticed someone handing him rubber gloves, which he put on as he walked closer. Rick was a few steps behind him, looking stunned and several shades lighter.

"This look like a warped version of a crucifixion to you?"

Tony watched Rick get even paler as he stood beside him. The smell of blood was strong but not overpowering. Someone must have opened the windows to dilute the odor with fresh air. He looked around the room, and sure enough, all the windows were open, but the curtains remained drawn to prevent nosy people from looking in. If it had been earlier than May, the house would have been freezing. Tony got control of his wandering mind and reluctantly looked back at the body.

"You know more about this than I do, Nelson. Does it resemble a crucifixion?" Tony knew fully well what it resembled, but figured if he could keep Rick thinking, the gore wouldn't bother him so much.

Rick cleared his throat. "Well, in a very warped way, yes, it does. There are the wrist wounds. The same thing was done to the back of the feet. But Christ wore a thorn crown, and nobody took the front of his scalp. The spear wound wasn't anywhere near as big either. I wouldn't be surprised if the perp was a religious fanatic, although it's not terribly realistic. It's just close enough to resemble it. I would check to see if this guy had some sort of record. Maybe to the killer, this guy had to die for his sins."

As if waiting for a cue, the man in charge stepped toward Tony and Rick. "We ran a check on him. Bradley Walker, but there was not much on the preliminary report, so there might still be something."

Tony and Rick exchanged glances. They both knew the man's criminal record meant nothing. If the person was crazy enough to kill, he or she would be surely crazy enough to concoct an excuse. Both men walked toward the body, trying not to disturb the crime scene too much. Tony searched the floor as Rick took a closer look at the body. Tony felt a small tingle at his back and turned around.

"Rick?" Tony said as he looked over his shoulder at his partner.

Rick looked back at him for a split second, then his eyes widened. He looked past Tony and walked over to stand beside him.

On the far kitchen wall, above the wooden cabinets, were symbols drawn in blood. They were up too high for any person to reach without a ladder. Tony heard someone swear before there was a flash in the wall's direction. He heard Rick whispering beside him.

"I guess no one else noticed that." Rick turned and walked back over to the body.

Tony stared at the symbols a little longer. He didn't recognize them as any language he knew; in fact, they didn't really look like a language at all. He looked down at the man in charge.

"Get some kind of linguist down here."

The man nodded and left the room. Tony turned away from the wall. There was little else they could do about it until the symbols were deciphered.

Nothing was out of the ordinary on the ground, except of course, the three huge puddles of blood. He looked around the room again, but saw no sign of a struggle at all. All the furniture looked untouched. He looked back at the body. *He should have struggled. Did he know the person?*

The wounds looked as if the victim didn't even try to stop what was being done to him. There were no defensive bruises on his arms that would suggest the man struggled against the binding ropes either. Then it occurred to Tony that the body was clean. Whoever killed him, also waited for the bleeding to stop, in order to wash the blood off his skin. If the killer took that much time and care, Tony was willing to bet there would be no prints.

Tony rubbed his temples and closed his eyes as Rick touched the side of the body. He hated fanatic cases. They were the hardest since there was rarely an easy pattern. When he opened his eyes, he found Rick standing right in front of him.

He was whispering again. “There are some things I think you should look at.”

Rick walked back to the body and Tony followed. They stopped about a foot in front of the body.

Rick spoke again. “Go stand on that side of the body.” He motioned to their right.

Tony did as he was told while Rick went to the other side.

Once he was facing the body, Rick gave him instructions. “Now push so you can see the guy’s back.”

Both men pushed the body out far enough so they could see each other. Tony turned to look at the man’s back where a gruesome picture was carved into the skin. It was so detailed, it must’ve taken hours. Rick let go of the body and walked around to Tony.

“I think it is supposed to be a Demon,” Rick said, as he started removing his gloves.

Tony stayed where he was for a few seconds and stared at the man’s back. *A Demon?* It must not have been a specific one, or Rick would surely have said so. Tony let the body fall back into place before standing in front of it again.

Rick came over and stood beside him. “I gotta get out of this room,” he said before hastily walking away.

Tony shook his head; Rick picked the wrong career. Tony’s eyes were drawn to the large hole in the man’s chest. It looked as if it were right above the man’s heart, but that should have caused more bleeding. *Where was the flesh? How could it have been so neatly removed?*

He looked back at the ground. There wasn’t nearly enough blood there, and the scene was just too clean. There was no blood splattered on the walls and all the blood was wiped clean off the body. There weren’t enough bloodstains on the floor, or the ropes. As for the wounds, there were no jagged edges, the lines were perfect. The hole in his chest was a circle, only slightly bigger than Tony's palm. He should have been able to see the front part of a rib, but it wasn’t there. Tony couldn’t understand how that was possible. He stood there another minute or two, then removed the gloves and dumped them into the garbage bag before walking out of the room.

The front room had pretty much cleared out. Tony looked out the back window and saw the majority of the officers in the backyard, so he assumed someone must have kicked them all out. Looking out the huge, bay window, he viewed some reporters out on the front lawn.

Rick was talking to the man in charge, near the front door. He must have been telling him what he found because the man was motioning for the tech taking pictures. Rick turned to Tony and indicated with his head that they should go outside.

As they left the house, they stood on the lawn next to the porch, but remained far enough away so none of the other officers, or the growing curious crowd of onlookers, and reporters on the other side of the caution tape could hear them.

Rick spoke first. “We can't question the neighbors right now. It would only fuel this circus. We will have to go with the initial reports Joan and his men collected; and come back later, when the buzzards are gone."

Tony nodded his agreement. The idea that the press would be following them door-to-door did not appeal to him either.

Rick stared down the street, and when he spoke his eyes were unfocused. "Who could have reported it? You saw how dead it was when we got here half an hour ago. None of the neighbors knew anything. Officer Joan said the report came from a woman who was calling in something she heard next door. The thing is: both neighbors are male. One is single and the other’s wife is on a business trip; and neither of their daughters live at home anymore. The call was dated early this morning, some time around five. The woman asked the police to go by in the late morning and ask the neighbor to keep it down. Can you believe they actually did it? They didn’t go over right after the call! They came by at about ten this morning. I bet he died in between the call and their arrival. Can you believe it? This could have been prevented?” Rick shook his head.

Tony took the opportunity. “There isn’t much we can do until the linguist translates that writing and the autopsy comes in. Let’s head back and write everything down and check into what Bradley did for a living.” Rick nodded and they headed for the car.

Before they crossed the caution tape, they prepared themselves for the onslaught of reporters.

They reached the car ten minutes later.

"Why don't reporters understand the meaning of 'no comment'?" Rick said angrily as he started the car.

"Okay," Tony said, pulling a note pad and pen out of one of his inside pockets, "what do we know?"

Rick turned a corner. "We know reporters are worse than a horde of buzzards."

Tony grunted. "I mean, about the case, Rick."

Rick sighed as if he dreaded discussing it. "We know it has something to do with religion, because of the way the man was killed."

Tony nodded and wrote it down, then added, "There was a lot of blood, but not nearly enough. He wasn't dead when those things were done to him, so there should have been a much greater quantity of blood. And some signs that he struggled, but I didn't see any."

Rick nodded and stretched his fingers on the wheel. "We know it had to take a lot of time. All of that couldn't have been accomplished in a last minute, rush job. It had to have been well planned. Then there's the report itself. That whole thing is off. There's the writing on the wall and on the victim's back."

Tony wrote down everything. "Writing on the back? After you left, I took a closer look at the hole in the chest. Again, there was not enough blood. I have a sneaking suspicion that something was done to the heart, but we won't know for sure until the autopsy."

Rick nodded. "Yeah, there were those symbols under the picture, too."

Their exchange of facts continued until they were a few minutes from the precinct. Then the car was silent. Tony was thinking about the man's body, and wondering if his lack of struggle meant the killer was someone he knew, or perhaps, he had been drugged? His thought was interrupted.

"What happened with you earlier?"

Tony could tell from the tone of his voice that Rick wasn't sure he should ask.

Tony sighed. "The lack of sleep got to me and I thought I was seeing a house I recognized from when I was younger."

Rick nodded, apparently satisfied with his answer. "Your childhood, huh? You know what Freud would say?"

Tony sat back in the seat. "Shut up, Rick."

Rick flexed his fingers on the steering wheel. "You need to slow down, Tony. Go to the game tomorrow. I hear they're playing the Yankees, and I know how much you hate the Yankees."

Tony snorted. *Like any diehard Mariners fan didn't hate the Yankees.* However, going to the game tomorrow didn't sound all that bad.

"You want to come with me?"

Rick shook his head, grinning. "I'd love to, but I can't; we're taking Rachel to visit her grandmother this weekend. I pick her up from daycare as soon as I get off work. You know, a 'parents only' weekend."

Tony smirked. "Which grandmother?"

Rick sighed. "Amanda's mother."

Tony laughed; he knew how much Rick's mother-in-law didn't like him. They pulled into a parking space.

Rick stopped the car, but didn't get out. He was staring at the steering wheel, and his face appeared solemn.

Tony turned in his seat. "What is it?"

When Rick finally looked at Tony, he received the stone-faced look of an interrogation cop.

"Tony, who's Chris?"

Tony froze. *How did Rick know about Chris?* He cursed himself, as he wondered what could Rick know about her.

"Who?"

Rick looked a little angry. "Don't act stupid. As you were running up to that house, I heard you say something under your breath, 'Hang on, Chris, I'm coming.' Who is Chris? I assume it's a woman, since you didn't sound like you were talking to a guy."

Tony stared for a second. He said her name? "She was the friend whose house I thought it was. She was one of my good friends in high school. During college, I lost track of her, which was okay with me because we got into a fight before she left." Tony glanced at his partner. "No, don't even think it. We were never like that. We were just friends, and the thought never occurred to change that."

Rick's smile disappeared and he straightened in his seat. "What was her name again?"

Tony gave him a weird look. "Chris, Christina Mirin; why?"

Rick frowned, but a few seconds later, he smiled.

"Just curious as to whether you talked about her before, but I don't recognize the name."

Then Rick gave Tony a huge grin, opened the car door, and got out.

Tony scrambled after him. "Rick, I know that look and you are not doing a check on one of my high school friends."

Rick grinned over his shoulder, but continued to walk. "Oh come on, Hollownton! I always wondered what type of person you would choose to be your friend, if you ever had any."

Tony caught up with him as they reached the doors to the precinct. "It was ten years ago."

Rick continued to grin. "Now if you were truly just friends, why are you so defensive about her, huh?"

Tony glared at his partner. He wasn't about to divulge why Chris and he no longer spoke. He screwed up and didn't want to relive the experience. Seeing Will, Tony swerved toward him.

Will looked up at Tony while his hands shifted through the pile of paperwork. Tony flipped his notepad.

"I need you to run a check on a Brad Walker, living at two-seven-two-three East Palor Way. I need it as soon as possible."

Will's eyes went slightly wider. "O-o-o-okay, Detective."

Tony flipped the pad closed after he was sure Will wrote everything down correctly and headed toward his own desk.

When Tony reached it, Rick was tossing the stress ball from hand-to-hand, and leaning back in his chair, smiling.

"What?" he asked, not quite sure if he wanted to know the answer.

Rick's smile grew wider. "She lives in King County, in Edmonds, to be exact."

Tony rolled his eyes as he shrugged off his coat. "I don't need to know that."

Rick laughed. “Oh, come on, aren’t you curious as to what she’s up to? I’ve got more information.”

Tony shook his head. “No, Rick, I don’t want to know; plus, we have a case to work on, remember?”

Rick's face changed and his eyes were glued to the computer screen. The stress ball rolled onto the desk, instantly forgotten.

"Oh, Tony, you're going to want to see this."

Tony felt the hair on the back of his neck stand up. This would not be good.

"Just tell me," Tony replied in almost a whisper as he sat down. A small part of him became encased in icy dread.

Rick scrolled the mouse further down and cursed several times before looking at Tony.

"She was abducted six weeks ago. Her Odyssey was found in a grocery store parking lot, only two miles from her home. There were signs of a struggle, and blood was found in the car. She was eight months pregnant. There are still no leads on where she could be. Her husband was the initial suspect, but he got dismissed quickly."

Rick was struggling to keep his emotions off his face, but failing. Tony could tell his partner was imagining Amanda in the same situation.

Tony vowed then and there that he would find Chris, or at least, find out what happened to her, and give her family peace of mind. Now that he knew she truly was in trouble, he wanted to do whatever he could to help. He was not there to help her before, so he needed to be there now. Unfortunately, Tony could only investigate the matter during his off time. The faster they solved the crucifixion murder, the faster he could look for Chris.

"We need to work on the murder at hand." Tony knew his voice came out clipped, but he didn't even try to correct it.

Rick sighed and gave Tony one last look before turning back to his screen and clicking a few keys.

“Bradley Reese Walker, no criminal record.” Rick scrolled down the page he was looking at. “We know where he lived. No significant other or offspring, and his family are all out of state. Worked as a nurse for a Swedish hospital on First Hill. There isn’t much here, Hollownton. Almost completely lacking in information. I take it you gave his name to Will?"

Tony nodded.

"Good, that kid is adept at digging up clues in things like this. I still don't know how, when you consider his… underdeveloped people skills." Rick tossed the ball at Tony, who caught it. "Okay, Hollownton. Let's see what we can learn about the victim and his neighbors."

Chapter 3

Tony moved along with the throng of elated fans walking from the crowded stadium. There was a general euphoria after the Mariners swept the Yankees. What more could the crowd want? As he reached the bus stop, he looked at his phone. He had about five minutes, if the bus was on time, which it probably wasn't. He leaned back against a tree to avoid the mobs of people walking by, shaking his head at all the people who drove into Seattle. Didn't they realize fifteen dollars was a rip-off for parking when you could take the bus for only five?

Two women were standing a few feet in front of him. They had their backs to him, but he could hear their conversation and a grin spread across his face. The woman on the left looked a little overweight. She had dark auburn hair that fell in a curly cloud around her shoulders. Wearing a large Mariners jersey and dark jeans, she was shorter than the other woman by about four inches. The second woman was thin, with straight, jet-black hair that didn't reach her shoulders. She was in a black leather jacket and black jeans.

"Oh, come on, you have to be more excited than that. We just swept the Yankees."

He knew that comment came from the shorter woman, owing to her excited movements.

"I'm happy; I just don't see why I should be jumping up and down screaming."

The shorter woman made a big gesture again and Tony grinned at her.

"That's the last time I take you to a game, hon. You just know nothing about baseball."

A chill went down Tony's spine and his smile vanished. The shorter woman turned slightly and went still.

"Did you feel that?"

The taller woman nodded and looked up. She must have cursed because the shorter woman looked up too. Tony followed their lead.

Looking at the night sky, he heard the smaller woman say, "That's not a good sign."

The other woman said something he couldn't hear. All he saw were dark clouds, but after a second, he noticed the clouds were far too small and moving faster than an airplane. Tony felt himself going into a panic. His only thoughts were about logical explanations for what he was seeing. He swore loudly, bringing his head down.

"Interesting sky tonight," he said to a man standing near him.

The man raised an eyebrow and looked up. "Yes, it is unusually clear." Then the man moved away.

Tony jerked his head back toward the sky. The same small, black figures covered the sky on his right. *Why couldn't that man see them?* Was he just imagining things? No, he couldn't have because those women saw it too. *Did they know what it was?* He looked straight ahead of him. Both women were talking in voices so low, Tony couldn't hear.

His bus pulled up to the stop, which Tony appreciated. It meant he could sit down and maybe recover from whatever he thought he saw. As he moved toward the bus, he noticed the two women boarding also. Maybe he could get some answers.

After paying with the exact change, Tony scanned the bus before choosing a seat directly in front of the two women.

As soon as he sat down, he heard the shorter one change the subject. "It's been awfully cool lately."

The other woman didn't say anything. Tony felt his nerves growing taut with the need for answers. He waited ten minutes, during which nearly a dozen people got off the bus.

When he could no longer stand it, he turned in his seat to confront the two women. Both blanked their faces and the short one stopped mid-sentence. From that angle, Tony rescinded what he thought earlier; she was obviously pregnant.

"What were those things?" He asked the question quietly enough that only the three of them could hear.

The Asian woman glanced at her shorter friend. The pregnant one just stared at him, looking shocked.

He stared back at her. "What?" Now he was getting aggravated.

She looked at the taller woman, who appeared confused. "Cher, do you know who that is?"

The Asian woman frowned and looked at Tony.

The shorter one waved her arm at Tony's face. "It's Tony Hollownton, I can't believe it! It's Two-Tone."

Tony felt his jaw drop, and all of his other thoughts were instantly forgotten.

"What did you just call me?"

No one had called him that since high school.

The woman grinned and looked back at him. It clicked! Like a light flipping on in his head. He couldn't believe it! Out of all the weird coincidences. He happened to be sitting in front of Christina Mirin and Cheryl Young. How in the world could that happen? Wait, wasn't Chris missing?

Christina spoke first, pushing her auburn hair behind her ear. "You should have kept in touch, Two-Tone. I hear you're a cop." She gave him a wide grin.

Tony couldn't get over his excitement, and grinned right back. Both girls seemed okay. Why was that not in Chris's file? Rick would have mentioned if she came back. He felt a weight lifting from his shoulders, since clearly, she was okay. Why wouldn't they have updated their paperwork? He would definitely ask her about it; he just needed to ease into it.

"Yes, I am a cop, a homicide detective. Where did you two end up?"

Christina pretended to pout and Cheryl answered. "You would know if you'd kept it touch with your so-called 'good friends' that I'm a nurse and Chris teaches first grade."

Tony started laughing harder than he had in weeks. "You've got to be kidding me. They're letting her near little children? And letting you handle needles? What is the world coming to?"

Tony felt a punch connect with his arm. His eyes were closed, but he felt safe to assume it was Chris. It took him a few moments to stop laughing.

When he did, Cheryl spoke again. "Are you still coaching youth soccer like you did in high school?" Both women came to practice several times, but only Chris ever said anything about his own lack of skills.

Tony shook his head. “I don’t have the time. I work too many odd of hours to do any good.”

As the bus turned a corner, both of Chris’s hands went up to the back of the seat, trying to steady her pregnant body. Tony got a good look at both of her hands. On her left hand index finger sat the Ellensburg blue ring her grandmother gave her as a high school graduation present; but he saw nothing on her ring finger. After coming out of the turn, both of her hands disappeared again. Warning bells rang in Tony's mind. Something was most definitely wrong here. He knew Chris was married. His cop sense screamed that everything was not as it seemed.

Suddenly, he realized Cheryl was talking to him.

“Tony, hey, you there?”

He looked at both women and decided to test the waters.

“Yeah, I’m fine. Just a little surprised to see Chris pregnant and not wearing a ring. You were always the pushy, moral one.”

Both women looked down in silence. He watched closely as several expressions played across Cheryl's face. They were too quick, however, for Tony to read.

Chris looked up first and Tony knew he said something wrong. Her eyes were on the brink of tears. Tony swore in his head, then took a closer look. Unless something was drastically different, that was not how Chris looked when she cried. She was faking it. Anyone who did not know her though, probably could not see the difference.

Cheryl’s arms went around the smaller woman’s shoulders. When Chris spoke, the words were very quiet, almost whispered.

“He died right after the baby was conceived, almost seven months ago. I would still wear the ring, but unfortunately, it’s missing.”

Part of Tony felt awful. He didn’t want to bring up a bad memory. But another part of him held steadfast that something about her reply was a lie. He looked at Cheryl, but her face was hollow except for a sliver of anger. Her expression convinced him they were feeding him a lie. Tony felt the first ripple of anger unfurling in his chest.

Cheryl continued. “He was in the armed forces.”

Tony shut his eyes. Being unable to fake sympathy with his eyes, it was the next best thing. He intended to play along until they made a mistake. When he opened his eyes again, she was wiping hers to avoid crying.

"I'm sorry." It was all he could manage to spit out. *Why were they lying to him?*

She gave him a quick smile that somehow looked less fake than her crocodile tears.

Tony wanted to catch them off guard, so he changed the subject. "So what were those things in the sky?"

Both women visibly stiffened. Was that whole story concocted just to keep him from asking about the things they all saw in the sky?

Chris looked him in the eyes. "What did you see?"

Tony studied her for a second. There was a sharpness to her eyes he did not trust. But he described the figures.

When he finished, Cheryl looked worried. "Have you seen anything like that before?"

Tony looked at the two women, feeling confused, and answered, "Of course not."

Chris's face was smooth and expressionless as she shrugged. "We don't really know what they are. Just that they represent a very bad thing."

Tony was about to call Chris out for lying, but the serious look on Cheryl's face stopped him. *What was going on?*

"What else is bothering you, Tony?" Curiosity was evident in Chris's voice.

Warning bells went off in his head and he covered his hesitation in answering by looking out the window. His gut told him that discussing Chris's abduction would be a very bad idea. Tony did not know exactly why, but he learned to always trust his gut. Before he could come up with a believable lie, he got a weird feeling and glanced over at Christina.

She was looking out the window with her head cocked to one side. Tony almost jumped when she started laughing, and slowly turned her head until she made eye contact with him. The laugh sounded nothing like the laugh he remembered. Her amusement ended suddenly, as if a switch was flipped. A slightly mischievous grin slid over her face. If it were a living thing, it could have slithered over and bitten him.

Tony wanted to look at Cheryl and see what she thought, but he couldn't look away. All of a sudden, the chanting returned. It was faint at first, and the words were different. But he could feel power behind them, the same power he sensed before. It spread around him like a long coat. Tony felt the pressure building in his head. The air around him grew thick, and it was getting harder to breathe.

The popping sound brought sweet relief. Chris was still looking as him, but her eyes couldn't hold his. He was startled to find Cheryl had moved and was sitting next to him, giving him a hug.

"It's so good to see you again, Anthony."

Tony was confused. *Didn't Cheryl notice something was wrong? Was she trying to distract him? Did she make the chanting stop? Why had Chris been staring at him? Where had the chanting come from?*

An electronic voice announced his stop. Tony felt relief flooding over him. He wanted to get off that bus more than anything else. He proceeded to disentangle himself from Cheryl. Chris smiled sweetly at him. The contrast between the two was unnerving.

"What a coincidence. This is our stop as well."

Tony tried to leave as fast as he could, but Christina stayed right behind him. She actually followed him outside and onto the covered waiting area. He stopped and turned around, more than a little agitated. As he turned, she bumped into him.

"Oh, sorry, Two-Tone. I should pay more attention. Did I hurt anything?" she asked while starting to rub his chest.

Tony's mouth went slack. *Was Chris hitting on him?* That was freaking wrong. Her hand started to go lower, down to his stomach. Tony felt just too freaked to try and stop her, although his head was screaming at his body to move. Just as her hand started to delve lower, another hand grabbed it and twisted it back.

"Ow! Hey, Cheryl. What gives?"

Tony let out a shaky breath. *This was way too weird.* Chris was looking at Cheryl with a flirty pout on her face. Cheryl's face was like stone, without any emotions what so ever.

What was going on? Tony was so confused. Part of him wanted to bolt, and the other part wanted answers.

Chris started to squirm, but it wasn't from discomfort. It was more like she knew he was watching and kept trying to turn him on. Tony had news for her: it wasn't working. It was creeping him the hell out.

She stopped moving and turned to pout at him. "You'll help me, won't you? I don't want a bruise. It would look oh-so-bad for a teacher to have a bruise on Monday."

Tony thought she had a point and turned to speak to Cheryl, but the taller woman was glaring at Chris. That made him stop. Her look revealed pure malice.

"That is quite enough. Tony, go home."

Tony looked at Cheryl, puzzled, as the woman continued to glare at Chris.

Chris's face went blank and she turned to Cheryl. "I'm just playing."

Cheryl shook her head. "Play with someone else." Then she started to drag the shorter woman towards the building at the far corner of the transit center.

Tony followed them, but had a hard time keeping up. Not because he was slow, but they were moving almost inhumanly fast. There was a tiny alley between the trees and the building. Cheryl stopped in the alley and threw Christina against the far wall on the opposite end.

Tony heard himself shouting, "What the hell do you think you're doing?"

Cheryl ignored him and lunged toward Chris with a crooked, ten-inch blade. Tony froze, and tried to move, but something stopped him from leaving the entrance of the small alley, like an imaginary wall.

Tony could see the knife clearly from where he stood; but had no idea where it came from. The blade resembled a lightning bolt. It had odd shapes carved in black. Tony's brain argued with his eyes that, under the current lighting, he shouldn't have been able to see the black carvings, but his eyes insisted he did. What he could see of the hilt looked like any blade you might find on a gang member. He couldn't figure out where she could hide such a blade.

Chris was on all fours and looked up as Cheryl walked toward her. There was blood coming from somewhere in her scalp and trailing down her face. Lifting one hand up to her head, her fingers came away, dripping blood, before she put them in her mouth. Then she hissed at Cheryl, but it wasn't a human noise. Christina's eyes where shining like a cat's in the dark.

Tony's mind commanded him to help his friend. If Cheryl was doing the chanting, he couldn't just stand there and let Chris get hurt. She went though a lot, which seemed to have left her a little crazy, but she was still his friend.

Chris hissed again. She launched herself onto the taller woman, toppling both of them to the ground. Tony couldn't believe what his eyes saw, since he was pretty sure humans couldn't move like that.

The knife went spinning off and Cheryl didn't have enough wind in her lungs to keep chanting. Chris swiped at Cheryl's face with nails that looked more like claws. Cheryl dodged her at the last second so there were only slash marks on her left cheek. Then she started chanting again.

Tony was baffled. Within a matter of seconds, her hand shot out and the knife came flying towards her. When her hand gripped the hilt, she stopped chanting and thrust the knife into her opponent's chest.

"No!" Tony heard himself scream as Chris fell backwards.

He could suddenly move again and he began to run towards his dying friend. By the time he reached Cheryl, she was already standing. Her arm shot out and a hand wrapped around his upper arm. He turned to scream at Cheryl, intending to fight her off if he had to. He would not let his friend die alone.

She spoke before he could get the words to leave his mouth. "I wouldn't do that. Even in that state, it can still get you."

He looked at the serious expression on her face, which made him even angrier. He turned to call out to Chris, but his words died. The body of his friend suddenly began to age and wither. He stopped struggling as a black, winged shape, the size of a human, seemed to fly out from the body. It paused for a second, only two feet from the ground, flapping its wings before hissing at Cheryl again and soaring into the sky.

Cheryl walked over to the body and removed the knife, which she put into her pocket. It shouldn't have fit, but it completely disappeared.

She walked back over to Tony and stood next to him, facing the opposite direction. "Don't worry, Tony. That wasn't Christina. I think she was gone a long time ago." Gripping his shoulder sympathetically, a second later, she walked away.

Tony turned. "Hey! What the hell just happened? Was that the same black shape from earlier?"

There was no answer. He walked out of the alley and looked around. Cheryl was nowhere to be seen.

"What about the baby?"

The only answer he got was a sudden gust of wind that pushed him toward his car. He looked back and shook his head.

"Of course, the body would disappear. Maybe I imagined the whole thing." He walked over and unlocked his car. "Or maybe I didn't." He drove out of there as fast as he could.

Tony shot up in bed, covered in sweat, and a death grip on his blanket. His heartbeat was roaring in his ears and he fought to control his breathing.

He purposefully pried the blanket from his hands. Tony almost never had nightmares, and when he did, they were never paranormal. If the dream were his imagination's suggestion for fixing the Mariners' losing streak, it needed to meet reality.

Clearly, his mind was trying to deal with Chris's abduction. He had looked up her file, but didn't find much. On his way home from the game, he drove to the location where her car was found. Toward the back of the parking lot, where fewer witnesses could observe her. He was not sure what his next step should be, and felt weird about questioning her husband.

Why was she unmarried in his dream? Why did his imagination make her into a monster? Why would he dream of Cheryl killing her? Was Cheryl involved in the abduction?

Tony shook his head, hoping for more sleep. Forcing his body to relax, he turned on his radio alarm clock to the classical station and let the music lull him back into deep slumber.

Tony stood in a foggy room. At least, he thought it was a room. *Hopefully this won't be another nightmare.* After a second, however, he realized it was far too big a space. He couldn't even see the ground he was standing on through all the thick, gray fog. He knew he wasn't alone and felt pretty sure the other person was somewhere in front of him. The other person wasn't any kind of threat to Tony. Not in the sense that he couldn't take the person if he were attacked, but that whoever it was meant him no harm. He couldn't see who it was through all the fog, but sensed his or her approach.

"Hello?" he called out.

As he did, a figure started toward him through the fog. Tony noted it was obviously a woman, from the slender hourglass figure and the sway in her walk. The woman was about six feet away from him when she came into full view and Tony gasped.

Christina was walking toward him, dressed in what looked like dark red lingerie slip that didn't quite reach her knees, and she was, in no way, pregnant. Her reddish-brown hair cascaded like a cape around her upper arms.

She looked at his expression and laughed. "Tony, it's considered rude to gape like that."

Tony stuttered. "Are you dead?"

She grimly nodded. "Yes, if Cheryl did as she promised."

Tony looked at her, utterly confused.

She sighed. "I'm not here to explain that to you. It would take more time than we have. It was either this or have a Culeen imposter, I guess you could say, running around."

She looked behind her as if something might've been following her, but, seeing only fog, she turned back to him.

"Where are we?" Tony knew it was a stupid question, but it happened to be the only one that came to his mind.

Christina lifted her left eyebrow. "We are in your dream world. I came into your dream to speak with you. It was far too easy for me to get in, by the way. You should work on that. I created all this fog so if anyone else entered your dream, they'd have trouble finding either of us."

Tony felt the wheels in his head starting to catch up.

"What is a Culeen? And why are you here? And why are you dressed like that?"

She almost seemed to smirk at him, this was the girl he remembered from high school. Well, not quite, he corrected himself. She had the same expressions and personality, but her body was radically different from what he remembered. She was shorter, overweight, and would never have been caught wearing what she was dressed in now. *Why was he dreaming about her again? Why did part of him think he really was talking to a dead woman?*

"The easiest way to answer your first question is: those flying black things I see flying about your memory. As for your second question: I'm here to help you. I'm not supposed to contact living humans, being kind of dead and all, but you were my friend and now you're in trouble. You'd do the same for me."

Tony would have agreed, but couldn't. If he were such a good friend, why was he talking to a dead woman?

She must have read his thought because she laughed before reaching up and stroking his cheek. Her hand felt like ice against his skin, but her touch still comforted him.

"Don't worry so much about the past. I knew it was coming and prepared accordingly." Her hand moved away from his face before balling into a fist by her side. "You're going to have a tough time now, hon. There are some not-so-nice things that exist in this world; and several of them are looking for people like you."

Tony grunted. "What? Cops?"

She shook her head, making her hair move across her shoulders. "No that's not…"

She was cut off by a loud, high-pitched screech that could not have come from human lungs.

"Oh no!"

Tony looked at the woman in front of him, who seemed close to panic. She turned to him, as if surprised to still see him standing there.

"How are you expecting to survive, Two-Tone?"

She began shoving him backwards, and if she hadn't caught him off guard, he could have grabbed her. She looked a lot thinner than when they were younger; and it would have been easy to control her. She kept pushing him back so he couldn't stabilize himself. There was another screech, sounding much closer this time.

"Chris, what are you doing? And what is that?"

She pushed him harder and he lost his balance before slipping and falling over.

She was looking down at him with an expression of terror mixed with worry.

"Goodbye, Tony."

Before he could ask what she meant, she lifted her arm above his head and began to chant. Panic began filling him. A strange power covered him like a warm blanket. He could smell fresh fruit. This power seemed friendly, unlike before, and he felt himself relaxing.

She turned away from him, planting her feet between him and the strange noise. Tony looked past her at two large, black figures now moving towards them.

"Christina?" was all he managed to get out before he started to fall.

He was falling faster than he could fathom. Looking down in all the fog, he could faintly make out his bedroom and his sleeping body.

Then he heard a woman scream.

Tony looked up. "Christina!"

He could hear chanting in a deep tone while barely making out Chris's unwavering voice. He began to struggle, determined not leave his friend. He felt himself slamming into his body. Bolting upright in bed, with the sound of the second, more frantic scream ringing in his ears.

Chapter 4

Sunday was Tony's regular day for grocery shopping. So of course, not being one to go hungry, he went shopping as usual. He had to stop himself several times from ramming into other carts because he was so preoccupied with his dreams from the previous night. He couldn't sleep beyond the four hours that comprised the two dreams.

After about the fifth close call, he turned into an empty aisle to get hold of himself. He closed his eyes and rubbed his face. "Come on, Tone. It was just a lack of sleep manifesting itself. Get a grip; you just imagined seeing your friends."

He opened his eyes to see Cheryl staring at him from the other end of the aisle. She gave him a small smirk and he saw the scratches along the side of her face. Exactly where Chris had scratched her in his dream. She was leaning against a shelf.

"Hey, Cheryl?" he called out in shock.

But all she did was wink at him and leave the aisle.

He jogged to the end and swung out in the direction she was headed, only to slam into another cart. Tony cursed under his breath. He wanted answers and he couldn't see her anywhere. He stopped scanning the store, and instead, looked at the driver of the other cart.

It was a tall guy about Tony's age with dark blond hair and dark green eyes. He had a little boy with him, about three years old.

"I'm sorry, I wasn't looking. I was following someone."

The man's friendly face went solemn. "Oh? Well, next time, be more careful. You could have hit a child."

Tony nodded. He deserved that for following hallucinations.

"I am sorry."

The man nodded once, then maneuvered his cart around Tony. The little boy stayed where he was and just stared at Tony with one of those smiles only the very young seem to possess. He looked exactly like a younger version of the tall guy, except the shape of his face was different, and his hair was lighter. His little hands were clasped in front of him.

Tony heard the man holler over his shoulder. "Come on, Corbin."

The little boy continued to stare. If the kid hadn't been so cute, it might have been creepy.

"Why were you following her?"

Tony was surprised to discover the boy saw Cheryl.

"Because I need to talk to her."

The boy didn't move.

"Corbin, it's time to go."

The little boy continued to ignore, what Tony assumed, was his father.

"Why do you need to talk with her?"

Why did Tony continue to talk with this boy? Simple, the little boy saw Cheryl.

"Because she knows some things about a friend and I want to know them too."

The little boy's expression changed ever so slightly.

"CORBIN!"

The little boy blinked. "Why don't you know what happened to your friend? A friend should always know. You shouldn't have to ask Ms. Young. You should know yourself."

Tony stiffened. It hurt to realize this little boy was right, but the boy also knew Cheryl, he actually *knew* her. That meant she was in the store. And with those scratches on her face. Did that make his dreams at least, partially real? Tony felt himself going cold. Dreams didn't come true; that wasn't how the world worked.

Just as he was about to speak again, the boy's father came over and grabbed the boy's wrist.

"Don't talk to strangers."

As he began to pull the boy away, the boy answered him, finally looking away from Tony.

"But Daddy! He's not a stranger. That's Mr. Hollownton."

The man stopped dead beside Tony.

"Are you sure?"

The little boy nodded vigorously and turned to look up at Tony again.

Tony was too confused to speak.

"The woman you are looking for had to leave, but she'll contact you," said the man before he walked back to his cart.

"Wait!" Tony called after the man.

The man leaned over and said something to his son before the boy went happily running off. Then the man rose again and walked back over to Tony, raising his hand to prevent Tony from speaking.

"I cannot answer the questions you have. It is not my duty to try. Things are complicated; and you must accept that, sometimes, people just need to disappear. When that happens, you move on. You don't try to talk about it. It could cause trouble for both them and you. You will get your answers, but not as soon as you might like. Things don't run according to yours or my wishes."

There was slight bitterness in the last few words and the man's eyes were hard.

Tony kept silent as the man walked back to his cart and headed toward his son. Tony just stood there, watching them. What had he stumbled into?

Chapter 5

Tony spent three hours scrutinizing the crime scene photos that were fanned out on his desk. He simply couldn't seem to keep his mind on the case long enough to gather anymore clues. It wasn't just because the pictures were bad, which they were.

No, he was dreaming of his old friends, watching one kill the other. And meeting some weird guy at the grocery store, who knew Cheryl.

He spent most of his off time over the weekend trying to figure out what was going on, and what his subconscious was trying to tell him. All he managed to deduce was that the black things, called the Culeen, were bad; and he dreamed one was pretending to be Chris. And part of him had to believe Chris was dead.

Why did that kid at the store know him?

He felt as if a mountain just fell on top of him. Something took his friend and her baby, and probably killed them. He had trouble understanding why his subconscious was fine with that. He would never have tried to seek comfort for himself regarding his friend's death. He didn't believe in any supernatural stuff… period. But for some reason, his mind was using the paranormal to explain Chris's disappearance.

Tony heard laughter and looked up. Rick was leaning on a desk across the large room. He and several other officers were laughing heartily.

That was something else, which bothered Tony. Rick was doing everything he could to avoid working on the case. Not that Tony entirely blamed him, but it was still odd for Rick. Tony was probably acting strangely all day, and the religious undertones of their case might've made Rick nervous.

Tony ran his fingers through his hair. He didn't work on the case this weekend like he planned. Having very little to go on, he pushed the pictures aside and pulled a paper out of the manila folder.

It was the official report of what the translator stated was written on the wall. Even that was fishy. It took awhile to find a translator that understood the symbols. They went through two dozen people before finding her. She told them what the message said, but when asked about the people who used such symbols, she became less than helpful. All she said was only two, or maybe three groups used that language. When asked about the rare groups, she waved the question off. She said the people were so scattered, it was impossible to identify them. That was the extent of her help. He was later told that despite their persuasive techniques, they couldn't get anything else from her. In fact, they detained her for withholding evidence, but she just disappeared without a trace.

He looked again at the picture of the wall, and then at the translation.

LET THIS BE A LESSON TO THOSE WHO HELP THE NYM.

I WILL FIND YOU AND YOU WILL BE NO MORE.

That was it. All it told him was that there would be more killings, unless it was translated wrong and misunderstood. Whoever committed the murder obviously didn't like the Nym. Whatever that was, since there was no record available of any such group.

The translator also said the symbols found carved on the victim's back were a name, but she couldn't pronounce it.

With no way of knowing when the killer would strike next, there was also no clear evidence or motive that could point him in the right direction. The threat of more people having to die tore him up.

Tony dropped the paper on his desk and ruffled his hair. He was about to get up when he realized someone was standing beside his desk.

Turning, Tony saw Will, who wasn't wearing his normally nervous expression. Instead, he stood there, perfectly calm, as if waiting for Tony to notice him.

When Tony made eye contact, Will spoke. "I was just going to get lunch and I think you should come with me. You look like you need the company."

Will turned slightly to look at Rick, who was laughing across the room.

When he turned back, Tony answered, "I'm fine; thank you anyway, Will."

Tony wondered why Will invited him. And why he was so calm all of a sudden; and why he could sense something was bothering Tony, when his own partner couldn't.

"Tony, trust me, it would be in your best interests to come with me."

Tony looked up at Will's face. He was so calm, but the tone he used sounded harsh and stern. It didn't fit Will's personality. It bordered on being a threat, or trying to let Tony in on a secret without actually saying anything. Then there was the use of Tony's first name, instead of the usual, *Detective* Hollownton.

Tony sighed. He should eat something and his curiosity was getting the better of him. He decided he could stand being around Will for a while.

Tony stood and grabbed his coat off the back of his chair. "All right, Will, you win."

Will seemed to relax. "Good."

As they walked across the room, Rick looked up only once before returning to his conversation.

Upon reaching the door, Tony heard the captain bellow, "Will! Where do you think you're going?"

Tony watched as the insecure Will returned, and he almost rolled his eyes. So much for lunch.

"To lunch," was Will's terse answer. He didn't move or make any sign of retreating, but stayed rooted where he was.

The voice was the same hard voice he used on Tony moments earlier. The only difference was Will turned so he could look at the captain.

"Well, all right then." Binns walked back into his office.

Will turned and continued to walk out of the building. Tony just stood there for a second. Binns didn't yell at Will or give him a time limit. He just submitted to what the intern said, no questions asked. Tony shook his head. Things were just getting weirder by the moment. Tony put his hands in his pockets and pushed on the door with his shoulder. Will was waiting outside for him.

After walking to the Dragon's Lair in silence, they were seated almost immediately in a corner booth. Tony stayed quiet, waiting for Will to say something, but not until after they ordered did Will even look at him. Will's body language and posture changed. He wasn't the same meek geek Tony knew.

His voice didn't shake and sounded deeper.

"Tony, I'm going to talk about some weird stuff and you can't talk to your partner about it. Understand?"

Tony rolled his eyes; he didn't need to hear other people's problems right now. He had enough on his own plate.

"Sure, Will, I promise."

The taller man nodded and took a sip of his water. He seemed to relax more and there was almost the air of a teacher about him. Tony found himself wondering if Will regarded him as the student.

"Have you been seeing weird things lately, Tony? Or hearing things? Having weird dreams perhaps?"

Tony went still. *How could Will know that?* He hadn't told anyone about the chanting or the dreams.

"I'll take that as a yes," Will said, swallowing another sip. "Tell me about it."

Tony just sat there, looking startled for a few seconds. He debated whether he should be sharing anything with the shy intern, although Will didn't seem so shy at the moment.

He hesitated just a second more before deciding to tell the truth. It was as if he felt compelled to admit it to Will.

"I thought I heard chanting in a foreign language at the crime scene Friday."

Will gave him a wary look. "Heard? How?"

Tony shifted in his seat. "It was as if someone was right there next to me, chanting in my ear. The air seemed thicker and it got hard to breathe. Then there was a popping noise and the chanting stopped."

Will's face was suspiciously blank. "Do you remember anything else? Did you see anything off?"

A red flag slid across Tony's mind. Will was trying to extract something from him. He knew something, and Tony needed that information.

"No, just the chanting." Tony reflected the same blank expression he was receiving from Will.

Will watched him for a second. Tony could tell he was deciding whether or not to push for more information, but eventually chose not to.

"Any weird dreams?"

Tony did not like that transition. Will seemed so much more together than usual. He decided to answer, without really answering. He would appease Will's questions with ambiguous answers before asking some of his own.

"I've been thinking about an old friend recently."

Will lifted an eyebrow, which was most definitely not a "Will" expression.

"Have you not seen this person in a while?"

Tony nodded and answered before taking a gulp of water. "It's been about a decade since I last saw her."

Will's mouth twitched. "Do you have feelings for her?" The way he emphasized "feelings" made Tony grunt.

"No, not in the least bit."

Will seemed to be watching him a little too closely.

"Is thinking about her a bad thing?"

Tony shifted in the dark red booth and looked down. He felt compelled to answer, even though he wanted to drop the subject and get to the bottom of Will's nosiness.

"I think she's dead."

When Tony looked back up, Will's posture changed somehow. He looked sterner and almost intimidating. Tony thought that was ridiculous because Will was in no way intimidating, but that didn't make him feel any better.

When he spoke, Will's tone had a spark to it. "So you're seeing a dead woman?"

Tony shook his head. He never said anything about seeing her; and technically, he didn't know she was dead. *What was Will hiding?*

"Only in my dreams, not in day-to-day life. I don't know for a fact that she is dead; it's just a hunch."

Will took a deep breath as the waitress served their food.

Tony looked down at the orange chicken in front of him, and shook his head again. Christina used to order that; and refused to get anything else at the local hangout. Why did he order it?

When he looked back at Will, the man was aiming something green toward his mouth. When it was about an inch away, he paused. "So how long has Christina been visiting you in your dreams?"

Tony dropped his fork, as Will stuffed the bite into his mouth.

"How did you know her name?"

Will paused a second to swallow. "You must have told me."

Tony felt all the muscles in his body tense. "No, I didn't, I was careful not to. And I would put money on Rick not telling you."

Will's eyes went wide like an animal caught in the eyes of a predator. "Oh, crap."

Before Will could move, Tony's arm shot out across the table, grabbing Will's wrist as he growled, "Tell me what you know, and do it now."

Will was staring at Tony's hand, as if confused about what to do, before he calmly looked back at Tony.

"I was friends with this woman named Christina Mirin. Never mind how I met her. About a year ago, when I started my internship, I was talking about all the cops at the precinct; and when your name came up, she got really excited. She explained how you two went to high school together and were really close. A few months later, she seemed really worried and asked me to keep an eye on you because she wouldn't be able to."

Tony let go of Will's arm and he fell back against the booth. He was so utterly confused and shocked, he forgot all about the food. Chris knew Will? And before she disappeared, she told Will to keep an eye on him? That meant she knew she was going to be abducted. This whole thing was getting weirder by the minute. *What could she have been into?* As soon as the first case was over, he intended to question her husband. If she saw her abduction coming, maybe he did too. Or maybe he was the abductor. Either way, Tony might have found a lead.

"What did she mean by that? Keep an eye on me?"

Will looked confused for a moment. "She was abducted, Tony."

Tony heard his voice continue talking even though his mind was reeling.

“How did she know? How did she know she would be taken? What does she think I need watching for?”

Will blinked and gave Tony a confused stare. "Are you joking?"

Tony just stared back at the other man.

Will's eyes widened. "You're not joking! Wow… How do you not know? Wait, how did you not notice? I thought you guys were close?"

That punched Tony like a blow to the stomach.

“What?”

Will jumped slightly at the harshness of Tony’s voice. He looked genuinely confused, but there was undeniable wariness in his eyes.

"Chris always knew things she shouldn't; she just knew them. She knew things about people, though they never told her. She knew when things were coming. She was always like that. Didn't you ever notice?"

Tony took a deep breath and tried to think back. Yes, Chris would sometimes say things that wouldn't make sense until later. He always chocked it up to her being hyper-observant. There was never anything about the future. Did Chris believe she was psychic? Clearly, Will thought she was.

He shook his head “No, she was normal. Well, a little odd at times, but not inhumanly so. She never mentioned psychic visions, or dead people, or any nonsense like that.”

Will rolled his eyes and moved in closer as an elderly couple was seated by the hostess in the booth behind Tony.

“Ask her next time she appears to you. Make no mistake about it, Tony, she is visiting you. It isn't just your imagination; she is trying to help you.” Will took a long drink of water.

“Is that why you had me come to lunch? So you could tell me my dead friend told you to look after me? Oh, and she thought she was psychic? And you think she is visiting me from beyond the grave or something like that?”

Tony‘s anger at the whole situation began curling up through his body, and as it rose higher, he heard his voice getting louder.

Will gave him a stern look and put a finger to his lips. Then he stood up from the booth and walked over to the older couple behind Tony. Tony tried to return his breathing back to normal. That wasn't like him; he didn't just blow up in public, no matter how ridiculous and delusional Will appeared.

Tony could hear Will talking to the couple.

"I'm so sorry if we are disturbing you. We're writers for a new television show. We have been given a short deadline and are trying to come up with ideas. I'm sorry if my co-worker or I startled you, but you know how it is when a deadline approaches. Tensions just sky-rocket. Again, I'm so sorry."

Tony heard the older woman chuckle before the man said, "It's okay, son. I wrote for a newspaper back in my day, so we understand deadlines."

Tony heard Will thank the man and watched him walk back to their booth. He felt sorry that Will's delusions were affecting other people.

Tony leaned around the booth. "Sorry."

The man smiled and gave a brief nod, his white hair falling as he did so.

The woman grinned, "Good luck, young man, it sounds interesting."

Tony gave them a genuine smile and leaned back into the booth.

Will nodded approvingly. "They can only hear us when we raise our voices, so if you think we can keep it down to a low murmur, then we can continue."

Tony felt his eyes narrowing. How dare Will give him a lecture! He saw the corners of Will's mouth start to twitch. It took Tony a second longer to realize Will meant it as a joke.

Tony shook his head. "Yeah, there is no doubt in my mind that you were friends with Chris."

Will went slightly solemn as he gave Tony a very weak smile.

"Yeah, it was a big deal to be her friend, especially with the five-year age difference."

Will stared off as if reliving some memory, and Tony let him.

When he came back from wherever he went, Will shook himself.

"No, Tony, that's not why I asked you to lunch. She spoke so highly of you that I could have sworn you knew what she was. I guess she was more guarded than I thought. I brought you here to answer whatever questions I can about what's going on with you."

Tony sighed, feeling drained; and began to pick at his food. He didn't believe a dead woman was in his dreams. He didn't really want to believe she was dead at all. But he decided to humor Will, since the other man seemed to need it.

"I don't think I'll dream of her again." He startled himself with that sentence, even though the thought lurked in the back of his mind, but he dared not confront it.

Will almost smiled. "Tony, she came across the barrier of death to see you! Whatever it is, you will not stop her from returning."

Tony wanted to believe Will. But he really wished he could find his friend and somehow, against all odds, have her safe and sound.

Tony decided to shift the subject. He was playing a hunch. He wasn't sure why we thought his first dream would be of interest to Will, but something inside him felt compelled to share.

"I had a strange dream before that one. It started with the Mariners game I went to on Saturday. I dreamt that we swept the Yankees."

Will snorted and Tony ignored it.

"The weird part happened after we swept the Yankees." Then he launched into a retelling of the entire dream, and only stopped when the dream ended and he woke up.

Will listened to the entire thing in silence, keeping his face blank the whole time. Tony met lots of cops who weren't as polished as he at keeping a blank face. Only after Tony completely finished talking did Will speak.

"That is a pretty intense dream."

Tony could tell Will wanted to say more, but stopped himself. Then his eyes lit up and he smiled.

"You know, I think I know what your dream is telling you."

Tony snorted, "Oh? Do tell." He slid a forkful of rice in his mouth.

"You know how Chris loved old mythology?"

Tony nodded. Chris loved ancient myths and excelled in sharing them. She never seemed to run out of stories.

"Do you remember anything about the Culeen?"

The word rang a bell, but Tony couldn't jog his memory. He shook his head.

Will set his fork down and leaned in, getting more excited.

"The Culeen were a race of creatures exactly like you described the black winged things. They traveled in packs, like what you saw in the sky. They had these glands on the undersides of their jaws that produced a powder; and, depending on how powerful the individual Culeen was, it could basically make him or her a puppet master for any human they spat the powder on. It often only stunned their prey long enough for them to attack the human; or allow the Culeen to control them from a distance for up to a week.

"I think you were dreaming of the Culeen myth as a way for your subconscious to justify Chris's abduction. Since Cheryl is her best friend, your mind added her in there, and made her kill the Culeen, thereby freeing Chris."

Will leaned back, clearly pleased with his assessment.

Tony struggled to recall anything Chris might have said about the Culeen, but he honestly couldn't remember. Perhaps Will was right. His mind was trying to reconcile Chris's abduction, despite knowing her body was never found.

They didn't really talk much after that. Tony pondered how Will knew Chris; and for whatever reason, he believed Chris was psychic. He also wondered why both Chris and Will thought Tony needed their help. What exactly did she think he needed help with?

Things did not improve when Tony and Will got back from lunch and Rick informed them there was another crime scene.

The two men rode to the new crime scene exactly as they had for the first one. This time, however, the mood in the car was very different. Tony was exhausted and confused. Rick was just *different*. He was whistling and had a smile on his face. He wasn't worried about the crime scene at all, which disturbed Tony even more.

"You thinking about what we'll find at this crime scene? I know the last one was hard for you."

Rick shook his head, sounding almost chipper. "Nope, not at all. I mean you've seen one, you've seen them all, right?"

Tony was more than a little concerned. First, his partner spent the morning avoiding both work and him. Now, he was positively chipper about viewing a new gruesome crime scene. Had everyone lost their minds today? Those thoughts kept Tony preoccupied until the car was parked.

This time, the murder occurred in an apartment building. It appeared much more brazen than the house the first victim lived in. When interviewed by the officers that arrived before Rick and Tony, the neighbors of the first victim said they hadn't heard anything. In an apartment building, however, neighbors heard and saw everything. They should not fail to find a lead this time.

The murder was on the second floor of the five-story apartment complex. It didn't get reported until a neighbor came home after dropping a kid at school and complaining to the manager of a "peculiar stench." The manager didn't even get around to checking on it until one o'clock.

The building appeared to have been renovated sometime in the nineties. It was basically that generic cream color that became so popular. It wasn't hard to pin-point the right apartment since two officers flanked each side of the door. Both the uniformed officers looked new on the force.

There was a black-and-white sign on the door that read, "All are welcome here" with "welcome" written in big, pink letters. As Tony and Rick walked up, Tony flipped them his badge.

"We're from homicide."

The taller officer, the one closest to the doorknob, leaned in and nodded.

Once inside, Tony realized just how small the apartment was. There were officers standing around the main room in tiny clusters, and there was a level of tension that wasn't present at the first scene. *Probably because this second murder meant it wasn't a one-time thing.*

There was a small hallway to the right of where Tony and Rick were standing, and Tony motioned to Rick for them to head in that direction. There had to be a reason no one was standing on that side of the room. As they passed the first cluster of cops, Officer Joan came up to them.

"It was in the bedroom this time."

He continued to speak while leading them as though he were giving them a tour.

"Victim is about the same age as the other. No criminal record." As he reached for the doorknob, he turned and added, "Female this time."

The bedroom was small, and opposite the door was a decent-sized window with mini-blinds. Little rays of afternoon sun squeezed through the slats. Against the right wall was a full-sized bed with a dresser at the left and a nightstand on the right. The room had a pale yellow theme, which was nicely complemented by what little light came through the blinds. To the left of the window hung the body.

Tony stepped into the room. Standing with his calves against the bed, he was only about a foot from the body. The smell was overpowering, and Tony gagged. Joan was right beside him, handing him gloves and a white doctor's mask. Tony gagged twice more before getting the mask on. Then the smell of the sterilized cloth filled his nose, and he took a deep breath before looking back at the victim.

She was hung exactly the same way as the first victim, except she was a good two feet higher up, placing her head only about an inch from the ceiling. Her wrists and ankles were cut, and the front half of her scalp was gone. The rest of her long blond hair was matted together with dried blood and clinging to her back.

Tony looked closely at her head without actually moving closer. He blinked and stared again.

Her stomach appeared to be no more than a dark red mass. It seemed as if her belly had been ripped out, leaving only a gaping hole in its place. It was done out of passion, and not like the rest of her body where the killer used almost surgical precision. There were marks all around the outside of the hole, showing how the flesh was ripped. The skin was torn away, leaving the smallest strip of bloody flesh hanging on the left side. All the organs appeared to be just a bloody mess. Part of the small intestine hung from her body and touched the floor, like a rope ladder, leading up into her vacant belly. Tony stared at the mess for a second until his brain registered what it was.

The woman must have been pregnant because the baby was crudely removed; and not just the baby, but also the entire womb. As if killing the mother wasn't cruel enough. She couldn't have been very far along. Tony started gagging again and looked down at the ground. *How could anyone do such a thing?*

Tony's mind spun, and he felt horrified. It was one thing to kill an adult, but a child? In his mind, that was one of the sickest things anyone could do. As he fought to gain control of his anger, as well as his lunch, he noticed he was standing on the edges of a puddle of blood. There was no way to avoid it in the tiny room, but Tony still shuffled his feet. He saw another pair of shoes next to his.

He looked up to see Rick standing beside him, but he wasn't wearing a doctor's mask. One corner of his mouth was turned up ever so slightly.

"Looking for the baby? It's not here. They probably took it with."

Tony looked back at the body with the gaping hole in the stomach. *Who could do that?* Tony raised his eyes to look at the rest of the body. He concentrated hard to avoid looking at the childless belly when he noticed the same palm-sized hole above the heart as the first victim.

Gathering what remained of his nerves, Tony tried to look at the back of the body, but there were no marks there, no carvings, and no symbols. He glanced across the room above the bed, but of course, there were no symbols there either, or he would have seen them earlier.

As quickly as possible, he exited the room, ripping off the gloves and mask. As soon as he dumped them, he stuck his head out the kitchen window, but even that air wasn't fresh enough to remove the horror clinging to his lungs.

Tony did not go back in to see the body. A body was bad enough, but having the fetus carved out and removed was just a little too much for him to handle. Rick, on the other hand, seemed to be handling things just fine. Tony thought Rick seemed more cheerful as they were leaving than when they came in.

Returning to the car, Rick went back to whistling again.

"Did you see the symbols this time?"

Tony, feeling half sick, turned to his smiling partner. "What?"

Rick's smile grew like an excited child bringing home an art project. "There were symbols carved into the little scrap hanging from the wound. It said, ABOMINATION."

Tony stared at his partner. "How do you know that?"

Rick made a face. "Oh, come on, it's obvious, think about it… The baby was removed from the body. It was obviously a protest of disapproval about the baby."

Tony looked at Rick for a few more seconds, then turned away. Tony couldn't say anything to reply, and thought maybe, just maybe, Rick had cracked.

Once they were back to the precinct, Rick wandered off. Tony did not want to chase this new version of Rick, so he sat at his desk. Rubbing his face again, he tried to push the images out of his head. There was a new envelope on his desk. Opening it, he realized it was a description, as well as the pictures, of the first victim.

His name was Bradley Walker. The six-foot, blond, thirty-two-year-old nurse at the Swedish Hospital was also single and had a good standing with the law. There was not much more to him. He seemed to enjoy a relatively simple life. He didn't belong to any groups, which made the Nym thing even more puzzling.

Tony put down the paper to look at the only picture. Brad had a big smile. His eyes were such a pale blue, they almost seemed white. Medium blond curls reached the middle of his ears. The sight of this man's mutilated body flashed in Tony's head. He put down the picture, but the images stubbornly refused to go. Following the crime scenes in his mind was the moment the dagger plunged into Chris's chest. At that point, Tony placed the papers back into the envelope before putting them into his desk.

He yelled at himself mentally and brought the envelope back out, skimming down the page. Brad mostly worked a day shift. There wasn't much else there. His parents and one brother lived in Oregon. There just was not anything else that proved useful. He needed to call the family, and see if they knew anything that might help.

Tony was rubbing his face when his phone began to ring. He felt his heart jump as he reached for it, hoping it wasn't a cackling woman.

"King County Police Department, Detective Anthony Hollownton speaking."

"I swear, Detective, one of these days, you'll stop with all that formal crap and just say hello like everyone else."

Tony relaxed at hearing the familiar female voice on the other end. "Viggo, what have you got for me?"

He heard the medical examiner chuckle on the other end. "I have a pretty face and a sarcastic smile; take it or leave it."

Tony smiled; he liked Viggo more than most of the medical examiners in the county. He was all too aware that he was only one of a few people in the department who got her sense of humor. Not that ignorance ever stopped her from making a joke. She smiled to herself fairly often, and most people just stopped asking her why.

"I take that to mean you want me to come down there?"

"That's right, Detective, your order is ready… Dead body at table two."

Tony chuckled. "I'll be right there." It was a good excuse for him to leave the office.

"Okay."

Tony shook his head as the dial tone came on. She always did that, as if hearing the word, *okay*, automatically ended any phone conversation. Tony put the phone back on the cradle. He hoped she would have information for him, since he needed hard facts right now. He was willing to bet she did if she wanted to see him in person.

Tony smiled as he grabbed his coat. Hanging around Viggo made it hard for him to stay in a bad mood, since she was just naturally cheerful. Several officers complained that it was wrong for someone in her profession to crack a smile as often she did, but Tony liked that about her.

Morgan Viggo was in the front hall, waiting for Tony when he got there. She was leaning her back against the wall so all he could see was her profile. Eating what appeared to be a wedge of a sandwich, she wore the same pink tennis shoes she wore every time Tony saw her. They were the only visible bit of clothing besides her long, white lab coat that all the techs wore.

Her light brown hair was pulled back off her face into a tight bun, except for the bangs that hung over her rose-colored small, round glasses with points on the outer tips.

She joked with Tony one of the first times they met, saying, "If you think I have a dark sense of humor now, you should see me without my rose-colored glasses."

Tony felt sorry for her when the *Lord of the Rings* craze hit. Even though it was before they met. She must have been teased horribly for the similarities her name bore to one of the leading actors. Tony was told when she started, a few threats to the lower techs was all it took for the taunting to stop. And that was years after all the movies came out.

Another thing about her, which Tony found amusing, was she claimed to be happily married. She couldn't have been much older than Tony, but she refused to tell anyone how old she actually was.

Tony couldn't help the smile that crept onto his face as he strolled towards her.

"Don't you hate it when the sandwich gets smooshed, and the bread crumples up on itself?"

She didn't look up from her sandwich, and it was more of a statement than a question, but Tony answered her anyway.

"Maybe your husband just needs more practice at making your sandwiches. After all, he's only had… what? Five years to master it?"

Tony stopped in front of her before she put the rest of the sandwich back into a plastic bag and looked up at him, grinning. The bag disappeared somewhere in the long coat.

"Four, and I think you're right. Let the flogging commence until morale and sandwich-making skills improve."

Tony began to laugh.

“Luckily for him, he has other talents.” She patted her stomach as she moved away from the wall and turned down the hallway.

Tony, being a few inches taller, kept up with her easily as they walked to the second examination room. “Wow, congratulations, Viggo.”

She flashed him a genuine smile as she reached for the door handle. “Thanks, Detective. Where's Nelson?”

Several excuses flew through Tony's mind. "He's working some leads."

Viggo nodded but did not give any other response. Once inside the room, Viggo handed Tony a pair of latex gloves before rounding the table that held the remains of Bradley Walker. Tony glanced at Viggo; her expression was blank, but not quite peaceful. Tony had to hand it to her, she saw death everyday, but never seemed bothered by it.

“I have to admit the first time I saw it, I almost puked on the body, but truthfully, that was from morning sickness more than anything else.” She gave a slight giggle before turning her full attention to the body.

Tony just shook his head and pulled out his notepad.

“Okay, Detective, ready or not, here it is.” She pulled on the second latex glove so it slapped for effect. “I assume you’re smart enough to have his basic info, right?” She actually looked at Tony over the tops of her glasses.

He couldn’t manage to look insulted, so he nodded.

“Good boy, now the ETD is about six am, and your guy here died of blood loss, which is pretty much a no-brainer.”

Tony waved his right hand to get Viggo to stop and look at him. “Wait, wait! Six am? That’s only an hour after the call came in. Are you telling me his death could have been prevented?”

Viggo shrugged, “Scary, ain’t it?”

There was no semblance of a joke on her face. Apparently, that thought already occurred to her. Tony could see the worry in her eyes. In that moment, he knew they were both worried about victim number two.

Tony watched as Viggo shook her head and blinked a few times to clear her thoughts.

Plastering her smile back into place, she looked up at him. “Top or bottom, Detective? Which goes first?” She was making scale movements with her hands.

It took Tony a second to answer. Looking down at the smiling face of the medical examiner, Tony realized that her small, almost patronizing expression, which she was so well known for, was merely a cover. *No one was who or what they seemed.* Or was he really that poor a judge of character? Tony wasn’t sure which thought bothered him more.

“Detective?” Viggo was snapping her fingers. “I do have other bodies to examine today, including yours.”

Tony sighed, “Top.”

Viggo moved to stand above the head. “Head it is, and may I say, excellent choice, sir. First, we have the scalping, which goes from about two centimeters before the hairline, to the tops of the ears, before completing the circle at the top of the head. Now before you ask, I looked very closely at the skin to see what type of tool was used. It appears to be a puncture wound similar to an ice pick, if not an actual ice pick. Your perp heated the weapon up first, and with slight pressure, let it burn its way through the victim’s left temple.”

Viggo was leaning over the body, her right hand in a fist and slowly moving toward the right temple. Her face was intense. That was another thing that bothered some of the other cops, she seemed to get a little too far “into” her work

“From the angle it’s at, I would say your perp is probably left-handed because of the way the body was suspended. If you look right here…”

Leaning further over the temple, she pointed so Tony had to move much closer to see what she was pointing at.

“You can see the entry wound and part of the burn from the initial contact. You can also see the burn all the way around the circle. In order to make the skin burn the way it did, that pick had to be extremely hot. I don’t know about the latest tools, but I’m guessing either your perp got burned or used protective gloves. So take that as you will. My guess is gloves, because I haven't lifted a single set of prints.” She made a dismissive movement with her hand, as if her gesture ended the subject.

Tony's hands flexed at the news. "So, do we have DNA?"

Viggo took a deep breath while bouncing on the balls of her feet. "No, there were no skin samples and no DNA."

She continued to bounce while watching Tony. He could tell she was waiting to be yelled at, but he knew it wasn't her fault. It made him angry though; the killer had to have left something.

"So there's no DNA anywhere on the body?"

Viggo clasped her arms behind her back. "No, and the crime scene guys didn't find any either."

Tony could tell Viggo was nervous, and it made him wonder how often people blew up at her.

"Okay, so the guy was careful."

Viggo let out a breath and smiled. "Your perp is most likely no more than five-nine, judging from the angles and stuff like."

Tony wrote that down, since he could ask questions when Viggo was finished. It was best to simply let her go through everything before she lost her train of thought.

"Okay, moving on." She elbowed Tony so she could stand on the right side of the torso. Viggo picked up the right arm so the wrist was at chest height.

"This lovely item, as you can see across the wrists, has rope burns; these burns tell us your vic struggled. The other three burns show the same thing. The burns on the ankles tell us that both ankles were tied together side-by-side. These burns are the first injuries; and I'm willing to bet that since he was conscious for them, he was probably awake for everything else. Which is, most definitely, a very unpleasant thought."

Viggo gave a small shudder and put the side of her palm next to the slice across the corpse's arm. "These cuts were done with a new weapon. The blade is at least seven inches long. You can see the motion used to slice open the arm. The edge near the hilt went down and in. Then the blade was pulled out though the cut." Viggo Demonstrated what she meant using the side of her hand. "These cuts severed the nerves, so this guy didn't have any use of his hands from almost the get-go, seeing how the cuts occurred right after he was securely tied. I think the wrists were cut more for effect than to actually sever the tendons. The ankles are the same way, and an inch below the rope, the back of the ankles were sliced open. It's the same motion as in the wrists, down and through."

She dropped the arm and it thudded on the examination table, Tony jumped.

"Now if you will be so kind as to stand on the other side of our guest, please." Viggo smiled up at him before leaning over the corpse's chest.

Tony shook his head as he walked around the table; Viggo definitely wasn't what people expected to find in a medical examiner.

"You'll want to put the book away, Detective; I'm going to make you touch things."

She giggled to herself as Tony sighed and put the notebook in his usual pocket.

"Take the jacket off, Detective. I don't want your fabric fibers contaminating my corpse."

Tony frowned at her as he took his trench coat off and hung it on one of the hooks next to the door.

As he walked back, Tony put his arms out. "Am I dressed appropriately? Or is this a black tie event?"

He heard Viggo's snicker before she looked up at him and grinned above her glasses.

"Not black tie, but if I weren't already married, I'd say shirts are optional. I'm told you have a very nice chest."

Tony's jaw dropped. *Where did that come from?* Tony was antisocial; so it must have come from one of the other cops at the gym.

"Who said that?"

Viggo looked up at him. "You mean they're lying? Bummer." She almost managed a straight face before she started giggling again. "I'm sorry, Detective, but it's not your body I'm interested in. Mr. Walker's, on the other hand, I find fascinating."

Tony scoffed; rolling his eyes and Viggo leaned back over the dead body.

"Okay,,. I give. Why is his chest so interesting?"

Tony leaned over the body so he was only about a foot away from Viggo.

"Well, Detective, I'll tell you, or better yet: put your hand in the hole."

Tony looked at Viggo, raising an eyebrow. "Excuse me?"

Viggo sighed, "Not deep, Detective; you don't have to go fishing. Just stick your hand in, put these gloves to good use."

Tony gave her a look before he made a fist and slid it into the hole. When he got near the edge of the glove, he stopped. He didn't feel anything. There should have been ribs and the heart, but nothing was there. Pulling his hand out, Tony cursed.

Viggo nodded, "Exactly, the heart has been completely extracted, and there are no pieces. As I'm sure you also noticed, there were no ribs in the way."

She leaned back and Tony followed suit. From where she stood, she grasped a flap in the skin, which Tony hadn't noticed before. She pulled it over the torso until the chest was bare with the skin flap hanging over the table.

Tony looked at Viggo from across the table. "That's kinda gross, you know. You could have just removed the skin."

Viggo shrugged, still looking at the chest. "But then I wouldn't have the hole; having the hole means I can limit the number of objects that could have been used. Now shut up, and look."

Tony followed her hand until he was looking at what was behind the hole, or rather, what *wasn't* behind the hole. Tony swore again. Sure enough, the heart was missing, but everything else was where it should have been, to his limited knowledge anyway. The only other thing that was missing were the front parts of the ribs that protected the heart.

"Not that you need me to tell you, but the heart and rib pieces are the only body parts missing. There are no fragments anywhere. There are no tear marks, on any of the tissue that would have been connected to the heart; and it's the same with the ribs. It's as if he never had them to begin with, which you and I both know, is impossible. I don't have the vaguest idea how it was done, and surprise-surprise, I've never seen anything like it. The only thing I can say is that the hole is about the size of a human fist, and that's all I got. There should be cuts or saw marks on the bone, but there aren't. I also checked the skin for the same burn marks as the scalp. Those are not there either. It almost looks like the skin was sliced with a finger nail. Which is both gross and all but impossible."

Tony stared down at the chest, but didn't have any ideas either. He straightened back up and removed the gloves. "And the markings on the back?"

Viggo shook her head. It wasn't until he disposed of the gloves that she answered him.

"I'm sorry, Detective, it's a burn and one that took a lot of time for it to get that much detail. It was the last thing done, even after the heart was removed. If the body remained hanging on the wall, I can't think of any plausible reason for doing it. It was. without a doubt, post mortem. Unless the killer was carrying a giant brand with him, which would have been mighty suspicious if anyone saw it, I don't know how it was inflicted."

Tony got the pad and pen out of his trench coat to jot down what little information he had. This case was going almost nowhere, and he had all but given up on getting any assistance from his partner. Tony knew he had to do this all alone.

After he turned the engine off, Tony leaned back in the driver's seat, staring at the side of the precinct. Before he left, Viggo assured Tony that the killer was very patient because what was done to Brad Walker took some time and planning.

Tony closed his eyes. He couldn't think of the vic as a person, just a body; and now, one whose death could have been prevented. Tony groaned and rubbed his face. He had too many unpleasant images and too many ideas bouncing around in his head.

He couldn't help it; his outside life was affecting his job. This was why he didn't have a life outside of work because it only got in the way. Even if he could get past Chris's probable death, and the dream image of that black thing, shedding her body like a snakeskin, he still had very little information on her case.

It should not have been so difficult. The images of the latest victim, with her womb in shreds, flashed through his mind. Tony tried to gain control of his thoughts before his stomach did more than churn. He couldn't get anything else done today, he was sure of it. Usually, at this point, he would be brimming with possible theories, but he had none.

Tony checked his watch. It was almost six. He wasn't sure where all the time went, although he probably spent a good chunk of it in traffic. As he stepped out of the car, Tony opted to quit for the day. His head was thumping. He knew he needed to go over the initial statements from the neighbors, and to re-question the neighbors of the first victim. However, he could barely concentrate on walking into the precinct. Maybe a good night's sleep would fix everything; and maybe, just maybe, nothing else would happen until tomorrow. Somehow, he doubted it.

Tony told the captain he was leaving for the day. Binns got angry and said crime doesn't skip out early just because someone's having a bad day. Then he looked up at Tony's face and agreed to let him go without further argument.

As he was leaving, Tony spotted Rick chatting away with some female officers. Then he saw Will, who was watching Tony's every move. They made eye contact, but Will shook his head and looked back down at his work.

Tony screamed at himself all the way home. He was doing next to nothing to solve this case, although granted, he was doing more than Rick, but still. Tony just couldn't determine why his work ethic had vanished. There was too much garbage flying in his head; so when he got home, he waited another hour before swallowing a sleeping pill and getting right into bed.

Chapter 6

Tony felt a warm body in front of him. Opening his eyes, he pushed onto his right shoulder. He was lying on a queen-sized bed covered in gold sheets, and spooning with a woman he presumed was his wife. All he could see of her was her long, sandy brown hair. He could tell she was sleeping and tried not to disturb her. The pale morning light shone through the light brown curtain, making it possible for him to see the bedroom was empty of any other people. Tony lay back down and closed his eyes. This was a good dream, and more realistic than most, but that was fine with him. He snuggled closer to the woman and inhaled her soft, floral scent. He felt his entire body relax, and after the day he had, this was exactly what he needed. Just then, the door burst open and he heard lots of chatter as only young children could make.

Tony felt the woman stir and wake; he groaned. She must have heard him because she laughed and he felt a slender hand patting his arm.

"I know, but the girls do love Christmas."

When a cry from another part of the house pricked his ears, he heard the woman moan and watched her sit up.
"Well, the little prince is up. I'll take care of him, but you're in charge of coffee." She didn't wait for his reply, but brushed past the two brunette little girls now standing inside the room, stroking the tops of their heads as she passed them. When she reached the doorway, she turned and leaned on it, looking right at him.

Tony was struck by how beautiful she was. She had big, bright, blue eyes; full lips, and her hair trailed halfway down her back. Her long, slender figure didn't offer the slightest evidence that she had birthed all his children.

She smiled. "Merry Christmas, Anthony." After gracefully blowing him a kiss, she left, while one of the little girls chattered away behind her.

The other little girl grinned at him. She looked about six and was missing one of her front teeth. "Merry Christmas, Daddy. See what Santa put in my stocking?" She lifted up a small, black teddy bear. "Isn't he cute? His name is Mr. Fluffykins."

As she said it, the little girl who left came back into the room.

"Nuh-uh! Mine's name is Mr. Fluffykins!"

The two girls started to argue and Tony realized with a start they were twins. He rolled over to the other side of the bed and sat up. There, standing next to his legs, as if waiting for him to see her, was a little girl with huge brown eyes that couldn't have been older than four. In her hands was a weird-shaped object that she obviously wrapped herself. When she spoke, it was the most angelic voice Tony had ever heard.

"Merry Christmas, Daddy. I made this for you."

Tony's heart melted. He leaned down. "Thank you, sweetheart; let's put it under the tree." Then in a fluid movement, he stood up and tucked the little girl under one arm.

She giggled. The two older girls were still arguing as Tony passed them on his way out.

It was about eight in the morning, and all the presents had been opened, littering the living room floor in crumpled paper. Three giggling, little girls sat by the tree, playing with new Barbie dolls; and his wife sat in the chair next to him, feeding a five-month-old baby boy.

Tony sat and watched them all, sipping his hot chocolate, completely at peace. This was a good dream, and he never had any like it before, but he hoped that would change. He set the half empty Christmas mug on the table between the two huge, black leather chairs.

As he did so, he heard a woman clearing her throat, and looked over at his wife, who was fully concentrating on the baby. He looked at the girls, but they were paying no attention.

"Try again."

He almost jumped. Turning in his chair, he saw a grinning Christina standing behind him, her arms behind her back and still wearing the dark red lingerie. She moved one arm and waved, obviously patronizing him. He looked around again, but his family didn't seem to notice the woman. He looked back at her, about to say something, but she cut him off with a finger on her lips.

"They can't see me, Two-Tone, I may be in your dream, but I'm not part of it. Can we go somewhere quiet?"

Tony looked at his wife for a long moment until he heard Christina make a frustrated noise.

"Fine."

He watched her walk over and lean behind his wife before whispering in her ear, her hand moving around the other woman's head. When she straightened back up, his wife turned her head to him and smiled.

"You look so tired, Anthony; the girls won't be needing you to put things together for a little while; why don't you go take a nap?"

Sighing, Tony stood up, kissing his wife's forehead. He glared at Christina, who was still beaming at him and left the room.

Christina entered the room only seconds after Tony, and sat down on the bed, facing him, the huge grin still on her face.

Tony rolled his eyes. "What?"

Her grin only grew wider. "Such a family man. Your dreams show you what you really want, Tony; remember that. They are all adorable, by the way, and that youngest girl looks so much like you. There's no trace of doubt she's yours."

She laughed and Tony couldn't help but smile.

"I'm glad you're okay." He reached out and hugged her.

Christina laughed a little harder this time. "Two-Tone, I'm already dead. There isn't much they can do to me."

Tony let go of her and his smile vanished. "No, I don't know you are dead. You were abducted, but no body was found. You could still be alive.

Christina tilted her head. "Tony, okay, if you insist on being logical about this." She straightened on the bed and put her hands in her lap. "How often is someone abducted, and I am just guessing, but it must have been several months now, and later found alive? There was a lot of blood in the car."

He fought to ignore the sinking feeling in his chest. "No, you could have staged it and run away."

All she did was raise her eyebrows.

Rubbing the bridge of his nose, Tony forged on. "I understand you are my subconscious way of dealing with my friend's death, but I can't believe you're dead until I see the proof."

Chris blinked at him. "Subconscious, huh? I guess it wouldn't matter if I insisted that I am, in fact, not a figment of your imagination."

Tony shook his head. "That is my conversation with Will talking. Next, you'll claim you knew your death was coming because you were psychic."

"Who said that?" She looked almost disgusted.

Tony shifted, to look at her better. "Someone at the precinct."

There was a pause before she spoke. "Your partner?"

Tony gave her a confused look. What was it with these people and his partner? "No."

She relaxed slightly and dropped her gaze. "Then who?"

Tony sighed. "Will, the intern. It's what we discussed in our conversation. But you are merely a figment of my subconscious mind, so you should already know that."

Her head shot up, and her face lit up like a light bulb. Tony found himself wondering just for a second if she were real.

"So, he's okay then?"

Tony was slightly confused "Yeah, he's fine."

A sharpness slid onto her features. "Tony, what if I could prove to you that I am really here, and not just your mind's way of grieving?"

Tony frowned, crossing his arms. "And how would you do that?"

She leaned in and her hands clenched in excitement. "With something you can prove. Did Will tell you how we knew each other?"

Tony just shook his head.

Her face became more animated. "Good. We are cousins on my mother's side. That is why we have different last names. We are both only children, so we kind of adopted each other. Some of our cousins used to call him 'little mouse' until he went to college, because he was so small and meek."

Dread began creeping into Tony's stomach. Yes, Will was meek, but the rest of that was nothing he heard before. He was almost positive Chris from high school never spoke much about her family. This could quite possibly just be information floating around in the recesses of his brain. Nonetheless, he was sure it was *new* information.

"Okay, let's assume this is not something Chris told me when we were younger…"

"Will is engaged! He became engaged six months ago to a girl he has been seeing for three-and-a-half years. He proposed on the Ferris wheel on the pier!"

Chris cut in before he could finish his train of thought. Tony knew then that he might be speaking to a dead woman. The idea was chilling. All he had to do was verify that information with Will, and everything he knew about the world would be turned upside-down. Part of him really did not want to know.

He let out a few curses. "Okay, so if you're dead, aren't there other places you should be? I'm sorry, Chris, but why are you here?"

She looked as if she were ready to make a snide comment, but thought better of it. Instead, she exhaled. "So you believe me?"

Tony sighed. "I am suspending disbelief until I can talk to Will."

She grinned with relief. "That is all a girl can ask. I'm here to try and help you. Before I died I… I had dreams about you being in trouble and needing help. I knew I had to help in any way I could. But as you can tell, things did not exactly pan out ideally. So, from time-to-time, Cheryl might pay you a visit and try to help you, as a favor to me, and as a friend to you. However, she is rather busy, and not in the safest situation herself, so she will only help when she can. That's why I am visiting your dreams. I'm here to help you in any way I can."

Tony thought for a second. He was not sure whether he should mention he encounter at the store. "Why do I need help?"

Chris sighed and ran a hand though her hair. "Because bad things are happening, and you're a very powerful individual, whether you believe it or not. You need someone to help you, for lack of a better word, and train you on how to defend yourself. Normally, we would do this very slowly, and ease you into it, but as you can see, I am no longer available."

"So you're telling me Cheryl isn't safe, for some reason, which I am sure you are not going to tell me; and you have some kind of psychic power that told you that I have powers? And having said powers puts me in danger, even though I have no knowledge or belief that I could possess such powers? Does that about sum it up?"

Tony may have been able to swallow talking to a dead woman, somehow, as absurd as that sounded, but the rest of it was far too difficult to believe. He gave her a look that told her exactly what he was thinking.

"I know, it sounds insane, but think about it, Tony. Haven't there been times when you just knew something was off? When you knew a suspect was lying? When you knew to turn left, instead of right?"

If Tony were truthful with her and himself, the answer would have been yes. But that was just good cop sense, and not some supernatural power. Normally, he would have asked Rick if he thought his cop sense was better than average, but Rick wasn't exactly himself yesterday.

Sighing, he rubbed his face. "Look, Chris, the idea that I might actually be talking to a dead woman is crazy."

He held up his hand when he saw her start to protest.

"But I am going to verify what you told me with Will. If you are indeed talking to me from beyond the grave, then we can discuss why you think I might be in trouble. But until then, I am capable of looking after myself."

She looked extremely tired. He started to ask if she were okay, but she cut him off.

"That is completely reasonable. I just don't want to wait too long, and I'm not sure how consistently I can visit. I have to get going; I am not strong enough to stay very long." Then she stood up a little too slowly and headed to the closed bedroom door.

As she reached it, Tony asked. "What is it that put you and Cheryl in danger anyway?"

She turned to him as she stepped out of the room.

"Don't worry, you are totally different than Cheryl and me, if that's what you're worried about. Hearing the name of our condition won't do you much good because you won't find any information on it, but it's because we are Nym."

Then she left, leaving Tony yelling her name behind her.

Chapter 7

Tony awoke from the dream, his body tight with tension. He sat still for a moment and realized his cell phone was going off, which must have been what woke him. He groped blindly for it before snatching it up and holding it only inches from his face so he could see the number on the glowing screen. It was the captain. Tony tapped the screen to answer. A whole new wave of tension ran through him.

"Hollownton? It's about damn time! I've been trying to get a hold of you and Nelson for the past fifteen minutes. Get down here now! There's been another attack; only this time, the guy survived and there's a witness."

Rushing with adrenaline, Tony mainly registered that they had a witness, which could be very good.

"I'll be there in ten."

Tony was hanging up the phone when he heard the captain say something else.

"What, sir?"

There was a pause, and the other man's voice sounded weary.

"The newest victim is Will."

There was another pause before the dial tone came on. Tony just sat in the dark for a minute. *The victim was Will.* That meant Will knew much more than he told Tony. *Was that why Chris was so surprised to hear Will was okay? Did she know?* Dread and something close to fear colored Tony's thoughts. He had to talk to Will.

When he got down to the precinct, the atmosphere was a mix of sadness and anger. The air was too full of emotion for three am. The anxiety he sensed was almost unbelievable. But it was understandable, since the killer went after one of their own.

The captain swiftly approached Tony and started walking him into one of the interrogation rooms.

"I know this isn't your area, but I want you to talk to the witness. She refuses to say anything if there is anyone outside the room listening in; and even then, she barely speaks. I figure she'll talk to you since you've actually seen the other victims."

Tony looked at the captain's face. He appeared worn out, like he hadn't slept in days.

"So no one else will be listening? Where's Rick?"

Binns stopped in front of the door to Interrogation Room One.

"No, no one else, so get her testimony on tape. And I haven't the foggiest idea where Nelson is; he's not answering any calls. After I got a hold of you, I sent two uniforms out to his house. I will let you know when they report in. He'll be out of a job here soon if he continues to push my buttons."

Tony wanted to find his partner and shake some sense into him, but he cleared his head; he had other more important things to worry about. Rick was digging his own grave. The captain opened the door to the room, and Tony took a deep breath as he hoped for good luck.

The tiny room had all white walls except the black, two-way mirror on the far side of the room. There was no one behind it. The tile floor was off-white, and a wooden table was placed horizontally in the middle of the room; with two metal chairs on each side. The one closest to the door was empty, but sitting in the other was a woman who could not have been any older than twenty-five.

The woman before him looked devastated. Her cheeks were streaked with old tears. Under different circumstances, Tony might have described her as perky and bright. She had short, stylish, blond hair that looked wilted from the long night. Her eyes were probably a bright, sparkling blue, but now looked glassy. She seemed like the type of person who smiled easily, with a smile that could've been contagious, but not today. Today, she looked utterly defeated.

Tony couldn't really blame her under the circumstances. However, he couldn't stop wondering how she ended up with a guy like Will. That is, assuming they were together, which he did, simply judging by her expression. Chris's words came back to him and he looked down to see a ring, but her hands were concealed under the table. Tony shut the door behind him as he strove to restrain the shock and fear coursing through his body. He was being visited by a dead woman.

The woman watched him with watery eyes as he sat down across from her.

"You're just going to ask me the same questions as the other two did. Why am I still here? Why can't I be with Will? He needs me!"

Tony's heart went out to her and he held out his hand. "I'm sorry you've been delayed. What is your name, by the way?"

The woman took his hand, using the one that didn't have a Kleenex in it. There it was, flashing under the tissue: a diamond engagement ring. Tony struggled to look her in the eyes without giving away his thoughts.

"I'm Tiffany Watson."

She had a very firm handshake as she made eye contact, despite the unshed tears in her eyes.

Tony nodded as he lowered his hand. "It's nice to meet you, Ms. Watson. I'm Detective Hollownton."

Her glistening eyes widened as a small, tentative smile appeared on her face.

"Anthony Hollownton? You're *the* Tony Hollownton?"

Tony nodded, feeling slightly confused.

Her smile grew. "Oh, I've heard so much about you, enough to feel as if I already know you."

Tony nodded again. "From your boyfriend?"

She made a kind of laughing noise and opened her little, black purse, pulling out a photo. "Not boyfriend, fiancé." She handed him the picture.

There was his confirmation, not that the ring wasn't evidence enough. But her words helped solidify things in his mind.

The picture she showed him was of Will and her. The couple were on a beautiful lawn in front of a cream-colored house. She was grinning, and her whole face shone. She was wearing a red sundress. Behind her stood Will with his arms around her shoulders and his face against the side of her head. He appeared the same except his hair was spiked, and he wasn't wearing glasses. He had a very masculine smile, and was clad in normal, casual clothes. The way Will carried himself in the picture was completely different to the Will Tony knew. In the photo, he seemed very relaxed and oozed confidence, and could've been the type of guy Tony would have even liked to hang out with, if Tony did that. Clearly, the man in the picture was not the same guy Tony worked with.

She pointed to the house that was visible in the picture, "That's his cousin's house. This was taken at her last birthday party." Then she took the picture and gave it a kiss before placing it back in her purse.

Tony just sat listening. If he could make her comfortable, perhaps, he could get answers from her. At least, that was his logic. In reality, his head was spinning. *Will's cousin was a she.* What more confirmation did he need? Tony tried to pay better attention. Yes, Chris was dead; and yes, she was actually visiting him from beyond the grave. Yes, she was related to his case somehow. But right now, he needed to concentrate on catching the killer.

She looked back up at him, and the small smile returned to her face. She wiped her eyes.

"She talked about you too. More than Will did. As if she were the one that saw you everyday." Tiffany gave a little chuckle.

Tony heard what came out of his mouth before he registered that he was saying it.

"Who?"

She waved her hand in the air. "Why, Christina, of course."

Tony's stomach dropped. There was no other way to rationalize the dreams.

Tiffany leaned across the table and Tony followed suit.

"You've been her friend for years, so you know their little family secret, right?"

Tony leaned back and nodded. He wasn't sure he liked where this was going.

"Amazing, isn't it? That much power?"

Tony really did not want to hear more about Chris's psychic gift. He was having enough trouble accepting the idea that she really was visiting him. Her so-called possession of telepathic powers was a bit much. He worried others might walk into the observation room, and feared they would think he was wasting time while a killer stayed on the loose out there.

"Tiffany, I have to ask about what happened earlier."

She shifted uncomfortably in her chair as he turned on the tape recorder.

"Explain everything that occurred last night from start to finish."

Tiffany fidgeted with the tissue in her hand, but kept eye contact.

"I was out with some friends of mine. I've already given their names. Anyway, I promised Will I would stop by tonight, because he said he had something to talk to me about. I'm not sure what it was. So I got there about two, and was letting myself in. I have a spare key. As I was unlocking the door, I heard weird noises, then a door slammed, then silence. I said a quick prayer and went in with the pocketknife Will gave me, which I always keep in my purse. I held it out in front of me. When I saw there was no one in the apartment, I went into the bedroom and found Will hanging on the wall with his arms and legs tied, and his wrists slit, and that's when I called nine-one-one.

"That's all, I didn't see anything or anyone else. I did not hear anything else except the door slamming. Will does not have a back door, so I guess the door could have been a window. That's all that happened. May I go to the hospital now?"

Tony stood up and turned off the recorder. "I'll see what I can do."

Though she was vague on the details, it sounded like she really might have just missed the killer. He wanted to talk to Will before checking out his apartment.

As he was getting up to leave, Tiffany grabbed his arm. "Off the record, he was talking to me before the ambulance got there. He told me he would survive because of what he was. He also said his attackers didn't know that, and probably expected him to bleed out."

She let go of his arm and leaned back in her chair. "Just thought you should know."

Clearly, she thought Tony knew more about these superhuman abilities than he actually did. He wondered why Will did not admit to having any extraordinary abilities, himself. *Why did Will believe it would help him heal faster?* More questions he needed to ask him. *Was their family involved in some kind of cult? Was that why Chris was abducted?*

Tony nodded, and sat back down, turning the recorder on again. He watched as Tiffany stiffened.

"Was anything out of place in Will's apartment?"

She shook her head. "No, nothing at all."

Tony reached for the recorder "Thank you, Ms. Watson."

After he clicked off the recorder, he opened his mouth, only to close it again.

Her eyes showed concern as she said, "He'll be okay, so that's not it. What's wrong?" Tony sighed, not sure whether he should ask. "What happened to Christina? I mean, I know she's dead, but does anyone know what happened?"

Pain appeared on her face as she took a deep breath. "You don't want to know."

Tony straightened in his chair, and a thread of anger ran through him. "Yes, I do."

She only shook her head.

His fist slammed on the table. "Damn it! Yes, I do!"

She jumped, he startled himself as well.

He rubbed his face with his hands. "Please… tell me."

She sighed. "Fine, but I warned you. The way it was explained to me was the Culeen wanted her in the local community. I don't know what made them pick Chris, but they took her. There was a bonus because she was pregnant, and the Culeen hate Nym babies. But Culeen poison doesn't really work on the Nym. Christina had some kind of genetic immunity. That was probably why they killed her." She shuddered before adding, "Not to mention, she had contact with you, or she was supposed to. You are on the Culeen hit list too, Tony. No one is sure why." She kept eye contact with him the entire time, but began tearing up again and clutched her hands together.

Tony's head was spinning. Tiffany was saying the Culeen, which Will said were only a myth, were actually real. Not only that, but they hated the Nym people. He needed to find out what that meant. The last thing Seattle needed was some kind of gang war between people that most believed were mythical creatures. And apparently, they had it in for him. Was it because he was a cop? Tony now had more questions than answers, as well as a bull's eye on his back. He needed to find out much more about these secret groups.

"Thank you," was all he could say as he got up and left the room. He had to talk to Will. Hell, he needed to talk to Chris. He couldn't believe he intended to question a dead woman.

No sooner had Tony shut the door than the captain came up to him, giving him no time to think about what he just heard.

"Well?" The older man looked tired and impatient. "Did she give you anything?"

Tony handed him the tape recorder. "Let her go; we can always speak to her later. She knows very little. Now give me Will's address so I can check his apartment out."

Binns took the recorder, and Tony closed his eyes and wiped his face. When he opened them again, the captain was watching him, and after a second, he nodded.

"I'll get you that address," the captain replied as he turned and walked to his office.

Tony sighed again and moved toward his desk. He thought he might as well read more about the other victims to see if there were any similarities to Will.

As he unlocked his second drawer, he heard a female clearing her throat behind him. He saw flashes of Chris standing behind the couch in his dream. He turned to find Tiffany there about two feet behind him. Both hands were clasped in front of her, showing off her nails, which were the same color as her dress.

"Um, Tony, I know it's not appropriate for me to ask this, but would you go with me to the hospital? My car is still at Will's since I was driven here in a cop car."

Tony knew before she finished he would say yes, not only because it gave him a chance to question Will about the attack, but also because she was a woman in need of help. That was something Tony just couldn't refuse.

"Sure, just give me a minute."

Her relief was visible as he slammed the drawer shut. Standing up, Tony saw the captain approaching.

"Here, Hollownton." The older man handed him a small piece of paper that was ripped around the edges.

Tony took it and shoved it into his pants right pocket.

Binns turned to Tiffany and gave a quick nod, saying, “Ms. Watson.” Then he headed back to his office.

It was a ten-minute drive from the station to the hospital. The first eight minutes or so were spent in silence. Then Tony felt his thoughts wandering back to the interview. Tiffany showed him a picture of Will and her at Chris’s party, but she made it sound as if it were a long time ago. If memory served him correctly, her birthday was on the first of February, which was only about three months ago.

“When was the last time you saw Chris?”

She blinked at him for a few seconds, as if he must have startled her, but she swiftly recovered. “Sorry, It’s just that no one calls her Chris except Gavin and Cheryl. It caught me off guard. The last time I saw her,” she trailed off.

He took the opportunity to interject, “I’m assuming, Gavin was her husband?”

She nodded at him vaguely.

He didn’t show any surprise that Tiffany knew Cheryl, but wasn’t sure whether it was a good or bad reaction.

“About eight months ago, give or take.”

Tony nodded. “Have you seen Gavin since Chris disappeared?”

"A few days ago, but he’s laying low because of grief and the attack.” Sorrow slowly began seeping back into her voice. He parked in the hospital’s short term parking, and couldn’t imagine how Chris’s husband must have felt.

As he auto-locked the doors on his dark blue Trooper, he sensed, rather than heard, a rustling. Trying to look everywhere at once, he put one hand on his gun and the other on Tiffany’s back, so she could be maneuvered out of the way easier.

Then his eyes locked on to some movement on his left, where he noticed some bushes, which were perfect to hide behind. All he saw was something moving *above* a bush. It could have been a shadow, but Tony knew better than to ignore his instincts.

He could not see anything, but he knew Tiffany and he were not alone in the lot. His adrenaline surged and he whispered a string of curses under his breath. There was more than one being; he could feel it. Starting to jog, he urged Tiffany to keep up with his pace. He knew there was no way he could take on more than two, but at least, if they managed to get inside the hospital, he could see them and make sure Tiffany was safe. He began to move faster.

"Tony? Tony, what is it? Four-inch stilettos are not made for running."

Wasn't she scared? Didn't she realize what was going on?

No, a little voice in his head replied. She obviously couldn't see them.

As they reached the doors, he ripped one open and he and Tiffany stumbled inside. At some point, he pulled his gun and pointed it at the shutting door. He could hear Tiffany chattering at him, but her words didn't register.

"Get back!" was all he could manage to say before he concentrated on the black figures outside, which were now moving toward the hospital doors.

He could make out about a dozen figures, slithering, creeping, or just plain walking towards him. He sensed it was like a game for them, and they took their time, expecting him to fail.

Tony's adrenaline was pumping furiously through his veins. It was overriding the panic that told him there was no way to get out of this alive. These were supposedly mythical creatures with poisonous venom, and he had no idea how to fight them. Tony only hoped he was the person they sought, but planned to take as many as he could down with him, just in case.

He faintly heard Tiffany praying behind him, although he could not make out the exact words. He was certainly not about to take his attention off the creatures outside to find out.

The first of the snarling black figures reached the lit entryway. Tony aimed his gun at the creature's head. As his finger began to curl around the trigger, there was a popping sound so loud, Tony feared his eardrums might burst. He put his arms up to cover his ears, but the extreme pressure turned to burning. He didn't remember falling to his knees, or closing his eyes. Dropping his hands on the floor, he was still clutching the gun as he tried to maintain his balance. Underneath all the pressure, Tony could swear he heard that damn chanting. He concentrated on it, picking it out of everything else going on around him.

As quickly as it came, the pressure subsided, and the chanting stopped. Tony could hear normally again. He concentrated on his breathing. He felt almost positive he was still alive. He swung into a crouch, aiming his gun at the doors. There were no glass panes in them; as if the windows were deliberately removed. They were shattered so completely, there was nothing left behind in any of the frames. Outside, the parking lot was empty, and there were no Culeen that he could see anywhere. Although there were no more immediate threats, Tony's adrenaline kept pumping.

He felt two hands on his back. "Tony? Tony, are you all right? Did some of the glass hit you as it shattered?"

Still holding his gun, he stood up and searched the corridor. There was nothing to see: no shadowy figures, or angry creatures anywhere. *Where could they have gone?*

"What happened?" he demanded, turning toward the entryway. He leaned out one of the doors with his gun poised in a low, ready position.

Nothing looked out of the ordinary, but a thin layer of shattered glass. There were no glass shards inside, as if the panes were just pushed out. He scanned the parking lot from where he stood; but saw nothing except a few light poles and his Trooper.

As he leaned back inside, something caught his eye. When he looked directly at it, there was nothing. He blinked and shook his head; something was very wrong with this picture. He opened his eyes and glimpsed something from the corner of his eye. He tried to look without concentrating too hard. *Steam.* It was steam, as if someone were putting out a fire. He took a deep breath and unfocused his eyes, and the only word that escaped his mouth was one long curse. With his eyes unfocused, he could see at least half a dozen places where steam was rising up from the asphalt into the sky.

Refocusing his eyes, he turned back to Tiffany, who appeared at least one shade paler.

"What happened?" he repeated as he approached her.

She blinked at him with a puzzled expression and took a step back. "Y-y-you were freaking out about something, and pushed me in here so hard, I nearly fell over. Then, when I asked what was going on, you yelled at me to get down and pointed your gun at the door. You stood there for a second or two, then aimed your gun and said something about chanting."

Tony was looking outside, but his head snapped back at her last words. "What!?"

She nodded before continuing. "Yeah, you were just standing there with your gun pointed outside at nothing. Then, all the outside light bulbs and the glass in the entryway shattered. It must have been just the outer shells that burst because the lights were still shining. When the glass exploded, you fell to your knees and covered your ears, groaning as if you were in pain. The lights were shining so brightly, I couldn't even see you after that. Then, about a minute later, you stopped groaning. It was as if someone hit a switch because the lights went back to normal. Then I ran over to see if you were okay. I mean, you were so close to the glass, but you don't even have a scratch."

Of course not, Tony thought, although nothing actually made any sense. *Why couldn't she hear the chanting? Or see the Culeen outside? Where did they go?* Was Tony losing his mind? He did not want to spend too much time on that last question although he was leaning toward the affirmative. Frustrated, he headed further into the hospital. Maybe Will could give him answers.

It took Tiffany a second or two to catch up with him. She didn't look frightened or intimidated by him.

"If I did everything you say I did, why aren't you afraid of me?"

Tony knew the question was harsh, but he didn't have the patience to put it nicely. He heard her make a noise and turned his head to look at her.

She was chuckling at him, or trying to repress it and failing.

"What?!" This time, he knew he sounded much more irritated and gruff.

She managed to control herself and grin. "Tony, I'm not a virgin."

He nearly stumbled. She started laughing again.

"Let me rephrase that. I've been around the Nym long enough to see all manner of weird things. After a while, you get used to it. I'm just surprised you haven't, and that you reacted in pain by the chanting you heard. I have never heard of that before; although I never heard chanting except when one of them was directly in front of me.

"Granted, you looked kinda scary and were pointing a gun, but I knew it wasn't at me. So yes, I was scared, but then I put two and two together, and I just couldn't be scared of four."

She shrugged, no longer laughing.

Tony wasn't sure how to respond to that, so instead, he shelved it to the back of his mind with the other bits of information he intended to chew on later.

As they reached the nurses' station, Tiffany went ahead of him and smiled at the nurse, whose dark eyes and wrinkled face seemed hardened by years of seeing death.

"Hi, I'm here to see my fiancé, Will Nylan."

The older, gray-haired woman's eyebrows rose. "It's way past visiting hours; try again tomorrow."

Tony pulled out his badge and flashed it.

After a few seconds, the nurse nodded. "Room two-seventeen. Just take the elevator and turn right."

Tiffany smiled and bowed her head, "Thank you."

Tony walked about a step behind her to the elevator.

"You know, usually I ridicule the people who only ride the elevator up one floor. It's a shame Christina isn't here to make fun of us," Tiffany said, shrugging her shoulders. There was a visible, little twinge of pain at her statement, but she didn't retract it.

Tony's chest felt a little pang, which was fast becoming a familiar feeling.

Once the doors shut, Tony turned to look Tiffany in the face. "I want to meet him."

She went solemn, staring at the floor. "I don't know if that is an option."

Tony felt his face hardening. At least, she didn't pretend not to know what he meant.

"Why not? He could be important."

The doors opened and she stepped out, waiting for him to do the same before finally looking at him.

"It's not my choice, Tony; he contacts us, not the other way around. I can inform him of your wish, but I cannot guarantee anything. Gavin just hasn't been the same since… you know." She looked at him, her eyes pleading for him to accept what little she could offer.

Tony stayed in the elevator to calm himself. He wasn't angry with Tiffany, since she seemed pretty open with what she knew, but that was almost as bad as talking to one of the Nym. It left him frustrated and with very little to go on.

"Fine, call him and let him know that if he does not meet with me soon, I will go through all the official channels and he won't have any choice."

Despite all the hoops he might have to jump through, he would do it in a heartbeat.

Tiffany nodded sadly before walking into the hospital room.

What if the killer was the husband? What if he were somehow involved in killing her? Or arranged it and now was killing others? Did all the victims know Chris? Will did.

Those thoughts tugged at his brain. He did not want to believe that Chris would marry a man like that, but ten years was a long time. Either way, he and this Gavin needed to talk. Tony took a deep breath and pushed thoughts of Chris aside. Right now, he wanted his whole head on the case.

With a nod at the young uniform standing outside Room 217, Tony knocked on the door before entering. The door was partly open, but he remained polite anyway. The room had two beds, but only one of them was occupied.

In the bed nearer the door, Will was sitting up with a thick amount of gauze around his wrists. He looked very pale, but otherwise appeared normal. Tiffany sat in a chair facing the door, as close to the bed as possible. She was pressing Will's hand on her cheek. Tony almost felt bad for disturbing them.

"Grab a chair, Tony," Will said without even turning his head, which startled Tiffany.

Tony shut the door and sat with his back to it. *Not exactly safe,* he thought, but he did have a good view of the window; at this point, the window seemed as much a threat as the door.

Tony's first question was intended to be about the attack, however, that's not what came out.

"Why didn't you mention you were Nym after the translation came back from the first crime scene? Hell, why didn't you tell me you and Chris were related?"

Well, his professionalism just flew out the window, and Tony scolded himself.

Will turned to look at him. Tony's face was cold and blank.

"I don't advertise such things when there are beings out there that clearly hold a grudge. How did you find out?"

Will turned his face just enough to shift his gaze onto his fiancée. Tony felt the stirrings of anger, but he kept it in check. Before he could answer, however, Tiffany jumped in. She was looking Will in the eyes with a determined expression.

"Tony is not some stranger off the street. He deserves to know what is going on in this world, whether you see fit to tell him or not. The Nym are horrible about secrets; and these secrets could have put him in danger."

There were a few seconds of silence during which the two lovers seemed to contest the other's intentions. Will's shoulders slumped and he leaned back in the bed, moving his hand to hold Tiffany's hand, instead of her face.

With a sigh, he turned back to Tony. "She didn't want you to know, Tony. She didn't think it was wise for you to know the connection. I know she's dead, but it was still her wish." His voice seemed tired and strained. "As for being Nym, that's just something you do not tell a lot of people. Every Nym child learns that before they can even speak." Will looked away and stared down at the bed, an old pain appeared on his face.

Tony rubbed his chin. "Will, Tiffany didn't tell me you were Nym, or that you were even related; Chris did."

Will and Tiffany both looked at Tony with twin expressions of shock.

"When?" Tiffany's voice sounded hesitant.

Tony took a deep breath before answering. It was one thing to *think* a dead woman visited him, and quite another to say it out loud. "She visited me in a dream."

Tiffany tugged Will's arm so he looked at her, and asked, "Can she do that?"

Will shrugged, then winced. "Though I have never witnessed it firsthand, we have an aunt that claims she can do it. The real question is why." Will looked back at Tony, with more admiration than before.

Tony sensed Will knew more information than he was offering. But he did not have the foggiest idea what to ask. Ultimately, Tony decided to change the subject.

"Will, I need you to tell me everything about the attack. I mean *everything*; none of this asking the right question stuff." Tony pulled a small, black notepad and pen out of his jacket pocket.

Will shifted slightly and looked down at the bed. "I was reading a book written by one of the most popular Nym writers from the time I called Tiff, which was about nine, until the attack, at about one am."

Tony noted the times.

"Then, at about one, I," he suddenly became quiet and began to fidget with the hospital blanket with his free hand. Tony continued to look at the man's face, which seemed to tighten. Before Tony could push him further, Will turned to him, looking more like the intern he pretended to be: insecure and scared

"Tony, some Nym can sense trouble before it comes. I knew something was coming for me about five minutes before the knock on my door, and I prepared." Will went quiet again.

It took Tony several moments to figure out what the other man was implying. "They didn't know you were Nym?"

Will slowly nodded as Tony continued. "The other two victims had no warnings, so they couldn't protect themselves?"

Will nodded again. "Yes, and because I was able to, it will raise questions, along with the whole true sequence of events."

Then it hit Tony. Will's survival compromised his story.

Tony took a deep breath. "Okay, Will, tell me everything and then we'll see if something needs to be left out."

Will visibly relaxed and turned back to the bed. Tony took another deep breath as he closed his notepad. There was nothing he could safely write down, not yet anyway. If Will thought his membership in this secret society of psychics would cause him trouble at work, then Tony intended to humor him. Plus, who would believe a report that mentioned mythical creatures and psychic societies anyway? Tony was about to lie during an investigation, which was something he swore never to do, but there it was. If his growing hunches were correct, he wasn't sure how he could arrest a Culeen anyway.

"I sensed something evil coming for me. I knew that it was not just some rogue Culeen, running amuck. It was something much worse. So I put down my book, closed my eyes and concentrated. I'm not very skilled at it, but strong enough that I could sense what was coming. I felt the presence of two Culeen, each with a person they took control of. Then I touched something more powerful. It was like a black hole: there was no power, only a presence. That's how I knew it was bad. If it could shield itself that well, then it had to be pretty powerful.

"So I pulled my power back in before they could feel me checking them out and went into my room to grab a baseball bat. I brought it out and leaned it on the table, then grabbed my, for lack of a better phrase, spell book, and cast a spell over me and my apartment, preventing any information from getting to these creatures. As poorly skilled as I am, that took up most of the extra time the early warning allowed me. So once it was done, I put the book back and stood in my living room, holding the bat, and ready to fight. But they caught me off guard by knocking."

"Knocking?" Tony repeated.

Will nodded. "Yeah, I thought it was weird too. It's too polite for the Culeen. I could feel them outside my door, so I grabbed the bat and looked out the peephole. There were kids standing out there! Well, Girl Scouts, to be exact, three of them, dressed in full gear. They all looked about twelve. Anyone with any sense would have found that off. I mean Girl Scouts at one am? Really? Since I knew that was not what they were, I managed to push past their glamor and see what they really looked like. The two Culeen were side-by-side, a behind two trucker-looking guys. They were all flanking, what I understood to be, a Demon."

Tiffany gasped and tightened her grip on Will's hand. Tony wasn't sure how to react. That sounded pretty farfetched. "Can you describe it?"

Turning his head back to the bed, Will shut his eyes before struggling with the memory. When he spoke again, there was only the slightest hint of anger, but his eyes remained closed.

“They are not Demons in the religious sense. That is just a nickname of sorts, although there are some among us who disagree. They look exactly like what you would imagine a Demon should. There are two sub-species of Culeen: your run-of-the-mill, spitting, mind controllers; and their more powerful sister species, commonly known as Demons.

"Demons are ugly, black, wingless and almost twice the size of an average Culeen. They do not have to spit on you to glamor you. You might think you are looking at a beautiful woman, but in actuality, it is a Demon Culeen. They can also do the same sort of magic as we Nym. They are the more dangerous of the two, but there are fewer of them. I read a report once that estimated only one out of every hundred Culeen was Demon. Nym are able to see passed the glamor, and detect what they really are. But being as weak as I am, I have to put more effort in to it."

Tony wasn't sure how to handle Will’s information. On the plus side, it meant there was physically someone he could charge with the crime. However, that person might not be human. Part of Tony wanted to get up and leave now. Could it actually be possible that there was a mythical species running around? Or was this merely a drug-induced culture war between two secretive groups? It couldn't be an illegal substance, or Will could never have passed his drug tests. Tony wouldn't ask, but Will probably would not admit to drug use anyway.

"Once I saw past their glamor, I told them to go away. The Demon spoke in a throaty woman’s voice, saying ‘Now, little Willy, is that any way to play?’ Then she waved her hand and the door’s bolt slid open. I backed behind the door as it opened and managed to knock out one of the Culeen before it noticed me. I got the other one in the arm before the Demon had me floating in mid-air, as if it had me by the throat. Then it sent me flying into the nearest wall. The whole time they kept talking about how naughty I was to help the Nym; and going on about how weak the humans are.

“One of the Culeen was still conscious. They took some ropes the Demon must have hung from its arm before they tied me to the wall with a weird-looking staple gun. The Demon pulled out a long, thin knife and kissed it, saying some sort of spell I couldn't understand. Then, very slowly, it slit my wrists, as if to get it exactly right. I'm going to refrain from describing just how painful it was, but there must have been a pain enhancement spell on the knife. It was nearly through my second wrist when the Culeen frantically alerted the Demon that I wasn't bleeding as much as I should have.

"The Demon stopped what it was doing, stood up, and smelled me, saying, 'He has a human smell to him, but that means nothing.' It then licked the side of my wrist, and whispered 'Nym' like a curse, as its tongue began to burn where the blood touched it."

Will shuddered. "I think it enjoyed the feeling. Then it was swearing, I think, but I couldn't really understand it. Tiffany was standing outside and the Demon went still, and whispered, 'Company.' Before I knew what was happening, it bit into my side, and said, 'Someday we will finish playing.' They left through the window with the unconscious Culeen floating behind them, and that's when Tiff walked in."

Will finally looked back up at Tony.

"Okay, Will, a few more questions: first, how did it know your name? Second, explain the naughty thing. Third, Why would there be a spell on the knife? Fourth, why wouldn't you bleed as much? Fifth, why would its tongue burn, and why did it take a chunk out of your side? Sixth, Why did they leave just because Tiffany came? Finally, why not just kill you?" It all came out in one long breath.

Will squirmed in the bed. "There are reasons we keep so many secrets, and I do not want Tiff to hear them. I don't want to endanger her any more than I already have." Will sound tired now as if there wasn't much fight left in him.

Tony looked over at Tiffany. Her face was all for Will, in an expression of pure love. "Okay, baby, I haven't eaten in a while. I'll go down to the cafeteria."

Will turned to her and smiled with sincere gratitude as he lifted her hand to his mouth and gave it a loving kiss.

She stood, reluctantly pulling her hand away. “Tony?” It wasn’t until after she spoke that she turned to him. “I assume you're going to Will’s next? I would greatly appreciate a ride so I can get my car.”

Tony looked into her sad blue eyes and nodded. She forced a smile and walked away. Tony didn’t turn to watch her leave, but waited while Will did.

The room was silent for about half a minute before Will took a shaky breath. “God knows how much I love her.” He finally looked away from the door, his face blank.

“To answer your first question, I don't know. I have never met a Demon Culeen before. My best guess is that it has spies or informants somewhere. Next, I assume it has some agenda to kill off people who are friends or helpers to the Nym. I guess it did not realize I was Nym. It could have been trying to gain information about the local Nym community. But I doubt it, because I wasn’t asked any questions. Most of the Culeen and the Nym have been at war with each other for hundreds of years, although I do not know how it started."

Images of the wall in the first victim’s kitchen popped into Tony’s head. This was a connection he could use.

“The spell it cast I don’t think was just on the knife; it could have been on the whole room. I can’t be sure. All I can really tell you is: there was a spell at work. The lack of bleeding was because I’m Nym, and we just heal faster, so my blood began to clot, and that’s all. Nym blood, for one reason or another, burns the Culeen. The stronger the Nym, the stronger the burn. Their sudden departure, I think, was because they made a mistake when it came to me; and they didn’t know whether Tiff was Nym or not. It took a bite to mark me. Since I’ll heal, it will only leave a scar; but that scar could be used as an identifier, which could get me killed later.”

Will kept a blank face while he spoke; but now, he looked thoughtful. “I believe that answers all of your questions, unless I forgot some.”

Tony shook his head and pulled out his pen and pad again, writing as he spoke. “So let me get this straight. You called Tiffany at nine, asking her to come over, but since she was busy, she said she didn’t know when she could. So from about nine pm until about one am, you were reading on the couch. You heard strange noises coming from outside your door. You turned off the light, hoping to catch whoever it was off guard. As you rose to investigate, the door opened and three people entered who overpowered you. They hung you up on the wall; however, they were interrupted by Tiffany's arrival, so they left. They mistook you as a member of a secret society known as the Nym; and they claim to belong to a rival group called the Culeen. Is this correct?" Tony didn't look up from the pad of paper, but he was sure Will understood what he was doing.

"That's correct," Will said.

Tony looked at him. "Two more questions. First, I know it was rather dark, but what did your assailants look like? Second, how did they manage to leave without Ms. Watson seeing them?"

Will's face went blank. "There were two large white men, both around five-foot-ten with little hair; and the leader was a woman with long, auburn hair who stood about the same height." Will paused so Tony could finish writing. "Outside my bedroom window is the fire escape. If they knew the building at all, they'd surely know that."

Tony jotted that down and flipped the pad shut, putting it back into his pocket as he rose. "Thank you for your cooperation Mr. Nylan. You know how to get a hold of me if you remember anything else." Tony was ready to leave when he felt Will grabbing his arm. Turning back, Will looked worried.

"Tony, Chris always spoke very highly of you. Before she disappeared, she seemed worried, and said it was very complicated so she couldn't talk about it, even to me. Thank you for doing this; I know how hard it must be. You now know enough to be at risk. I wish I could return the favor, but I know nothing about your case." With the last word, Will released his arm, but kept eye contact a little longer before dropping his gaze.

Tony did not reply, but just left the room; he didn't have the faintest idea of what to say to that. Once he was back on the first floor, Tony followed the signs to the cafeteria. When he reached the cafeteria's double doors, he checked his watch. It was quarter to five and he almost couldn't believe it. He spent over an hour in Will's room and still had to check the crime scene. Tony pushed open one of the doors as he mentally kissed any chance at sleep goodbye.

He didn't see Tiffany immediately, so he turned to his left where all the food was offered. He headed straight for the pop, and passed the machine that held too many kinds of coffee. He needed a caffeine fix, but coffee was not an option. People always said his avoidance of, let alone non-addiction to, the bean-derived beverage, was pure sacrilege.

Tony shook his head to clear it as he paid the cashier. This case just kept getting more complicated. Opening his drink, he looked around, trying to spot Tiffany. She was sitting in the booth furthest away, next to a wall that was mostly windows, with a door leading outside directly behind her. She had her head down and appeared to be reading something.

As he joined her in the booth, he realized she was bent over a small e-reader. After a few seconds, she closed it up and carefully put it back in the olive green purse beside her in the booth. Sighing, she grabbed the warm beverage cup in front of her with both hands. Tony opened his bottle and took a swig. When he set the bottle down on the table, he heard her chuckle softly.

"That's a unique choice for this time of day." She brought the cup to her face and took a sip.

Tony grunted, "Oh? And what do you have?"

She put her cup down and smiled earnestly at him. "It's a soy chai tea from the Starbucks counter; would you like to try it?"

Tony grunted again and took a bigger swig of pop. "No."

She chuckled. After a few minutes of silence, Tiffany looked up at Tony. "I know you probably have questions for me or something, but before all that, I want to ask you something."

Tony raised an eyebrow at her. "Yes?"

"How did you meet Christina? I mean, I know it was in high school, but how did it actually happen? Christina would never tell us, she just got a faraway look and grinned."

Tony choked on the swig he just gulped. Tiffany giggled as he started coughing.

"Well, that's a better reaction than I expected."

Tony took another swig to calm his throat. "Why do you ask?" he inquired, trying to keep his face blank.

Tiffany grinned at him. "Her reaction to you; and besides, there are bets going around among some of the cousins."

Tony just looked at her. "Okay, well, it was the very beginning of freshmen year and I had just gotten a part in the play, as did Chris. Incidentally that was also the only play I tried out for, but that's a different story. Anyway, we were cast as love interests."

There was an eruption of giggling from across the table. "Oh, that's priceless."

Tony rolled his eyes. "Glad you like it. Anyway we were both fourteen; and we didn't have a kissing scene or anything like that, but still. I often tried to start conversations with her, but she would just get up and walk away, totally ignoring me. It wasn't until later that I learned she was just really nervous about the love interest thing.

"So, on the first day, we reached 'the scene' where we had to get all 'lovey-dovey' as the teacher put it. The teacher told us to hold on and got up to make a call or something. As soon as she left the room, one of the minor characters, this tall, tubby guy with blond, curly hair, stormed on stage and shoved me. It caught me off guard, and that's the only reason I fell. So, as I began getting up, this guy was yelling at me about how I tried to steal his girl, and now I had to pay.

"I got up and just as I prepared to pound him, this little brunette slid in front of me and started screaming at the guy. That totally caught me off guard also, and I took a step back. I realized it was shy, little Christina, yelling at a guy who had to be twice her size. If I hadn't been so confused and angry, I think I would have laughed. I remember hearing her say, 'You overgrown idiot! You'd think after shooting you down for the fiftieth time, you'd finally get the idea.'

"He then did something very stupid. He pushed her slightly out of the way and said, 'This is between me and him because your mine, not his.' Well, at that point, two things happened: One, I punched him hard enough to break his nose; and two, Christina kicked one of his legs out from under him. His fall made a very loud noise, especially with the applause that followed. It was loud enough to bring the teacher running in.

"All the kids defended me, and told her that the guy just randomly picked a fight with me. So there were no repercussions for me, but he got thrown out of the play. The next day at practice, Chris came up and introduced herself before shaking my hand. That same day, Cheryl came up to meet me as well. She was on the set crew and witnessed the whole thing. So, yeah, that's how I met Chris."

Tiffany was grinning, and when he finished, she clapped. Rolling his eyes, Tony grabbed his soda before sliding out of the booth. As it was, he couldn't get to the crime scene until six, and he had reports to fill out, as well as new information to process. Tiffany stood up too, grabbing her coat.

As they reached the lobby, Tony noticed the broken glass was already replaced. It seemed odd to fix it so quickly, but he didn't think too much of it as they headed outside. Tony kept his hand on his gun all the way to the car, but nothing happened.

Nothing jumped out at them.

Nothing seemed off.

As he unlocked the doors, he got a weird feeling on his right side. Tiffany was getting into the car and he turned. There was a lamppost behind him, about seven spaces away, and he detected a movement in the light, like it had a presence. At first, he could have sworn there was someone standing at the edge, but no silhouette was visible. Shaking his head, he climbed into the car.

This time, their entire drive was wrapped in silence. Tiffany just sat looking straight ahead, with one thumb rubbing her purse. Tony didn't feel much like talking either, so he let the silence be. Although the sun was just beginning to rise, there were plenty of cars all over the roads.

Will's apartment complex surprised Tony. It was north of the city on the edge of a suburb. The complex looked less than five years old, and appeared to cater to the upper-middle class. He didn't even question how Will could afford to live there. Tony noted the nice cars as Tiffany directed him toward the back of the complex.

"You can park where my car is now; just let me move it." Tiffany turned back to him once she was out of the car. "It was nice to finally meet you, Tony, and thank you. You know which apartment is his, right?"

Tony nodded and she shut the door. Tiffany walked to a nearby driveway with a red Volkswagen Bug parked in it. It looked fairly new. As the Bug pulled away, Tony parked in the driveway and fished the address out of his pocket. The apartment was on the fourth floor, which seemed to be the top.

When Tony got to the fourth floor, he immediately saw which of the six doors was Will's. There was caution tape across the door and a lone officer standing outside. Tony didn't recognize the young man with blond, curly hair as a rookie from the precinct, but felt positive, judging by his appearance, the guy had to be a rookie.

The rookie looked too calm, but stood stock still as Tony approached.

"Sir," was all he said as he opened the door for Tony.

The living room to Will's apartment looked unharmed. There were two oversized cream-colored chairs and a matching loveseat with a glass table in the middle. To the right side of the room stood a counter that divided the living room from the kitchen. The kitchen was modern and mostly silver and black.

The rookie stepped up beside him. "It's kind of odd, sir. Outside, they identified the blood as Mr. Nylan's and there is no other evidence at all, no fingerprints, or anything. Oh, but there was this, it was copied so I could give it to you."

Tony turned to the rookie whose outstretched hand held a small piece of paper with an address on it. It didn't make any sense. Tony never received a *copy* of the evidence.

"Where's the real thing? It could be important."

The rookie shrugged and smiled, lighting his face up and making him look even younger. The youthful, grinning face reminded Tony of the cherub stereotype often used in cartoons. Tony mentally shook himself as the rookie spoke.

"You never know, but someone will probably lose it, so you might as well make a copy." The rookie walked into the bedroom.

Tony followed the rookie and was about to demand what the guy was talking about, when he walked through the bedroom door.

Tony heard an echo of Will in his head: *Cast a spell over me and my apartment so no information could be provided to these creatures.*

It looked like he'd done too good a job. Tony walked into the bedroom, but stumbled as the chants began again in his head.

"Are you okay, sir?"

Tony nodded and tried to ignore the feminine voice he was hearing.

The rookie just smiled at him. "It's okay, sir, you get used to it."

Tony knew the rookie was referring to the blood, so he didn't say anything. It was hard, but he concentrated on the blood as he tried to get to work just to drown out the chanting voice. There were puddles on the carpet, although they were nowhere near as big as the others, and blood trails on the wall. That went along with what Will said. He looked at the holes in the wall. They were very deep and would have taken a lot of strength to make. Will said the leader was powerful. Tony knew after about two minutes of inspection that it would do him very little good.

He walked out of the room with the rookie on his tail. As soon as he crossed the threshold again, the chanting stopped dead. Tony felt his body relaxing and it was much easier to concentrate. He really needed to ask someone what the hell that was; but at the moment, he was almost too tired to care.

"Weird, huh? How he was able to survive that? Makes you wonder just how many could."

Tony didn't even turn. "Yeah, quite a miracle."

Once they were back outside the apartment, Tony turned to dismiss the rookie. "Look you can…"

The door to the apartment was closed behind him, but no one stood out in the hall. That woke Tony up. He reached out to the door, but it was locked, and there was police tape across the doorway.

"What the hell?"

He pulled out his cell phone and called Binns, who answered on the second ring.

"Binns." The captain never answered properly, like he was inferring, *you already know my rank; so I'm not wasting the time to say it.*

"Captain, it's Hollownton, and I'm at the crime scene."

"About damn time you got there, Hollownton! I had Winston out there waiting for you until after five-thirty! Where have you been?"

Tony opened his mouth to say he was here, but paused and looked down at his watch as he swore. It was six-forty-five.

"I take that to mean you haven't been watching the time. Damn irresponsible, Hollownton! Not that it matters anyway. Nothing was found, and I mean *nothing.* Even Will's blood was inconclusive."

Tony put his hand in his coat pocket, where he put the paper, which was still there. His body tensed. "Absolutely nothing was found? No blood? No papers?"

"What did I just say, Hollownton? Nothing was found. Now figure this thing out!" With that, the captain hung up.

Tony stood outside the door, his blood pumping ice. Nothing was found, and there was no one here to meet him; yet, he had an address, and a rookie let him into the crime scene.

Tony sat in his car. He couldn't decide what to believe. Reaching into his pocket, he pulled out the address again and looked at it. Tony didn't recognize it except that the zip code was about an hour away and near the national forest. His body was tired, but his mind would not let him sleep. Going back to the precinct seemed his only option. Starting the car, he sighed and tried to keep track of everything he knew, or thought he knew, about the case.

Chapter 8

Tony found himself in the bedroom he and his dream wife shared. This time, he was alone and reading a newspaper. He folded it down and jumped, banging his head against the wall. At the foot of the bed stood Chris in her usual attire, with her arms crossed under her chest. Tony rubbed the back of his head.

Amusement and sympathy played across her face. “Hello Two-Tone! Sorry about that. I wouldn’t have done all this,” she waved, indicating the room around them, “but when I left last night, you were freaking out and I got worried. I really shouldn’t be back so soon, but as I said, I got worried.” She glanced at the newspaper. “Anything worth reading?”

Tony softly leaned his head against the wall. He focused on his breathing to gain control of himself before he yelled at the woman in front of him. “First off, why do you keep running off? How are you supposed to be helping me? Tell me everything about the Nym.”

The look on her face told him he was talking like a cop at an interrogation. She blinked and seemed to recover, as Tony cursed himself. She went from being playful to defensive in a nanosecond. Her nails were digging into her arm and her left hip shifted forward, moving her upper body a few inches further from him. The changes were subtle and most people would have missed them, but Tony knew better. He also knew it meant she would become more difficult, which was not what he needed right now.

“I told you I wasn’t supposed to visit the living, but you’re my friend. I’m not sure how I can help you other than to give you all the information I can, and just be there for you. Why do you want to know about the Nym so much?"

Tony balled his hands into fists. She was giving him very little information about anything, and in this case, lives were at stake. “It’s important, okay? And those aren’t answers. I want real, full answers to what is happening.”

She physically took a step back and stood there, tense, as she watched him as if he were a predator. Then she went blank. Tony knew she was getting angry. She would probably leave without giving him any information at all.

"Tony, I don't know what's going on with you, but perhaps I'll come back in a few days, when you've calmed down."

She moved quickly towards the closed door. Tony felt himself boiling with anger. She could not just leave.

"No!" he growled as she reached for the knob.

There was a new power behind his voice. As soon as she made contact with the doorknob, it was as if she got electrocuted. Tony saw a flash of something blue that his mind did not really comprehend. It was too fast to get a good look at, but it still gave Tony a sinking feeling.

Christina flew back across the room and slammed into the far wall. Tony's concern for her replaced his anger as he leapt off the bed and fell onto his knees, straddling her legs in less than a second. He put his hands on either side of her face. He was positive she was just unconscious, then wondered if the dead could even lose consciousness. His answer came when she stirred and let out a moan. Her eyes fluttered open.

Once they focused on him, they were filled with fear and anger. "Where did you learn that?"

Tony could tell there was plenty more she wanted to say, but was holding her tongue, which was probably a good thing. "Learn what? What was that? Are you okay?"

Tony watched her closely as her curiosity and confusion replaced fear and anger.

"You've blocked me, Tony." She said it as if it should have made sense to him.

When he just looked at her, she sighed, and her face tired.

"I'm fine, Two-Tone. What happened is you somehow gained control of your dream world. I can't leave until you let me. Since you don't want me to leave, I can't. It also means that no one can enter your dreams without obtaining your permission either. Which, for the most part, is a good thing; except for me wanting to leave."

She wasn't trying to get up or make him move. She just sat against the wall, looking up at him.

"So that electric shock, or whatever, happened because I don't want you to leave yet? Why didn't that happen yesterday?"

Christina shrugged. He slowly stood back up and offered Christina a hand. She glanced at it, then up at his face, before standing. Once upright again, she crossed her arms and leaned against the wall. Tony shook his head; she was the same as in high school.

"So, since I'm stuck here, what do you want to know?"

Tony's first impulse was to yell at her, but instead, he sat down on the nearest edge of the bed. "Well, we'll start with your reaction to my not letting you leave; you were bluish or something."

Tony watched Christina push off the wall as she moved farther from him. She stared at the floor, with a worried expression. "What exactly did you see, Tony?"

He sat for a second just looking at her, knowing he wasn't going to like her answer.

"Just a flash of light blue. It was blurry, but bigger than you."

She was chewing on her lip and still not looking at him.

"Why?" he asked.

Her arms moved around her, turning into a self-soothing hug. "What you saw was something most people have no idea exists. And for those that do, extremely few have the ability to see it on their own." She stopped moving and looked up at him. It seemed as though she were only moments from a panic attack. "Tony, you saw a Nym."

Silence filled the room, and a sense of dread churned Tony's stomach. "Okay, you mean you are a Nym, and I saw you get an electric shock?"

Chris started to fidget. "Yes, well, I am Nym. The thing is: Nym are not exactly human. But we can look human. It's what makes us fit in so well. The Culeen only have one form, and that's why they use glamor and tend to only come out at night." She paused for a second before taking a shaky breath. "The Nym have the human form, which is what you're seeing now, and their more powerful form. Most Nym, when exposed to power, jolt to the other form. That's what you saw: my other form." She wrapped her arms around her waist.

Tony exhaled slowly. His first inclination was to adamantly deny everything Chris was saying, and chalk it up to his imagination. But the heavy weight in his stomach told him he couldn't. He wanted desperately to believe that paranormal things did not exist in this world. But he didn't think he could continue to believe that if he were to solve the murders.

When he spoke again, his voice was barely above a whisper. “Show me, Christina.”

Tony watched in dread-filled horror as her skin drained of its color. Normally pale, now she was white, as if someone removed all her pigment. The blue light he saw seemed to be emanating from her veins. He could see most of them clearly and they glowed under her skin. Her eyes were bright green. If he’d seen that shade of color any other time, he would have thought they were contacts. The size of her eyes changed as well: they were huge and almond-shaped, but didn’t look out of place. Her lips were as white as the rest of her skin, and her long hair was the same shade as her eyes. However, within her hair were many other colors that played hide and seek with the light. The last startling change was the appearance of enormous, off-white wings. Tony never saw anything like them. There were about two dozen very long feathers per wing. Looking more closely at them, he noticed they had a tint, the same green as her hair and eyes.

Tony blinked and beheld her whole transformation through the panic that veiled his thoughts. There was a slight pull in his chest, which he identified with his friend. Although she looked so different, he could still see the Chris he knew. Then he noticed how shallow her breathing was, and assumed she was about as panicked as he was. Something about seeing how worried she was calmed Tony. Either he was having a psychotic break, or his need to comfort his friend overcame his own fears.

“Okay,” Tony said as calmly as he could. He did not know when he stood up, but he sat back down on the bed.

She looked at him, somewhat confused. “Okay? What do you mean ‘okay’?” Her voice rose about two octaves with the change, but it also sounded richer, and like there was more substance to it.

He shrugged. “Just okay. I’m not going to run away screaming. But I am not comfortable with the idea either. Part of me needs to verify this…” he waved at her, "with someone from the outside world before I fully accept it. I mean, let's be honest. It is one thing for you to believe you are psychic, but it's completely different for you to be verified as not human."

In the blink of an eye, she looked like the Chris he remembered. Her eyes were shiny, but Tony could tell she was restraining her tears. She glanced at the space next to him, and clearly seemed at odds whether to sit beside him. Tony couldn't blame her. While he was struggling with what she just showed him, part of him really did not want to be near her. He felt guilty about it, but it was a hard pill to swallow. She seemed to settle on giving him more space because she moved down the wall and sat with her legs curled to one side, and her skirt covering her knees.

Tony closed his eyes; they had to get down to business. He needed information that would help him solve the case and he was not sure how much time he had.

"Chris, I need you to answer all my questions in full. It's extremely important." He added the last part because he knew she would take it seriously.

She folded her hands in her lap and her face crinkled with concern. "What are you not telling me, Tony?"

Tony took a deep breath. "Do you know what's going on in the Seattle area, Chris?"

Her face crinkled even more. "No."

This would just make it harder for Tony. "People are being killed. They are being strung up as if crucified in some twisted way."

Tony watched a variety of emotions crossing over his friend's face as he told her about the attacks. At some point, she crawled onto the bed, careful to keep space between them. When he got to the female victim, his description became as vague as possible.

Partway through, Chris stopped him. "Was the baby completely removed?"

That caught him off guard, since all he said was there was a stomach wound. She wasn't even looking at him. Instead, she looked at the wall from the foot of the bed with a faraway glaze to her eyes.

When he did not respond right away, those faraway eyes turned to him. "Tony?"

Her eyes looked back at the wall and deadened. Her whole face appeared to have shut down. “Were there any markings on her belly?”

Tony began to worry, not only about Chris, but what she was about to say. “Yes, there were symbols, just like before. They haven’t been interpreted yet, but my partner thinks they said, ‘abomination’.”

Her eyes focused then and snapped back to Tony. “Your partner could read it? Tony, he’s probably right, and that could be very, very bad. Has he been acting off lately?"

Dread churned Tony’s stomach again. "A little."

"Tony, you need to keep an eye on him. If the Culeen have compromised him, he is going to sabotage your case. But you can't go anywhere alone with him. It could be a trap."

Tony did not want to believe anyone had gotten to his partner. Rick was a good cop, as well as a friend. There were few people he trusted more. But he knew when to keep his mouth shut. If he argued, he might not get the answers he needed. So all he did was nod.

“The markings?” he prompted her.

For a second, he thought she wouldn't answer. She watched him for several moments before leaning back into the pillows and focusing on the wall again. Her face did not give anything away, but her voice was threaded with fear, anger, and sadness.

“They were a message.” Her hands tightened around his and began to tremble. “But not for you, and not for the police, For the Nym community. It happens often enough that any Nym knows what it means. The Culeen took that baby. It was removed from the mother’s stomach, probably as she died. The symbols…” Her hands trembled and her breath came faster.

Tony felt his pulse speeding up in reaction to hers; he watched her struggle to finish the sentence.

“The symbols mean the baby must have been part Nym. A child born of both Nym and human parents is considered an abomination in the eyes of the Culeen. They can’t understand why we would want to have relations with beings they consider food. They…they…they take the baby to whatever lair they are currently inhabiting and… mount it on an iron spike, like some sick decoration, a trophy for their cause. If the baby was taken from the womb, however, it is seen as a very special prize. The fetus is given to the leader of that particular group of Culeen, usually a Demon Culeen, and eaten raw."

Tony felt a wave of nausea as the world began to spin. His brain refused to comprehend what he was hearing, but she continued, and her breathing sped up further.

"It doesn't matter the age either, as long as it's not at full power yet. You just pray the child was dead before…" She stopped and began trembling so hard, her teeth chattered.

Tony wanted to comfort her, but the voice in his head wouldn't stop screaming. It was screaming so loud, it seemed to engulf the entire world. It took him a few seconds to force the screaming to stop while he convinced his stomach not to vomit. After mostly calming himself down, he swore not to think too much about it, if just so he could move on. But once he looked at Chris again, he knew moving on was not an option.

She was staring past him into space. Her face was like an open wound, making it very obvious a memory was playing out in her head. One of her shaking hands moved up and touched the back of her right shoulder. He saw her jump, then blink a few times before slowly looking into Tony's eyes.

"What, Tony?"

He didn't mean to curse out loud because she noticed him watching her and jerked her arm away from her shoulder.

"You! It happened to you!" It was all he could say.

She hesitated before nodding. "Will, too."

Tony closed his eyes and swore again. "But you both lived."

She nodded very slowly, looking past him again. "I don't think I can talk about that, Tony, now or ever."

The last words were so quiet, he barely heard them. She was broken, or close to it, and that scared Tony more than everything else going on. A very small voice in his head told him he still needed information from her.

"I need to know what their lairs look like."

Chris closed her eyes. "I know."

She took a deep breath. Her hands stopped trembling and gripped his. Tony didn't think she was aware that she was practically clinging to him.

"They're very dark. Most vampire lore comes from the Culeen's habits. Their eyes can't handle light very well. It hurts their eyes, but that's about it. Silver can also hurt them, but it needs a spell engraving to do a fair amount of damage. They scatter all over the places they've acquired. The back wall is usually decorated with the leader's throne, for lack of a better term."

She started shaking again. Tony could tell that was all he would get from her, not because she didn't want to tell him, but because she couldn't. He reached out and put a hand on her back. Chris flinched, but Tony kept it there and began to rub small circles.

She whimpered. "Can we move on please, Tony?"

Tony nodded. His thoughts shifted to what happened earlier, He vowed he would tell Chris what happened, since he was beginning to realize how close Chris and Will were. It might not be the best time, but he needed to get it over with. She needed to know.

"I have more bad news for you. The third victim is Will." He felt her body shuddering as a screech flew from her lips. Tony hurried to complete the news before she could do anything else.

"He's alive, and the healing powers you guys have are what saved him."

She smacked his chest hard and Tony winced. "Don't do that to me! Don't you ever do that to me!"

Then she bent over and started crying into her hands. "Thank you, God!" was all she managed to say.

She cried far longer than Tony expected. Her body visibly shuddered under his hand from the wracking, heart-wrenching sobs. Tony wanted to comfort her so badly, it made him itch, but he knew there was nothing he could say or do that could make things right for her. So he sat there, rubbing her back, and watching her breakdown. Tony did not remember ever seeing her cry in all the years they were friends.

When she seemed to be recovering, he took the chance to speak. "Tiffany confirmed you two being related."

Chris made a small attempt at a smile and nodded, trying desperately to recover. “I figured. Will would never go against his word.”

Tony didn’t reply, but changed the subject instead. “Why didn’t you tell me about all of this in high school?”

That surprised even him; he meant to ask about what attacked Will. Then he realized that thought had been bothering him for days. *Why hadn’t she told him?*

She blinked and sighed. “Tony, it isn’t exactly something you tell people.”

It hurt Tony that she hadn’t trusted him then. He began to shake, but not of his own accord. He looked at Chris, expecting to find her shaking him. She gave him that small smile again.

“That’s not me, Two-Tone.” She stood up and as she did, the room around Tony began to fade.

Chapter 9

"Hollownton! Hollownton! Wake the hell up!"

Tony lifted his head off his desk to see the captain glaring down at him and shaking his shoulders.

"Hollownton, there's a killer out there running around and you're sleeping!"

As the man stood up, Tony looked over the captain's shoulder at the clock. Nine am. He slept two whole hours! He swore as he got up and tried to clear his head.

"That's right, Hollownton, do your damn job! And if you see your partner, tell him he's in waist deep..." The captain's cell phone rang before he could finish. Binns turned and stormed back into his office, grunting into the phone.

Tony grabbed his coat off the back of his chair. He needed to question the day shift at the hospital about Brad, to find out his habits and maybe, how exactly he became involved with the Nym.

After three hours of questioning victim one's co-workers, all Tony learned was that Brad was extremely friendly and would go out drinking with the others from time-to-time. Until about two months ago Brad mostly worked the night shift with a "Doctor Horn."

Brad spent a lot of his time with one other day shift nurse that Tony had yet to track down. The guy's name was Paul. He was supposedly working on this floor, the same one Will was on. Beyond that, however, Tony had nothing. No one seemed to know much about Brad, a fact several of them didn't realize until Tony asked.

Tony was sitting down the corridor from Will's room, flipping through his notes, when he felt someone sit down beside him. Turning his head to the left, he took a look at the newcomer.

The man was huge, about six-and-a-half feet, and had muscles that could only be attained through heavy exercise. His head was shaved and his brown eyes stared at the wall straight in front of him. Tony took the hint and did the same.

"You the cop asking about Brad?"

Tony nodded, but remembered the large man wasn't looking at him. "Yes."

The man leaned forward, and out of the corner of his eye, Tony could see him resting his elbows on his knees.

"You won't find anything leading to his death; you should just leave. He was a good guy. End of story."

Tony was about to protest when the woman behind the nurses' station hollered down the hall. "Paul, check in on room two-seventeen; he just hit his button."

The man got up and walked down the hall to Will's room. Tony was tempted to follow and corner him. Then the name clicked. Paul was the name of the day shift nurse Tony was looking for. Perhaps this was the man who could give him the information he needed.

Barely a minute later, Paul came back out and headed straight for Tony. Before Tony could prepare what he planned to say, Paul sat back down.

"There were two Nym-friendly nurses on the day shift, plus, two Nym nurses and a Nym doctor on the night shift. Brad was one of those two nurses, and I'm the other. Brad had just been switched from the night shift. If a Nym ever comes into this place, one of us is always their nurse, and Doc Horn is always their doc. I don't know who the killer is, or how they found out about Brad, but I know the Nym are worried because I'm being watched over like a newborn." Paul turned to look Tony in the eyes. "The Nym are not here now. You'll have to come back tonight. That's all I know, man."

Puzzled, Tony watched the man for a moment. "Why are you telling me this?"

Paul shrugged his bulky shoulders. "Will said to tell you, and that you're a friend to the Nym. You can be trusted. It's good to know there's a cop on our side."

Paul nodded to say goodbye, and stood up. Tony grabbed the nurse's arm before he could leave. Paul looked at his hand, then at Tony's face. Tony took that as a cue.

"No, that's not it. I have questions, you can either answer them here or I can cause a big scene by taking you in for interrogation." When he finished, Tony let go of the other man's arm.

A muscle in Paul's jaw twitched, "Fine." The nurse leaned back and crossed his arms.

After another five minutes, Tony received no new information. Paul and Brad met here at the hospital and neither of them were aware the other knew about the Nym until both were assigned to the same doctor, which was odd. Then the truth came out. Paul told Tony that Brad dated a Nym some years earlier, and a few Culeen attacked them on a date. Paul didn't know the woman's name, or anything else about her. Brad was not seeing anyone the night he was killed, which was also his night off.

Tony sat there and absorbed everything. Will must've heard their initial conversation from down the hall and convinced the nurse to talk. He supposed a "friend" simply meant someone who knew about the Nym. Tony's doubts still lingered about whether it was some kind of cult war that had gotten out of hand. The existence of psychic people were one thing, but it was quite another to believe that warring, non-human species were wandering around.

Was that the reasoning behind the killings? Was this simply a gang war with outside casualties? But why? Why go after the people who weren't Nym? Why not go after the Nym themselves?

It was starting to make sense to him, which worried Tony. This was real life, not some movie. Tony stood up and said, "Thanks, Will." He spoke softly and was somewhat relieved when he did not get a reply.

As he got to the staircase, Tony paused. Now would be the time to question Will about Chris's visits, and not being human. Part of him did not want to know the answers, but he believed it would be key to solving the case. Turning around, Tony walked back to Will's room.

The door was open, but Tony stood in the doorway. Will picked up the remote from next to his bed and turned off the television.

"I never liked those judge shows anyway." Will turned and smiled at Tony, saying, "Shut the door."

Tony moved into the room, shutting the door behind him and sitting in the same chair he sat in only a few hours ago.

Will folded his arms, "So what's up?"

Tony took off his jacket before answering, which made Will lift an eyebrow. “I need more information on some things Chris was telling me. We always seem to get interrupted.”

Will's eyes widened, “How many times have you seen her?”

Tony shrugged. “Three.”

Will sat up a little straighter. “Three? Three times? No one else has seen her at all.”

Tony felt his cop instincts kick in. *Why would no one else see the dead woman?*

Will shook his head. “I'm sorry, that's not what you're here for. What has she been telling you?”

Tony debated what to ask first. After several seconds, he settled on satisfying his own curiosity. He knew he was clenching his fists, but didn't force them open. He could feel the dread building. Tony was pretty sure of the answer; and had never wanted to be wrong so much in his life.

"She told me the Nym are not human. They are a different species entirely."

Will's face froze and every muscle in his body tensed. The silence that stretched between them seemed to last for ages. "Why do you think she would say that?"

Tony knew then that it was true. Part of his reality instantly shattered. What he knew about the universe was wrong. Just how many hidden species were out there, posing as humans?

Tony just ignored Will's question. "Is she lying?"

As Tony watched, Will struggled to decide whether or not to lie. "No, she wasn't."

The thick silence was back. This time, it was much longer and Tony grappled with the information. He did not know how it was possible. How could that have been kept hidden? The panic rose up from his stomach in a crashing wave that threatened to drown him. Tony wrestled with that passing thought and held onto it as much as he could. Tony could not let himself drown.

He was a cop on a murder investigation. Lives depended on him. He needed to push those thoughts aside to mull over later when there wasn't a killer running around. Besides, he still had no proof. Just because they told him they weren't human did not make it true. Not that he was going to ask for proof. Tony took a deep breath and directed his mind to something that could help with his case. "I need you to describe Culeen lairs to me in the best detail you can."

Anger and panic crossed Will's face before he could speak. "She told you about that? Why?"

Tony rubbed his face, thinking this might be a bad subject. "She began explaining about what is done with Nym/ human children. She unconsciously touched a scar. I kinda figured it out, and she just confirmed it. Said it happened to you as well. She sort of broke down while describing the lair, and I couldn't bring myself to make her elaborate in more detail."

Tony watched Will's face soften in relief and he folded his arms again, but this time, it was more like a hug. "Good; the less she has to remember about that, the better." Will looked back at Tony, and his face grew solemn. "She saved me. She saved my life and she was only twelve at the time." Will shook his head again, staring down at the bed.

Will did not appear to be as scarred from the event as Chris was, which only made him wonder more about what happened.

"They are always dark. Other than that first time, I've been in two other lairs, after they were vacated, of course. They are always found in remote areas, whether that may be a warehouse or a cave. There are a number of people searching out this newest colony's lair, but they haven't seen much success.

"If there are windows, they are usually blacked out or covered because the Culeen are just too sensitive to light. That and having them wander around during the day would obviously make them targets so they could be shot at. Most of the lair is like nests made out of various things, and there is no real consistency. They simply use whatever they can get their hands on. One wall will have a throne of sorts, that could be built out of anything as well.

"I heard in the olden days, they were made out of human bones, but that was before the huge human population surged and forced the Culeen to become more migratory. On each side of the throne against the wall is where the spikes would be, if there are any. Only the bigger groups, of fifty or more, usually start collections, although we don't know why."

Will went quiet before turning to Tony. "Looking for the lair may just be a waste of time for you. Trust me, as soon as those Culeen were spotted in the sky, people have been hunting them. A colony that size can't hide for too long."

Tony nodded. He made a mental note to check all the local, abandoned buildings. Then he stood up and grabbed his coat. He would come back later if the leads dried up, and ask about Nym hangouts; but for now, he decided to treat it as a serial murder and not a gang war.

It would have helped if Rick were with him. The load would have been so much easier if there were two of them. But he called and left messages on all the numbers he had for Rick, and the other man never picked up. Tony decided to stop by Rick's house on his way home. He wanted to make sure his partner was okay.

Will spoke as Tony slid on his trench coat. "Does she know I was injured?" Tony nodded and Will swore. "I was going to ask you not to tell her. There's no use in her hearing about something she couldn't have prevented."

Tony stuck his hands in his pockets. "Sorry."

Will just gave him a sad smile.

As Tony walked out of the room, he wondered what exactly he had gotten himself into. Hoping, yet dreading to find the female victim's file on his desk, Tony left the hospital.

Tracy Hurst was twenty-four years old. Her young face grinned up at Tony from the picture on his desk. She didn't look more than twenty. She was pale, which was common for a native Seattle-ite. Her honey hair was in a tight braid that hung over her shoulder, and she had small, forest green eyes. Her description stated she worked at a daycare not more than five minutes from the precinct. It had a strange name.

Tony flipped through the pages. *The Braided Tree*. Tony figured it must have been a reference to something, but nothing he knew of. Putting the papers back into the envelope, Tony got ready for his next stop: a city daycare. He shuddered, remembering what Chris told him about Culeen and Nym children. His thoughts chilled him. He had to solve this soon, especially with all those children at risk.

The outside of the triple-story daycare was welcoming. A three-dimensional tree covered the front of the building. The trunk of the tree had the appearance of smaller trunks, all braided together. Tony hit the leaf-shaped doorbell. After a few seconds, he heard someone come to the door and unlock it before a somewhat shaggy man stood in the entry.

He was perhaps four inches taller than Tony. Medium brown hair covered his ears and had a gentle wave to it. His face had a slight stubble, and he appeared to be one of those few people who didn't need to work out.

When he spoke, his voice sounded almost like a growl. "How can I help you?"

Tony pulled his badge out of his pocket. "Anthony Hollownton, King County homicide. I'd like to ask you and your co-workers about Ms. Tracy Hurst."

The man didn't even glance at the badge. "Prove it."

Tony was beginning to think the growl was just his natural voice, rather than any attempt to intimidate him. He also wasn't sure how he was supposed to "prove it," since that was what the badge was for.

From behind the man, Tony heard a child giggling. The man spun around as if to protect the child.

"Get back inside. You know it's not safe to be near strangers. Go. Move."

Much to Tony's shock, the little boy from the supermarket poked his head out from behind the man's leg.

"But that's not a stranger. That's Mr. Hollownton." There were more giggles and the boy looked up at Tony. "Why does everyone call you a stranger?" Tony had no idea how to answer that. His mind was still trying to comprehend the little boy's presence there.

The man looked at Tony, then down at the boy. "Are you sure, Corby?"

The little boy nodded vigorously.

"Okay then." The man ruffled the boy's hair. "Go finish your lunch."

The little boy beamed, "'Kay!" before running around the corner.

Once he was out of sight, the man turned back to Tony. "Sorry about that; you can never be too careful. Travis Benzin." He held out his hand as he said his name.

Tony put his badge away and took the proffered hand.

"Come on in," Travis said, the growl now softened, but not completely gone.

Tony felt sure it was what his regular voice sounded like. The man moved aside to let Tony in. Once both men were inside, Travis locked the door.

He turned back to Tony. "Again, I'm sorry; we really can't be too careful."

Tony understood, the general panic was high with the increasing crime rate and the very recently lost teacher, but this man made it seem like an everyday thing. Being a keeper of the peace himself, Tony felt a bit offended.

"Up until recently, crime was never that bad in King."

Travis cocked his head to the side, obviously confused. There was something almost wolfish about the gesture. After blinking a few times, he straightened his neck and replied, "You don't know, do you?"

Now it was Tony's turn to be confused.

The taller man continued. "This daycare. It isn't for everyone." He paused as if Tony should have understood what that meant.

Tony continued to look at him, waiting for a more substantial explanation.

Travis sighed, running a hand through his hair. "This is a daycare for Nym children only. There has to be Nym in the child's ancestry somewhere in order for the child to be accepted here."

Tony saw some pieces slipping into place. *That was how the killers knew how to find Tracy.* That also explained why the boy knew Cheryl, but not how he knew Tony.

Travis interrupted his thoughts. "I guess that means you didn't know. Figures. Nym are terrible with sharing. If Cheryl hadn't told me to expect you some day this week, I would have had no idea who you were."

Tony held out his arm to stop the man. "Whoa! Hold it! Cheryl?"

Travis nodded. "Yup."

Tony continued to look at him. *How did she fit into this?*

"She's my wife." Travis's mouth twitched with male pride.

"I take it, then, you're not Nym."

Travis shook his head. "Nope, just a Jesper."

Tony felt his panic spiraling again "A what now?"

Travis chuckled. "Wow, no one told you anything, did they?"

Tony simply blinked at the other man.

"You know what Nym are, right?"

Tony nodded hesitantly. He knew next to nothing, which was still much more than he wanted to know.

"When a Nym and a human have a child, that child has a fifty-fifty shot of being Nym itself. On rare occasions, a Nym has kids with a human psychic. Those children, if they turn out to be human, are called Jespers. The Nym blood enhances the psychic abilities that are already present. Those enhanced abilities stay in the bloodline, so a Jesper can pop up from seemingly normal parents if only one is a carrier. Perhaps, if it makes it any easier, you should just think of me as a super powerful psychic." Tony couldn't help the shock in his expression.

Why was this becoming increasingly complicated?

Travis waved his hand as if dismissing his explanation. "I know, it is a lot to take in at first. Both my parents are normal, but one of my grandmothers is a Jesper. I remember how hard it was for me to accept all of that, and I was only fifteen. But that's not what you're here for. The kids have another five minutes for lunch, then it's naptime. That would be the best time to talk with the other teachers."

Tony nodded, his head swimming as Travis turned to lead him down the hall. He was escorted into a room with about twenty children, ranging from infants to five-year-olds, most of which were sitting at two long tables. There were two other teachers, both female.

Travis told him to hang out until lunch was over before he left to help a boy in potty training. It didn't take long for the kids to notice Tony standing there. One Asian girl of about four, with large, black-rimmed glasses, began whispering.

After a while, she looked over at him and said in a high-pitched, scratchy voice, "HELLO!"

Every child of age three and up broke out into a fit of giggles.

One of the two female teachers, a tall, blond with glasses, put her hands on hips. "No May, no crazy lady voice! Finish your lunch."

The little girl giggled as she started sipping her juice box. Tony couldn't help smiling; it was good to see a bunch of happy children after all he'd seen in the past few days. It made things feel normal, almost.

After another few minutes, the other female teacher clapped to attract the kids' attention. "Okay, everyone, it's naptime so clean up your lunches."

Tony heard a squeal of delight as his attention was drawn once again to May. She ran to the closest trash can and threw in her paper bag, a little too violently.

Then she began clapping her hands and saying, or rather, almost singing, "Nap, nap, nap, nap."

She ran over to the other side of the very large room where blue mats were set out on the carpet. After choosing one in the middle, and still singing, she began to take off her shoes. Tony could not stop his chuckle from escaping.

The blond teacher came over and stood behind the girl. "May, are you forgetting something?"

The girl looked up at the teacher, appearing confused for a second, then she turned and started running toward, what reminded Tony of, kindergarten cubbies. When she reached them, she bent over and put her hand into one of the dark holes, but he could barely make out her words.

"My precious blankie," she cooed as she walked back over to her mat, her red blanket in hand. She curled up around the blanket, instead of getting under it.

When Tony finally stopped watching May, he noticed who was lying right next to her: Corbin. He was under his own much darker red blanket. Tony watched the teachers help all the kids get ready for naptime. The sight of something so mundane was quite grounding for Tony.

Once all the children were settled for naptime, the three teachers and Tony sat in the only adult-sized chairs across the room. They were arranged in a small semi-circle so the teachers could keep an eye on the kids without disturbing them. Tony had his back to the wall.

He was introduced to the women as Travis read to the kids. The woman on his left was the dark blond. Her hair was up in one big clip. The ends looked like a fountain spray above her head. Small glasses circled her dark brown eyes. Her name was Heidi Craig, and she was twenty-seven. She had worked there four years and was a Nym.

The woman to his right had a long, light-brown braid that went past her hips and huge, pale green eyes. She was only about five feet tall and nineteen years old. This young Nym worked there on her college breaks both this year and the one before. Her name was Nancy Omberson.

The two women informed him that Travis was thirty-three and worked there about seven years. Apparently, he was the first non-Nym to do so. Tony had his small notepad out, hoping he'd receive some information that could go into an official report, though he very much doubted he would get any. If he turned in a report describing combat between two imaginary species, he would lose his badge for sure. The three teachers looked at his notepad nervously.

"It's okay, I won't write anything supernatural in here, just the basic stuff, like how long she worked here."

All three relaxed visibly before Heidi answered him. "She worked here about three years, I think."

"Okay, I need to know her hours, and what she did socially. Plus, we know she was pregnant, so I need to learn everything about the father." Tony suppressed all the images that flashed through his mind.

Both women shifted nervously in their chairs and glanced at Travis. It was obvious he was the most dominant of the three. Tony noticed Heidi touch something through her blouse. It was a nervous gesture Tony recognized from the years he spent with Chris and Cheryl. He had no doubt there was a religious symbol underneath her blouse.

Travis cleared his throat before giving Tony direct eye contact. "Her hours were the same as Heidi's and mine: five-thirty to seven-thirty, Tuesday through Thursday. Socially, there wasn't too much. She mixed with Nym and non-Nym groups. She liked to go to clubs on the weekends, mainly The Rain, which is further downtown. I don't know too much else.

"When she met Max, one of the younger kid's uncles, she stopped doing all those things. I think she and Max were thinking long haul; I guess they were going to move in together next month. He would know about her friends and all that jazz. They were both ecstatic about the baby. We don't have a way to get hold of Max for you, but I would assume she had a number for him somewhere."

Tony continued writing. Travis paused until Tony finished.

"I assume you'll want to know which kid," Travis said, turning, and pointing to where May and Corbin were sleeping. "Max is May Kim's uncle. You already know Corby; she's lying right next to him."

Tony nodded. He was surprised, not that May was the child in question, but that it didn't surprise him.

Heidi added, "He knows which one she is." She turned from the children to look at Tony with a small smile, saying, "She's very vocal."

Again, Tony nodded; vocal was one way to put it.

"What is the best way to get hold of Uncle Max?" Tony asked, knowing perfectly well he could track Max down through police channels, but if there were an easier way, he would prefer that.

Plus, he didn't want the Nym community closing ranks more than they already were. He figured that would happen if he went outside the community for information.

Both female teachers looked at Travis, who shrugged before answering, "Beats me. He comes to the once-a-month family nights, which won't be for another two weeks. Other than that, I have no idea."

Tony nodded and scribbled some notes, so much for the easier way. When he looked up again, Travis was watching him.

"She was human; she was the first full human to work here, ever. It took awhile to convince the parents that a human could protect their kids just as well as we could. I wouldn't be surprised if this was meant to be an example to discourage other human teachers from working here."

Tony could hear the edge in the man's voice. Apparently, the Nym weren't very inclusive, even with their own. Tony wondered just how tight this community was.

"Have you heard about the other related death?" he inquired.

The two women shifted, confirming Tony's suspicions.

"Nancy!" Travis's exclamation sounded like a combination of a hiss and a growl.

Tony looked at Travis whose eyes were fastened on the young woman. He was just in time to see Nancy's eye color change back to pale green. He didn't get more than a glimpse before her eyes fully changed back. All he saw was the other color was darker.

The young girl seemed to curl in a little and her voice came out younger and softer. "I'm sorry, I… I just." She seemed on the verge of quaking.

There was a small voice in the back of Tony's mind, which suggested the eye color change was proof that Nym were not human. Tony jumped when he felt his cell phone go off. Pulling it out, he recognized the number as the captain's.

"Excuse me," Tony said.

As he was turning toward the far side of the room, Heidi spoke. "Go stand next to the front door; it's far enough away that Travis won't hear you."

Tony glanced at the other man and saw Travis giving Heidi a droll look. Nodding, he headed for the door.

Tony tapped the screen.

"Hollownton"

Hearing his name bothered Tony. There was something definitely wrong. He could tell from the Binns's voice.

"Yeah, Captain?" Tony could feel the tension through the phone.

"You've got a fourth vic, Hollownton. It was called in almost an hour ago and the impotent moron in charge of the scene didn't call us right away. She's in apartment forty-three in that old rundown apartment building on Saucer Avenue. You better be making progress on this freakin' case, Hollownton. Three unsolved homicides does not look good. Your damn partner is MIA and I got the chief breathing down my neck about this. I want a full report on my desk by the end of the day; you hear me, Hollownton?"

Tony struggled to refrain from cursing. "Yes, sir, I'll have a report done as soon as I view the crime scene."

There was a slight pause. "Good; because you'll be presenting that report to me as well as briefing a new detective, seeing as how you're alone now. She'll meet you at the crime scene. I need more than one mind on this case. If the two of you don't have this wrapped up soon, the case won't be yours anymore."

There was a click as the captain hung up. Tony just stared at the phone. Now, he was expected to break in a new detective? Right in the middle of a case? What could he tell her? It wasn't like he could explain how the Nym and Culeen were involved. Tony used some choice words under his breath before going back into the other room.

Heidi and Travis were waiting for him, and Tony took a brief glance around. Nancy was walking in between the mats, supervising the sleeping kids. Tony figured the two older teachers sent her over there just in case she had another slip. He could understand their secrecy, but a part of him was a little angry over the girl's unnatural behavior.

Finally, he turned to look at the other two teachers. Travis had his arms across his chest and didn't look too pleased. His expression suggested that if Heidi had not said anything, Travis would probably have listened in on the phone call. Heidi was standing with her hands clasped in front of her. Tony realized the woman was intentionally trying to appear harmless, and it made him wonder why.

Heidi spoke first. "I take it you have to go?"

Tony just looked at her, unsure if she were listening.

Her smile grew slightly wider before returning to the small curve it had been. “I guessed it because you didn’t ask more questions, even though I could hear you swearing as you came down the hall.”

Tony’s expression turned sheepish. “Sorry about that.”

Travis snorted. “Don’t worry about it; the kids couldn’t hear you.”

There was a short pause before Tony took his right hand out of his pocket, and shook Travis’s hand with a nod.

As Heidi reached out to him, her voice shook a little. “Was there another murder?”

Tony’s face went blank. “I am not at liberty to discuss that. I’ll be available by phone if anyone remembers anything else.”

He saw the woman’s face fall; she knew where Tony was going. Reaching into the inside pocket of his coat, Tony pulled out several business cards and handed them to Travis, who took them with another nod. With that, Tony turned and left the daycare. Even though Binns didn’t really give Tony much in the way of directions, Tony knew exactly where to go.

Saucer Avenue was in an area that passed for the lower end of town. Comprised of a four-block square, it was entirely made up of old, run-down buildings. Many of the houses still standing in that part of town were at least eighty years old. What once was designed as single family homes, now housed two or three families. There was a fair number of apartment buildings, few of which were up to code. The reason Tony knew exactly which building to seek was because the Saucer Heights apartment building on Saucer Avenue was pretty well known around the precinct.

About two years ago, the apartment manager was busted for possession with intent to sell. While going through his apartment, police heard a gunshot from one of the upper floors. They soon discovered several women on the top floor who called themselves “ladies of the night.” When a “john” refused to pay, they shot him in the leg. Later, after that situation died down, Saucer Heights simply became known as the only apartments on Saucer Avenue.

The drive was twenty minutes from the daycare. When Tony turned onto Saucer Avenue, he saw the telltale cop cars lining the street. A fairly large number of reporters, as well as a sizeable horde of neighborhood gawkers were also in attendance. That was one thing Tony came to expect in this part of town; people always came out in full force to view a crime scene.

Parking in the first available spot he could find, Tony walked two blocks to the apartment building. He strode slowly and deliberately, intending to make it seem like he was in no hurry. If the officer in charge tried to cause any problems, Tony would have to assert his dominance right off the bat.

When he was only a few feet away from the police tape, a younger officer, dressed in plain clothes, noticed him and walked to the edge of the tape. Tony had no doubt this was the new detective he was supposed to brief and work with. Tony put her age at about twenty-five. Her brown hair was pulled back into a short ponytail. She was extremely pale and a few inches taller than Tony. What caught most of his attention, however, was her enthusiasm. Her innocence shone brightly in her eyes, although she tried to conceal it. Anyone who took a good look, however, couldn't have missed it. Tony almost felt bad at seeing her. Enthusiasm and innocence were two virtues that failed to flourish for most homicide detectives. It seemed a shame she would choose that line of work.

She waited until Tony entered the taped off area before introducing herself. "Hello Detective Hollownton. I'm Officer Beatrix Bentley, and your new assistant, for lack of a better term. I've already taken all the victim's information. Would you like me to read my report so far to you?"

Tony wondered if she always spoke so fast or was just nervous; and really hoped she was just nervous. Tony shook her hand and motioned for her to walk closer to the house. As she followed him, she flipped open a small, black notebook and began to read from it.

"Victim is Jessica Abrams, age twenty-one. Her next door neighbor, a Mrs. Debbie Quates, called in after noticing a strange smell at noon today, when she was chasing one of her cats. Abrams has lived there three years, with no spouse, or significant other as far as any of the neighbors knew. She worked as a waitress at

George's Place, which is down at the southern edge of Seattle, right off the I-Five."

Tony nodded, he knew the diner, it was mostly known as a biker hangout or a rest stop for travelers on the freeway. Tony didn't exactly look forward to visiting George's Place. Sighing, he rubbed his face. The information she got would save Tony a lot of hassle.

"How long have you been here, Bentley?"

She crinkled her eyebrows as she looked down at her watch. "About twenty minutes, sir, why do you ask?"

Tony nodded again and started walking up to the building entrance. "Have you had a chance to look at the body yet? Or speak with the officer in charge?"

Tony watched the young cop's face appear vacant, but he glimpsed some anger in her eyes.

"No, sir. Since I am not a detective, he refused to let me speak to him, or allow me into the vic's apartment."

Tony understood her anger, since arrogant cops always got on his nerves too. "What's his name?" he asked as they wove their way through the random cops before climbing the stairs.

"Roads, sir."

Tony gave a small chuckle; he knew Roads. The man was about forty and dying to make detective. Trouble was: stunts like burned all his bridges.

As they reached the top of the stairs, Tony turned to Bentley with a smile. "Just watch this."

She looked at him, confused for a second before becoming expressionless.

"Detective Hollownton, what a pity to see you on such horrible circumstances."

Tony turned and gave Roads a dry look. The man was about Tony's height with very short, blond hair and small, beady eyes.

Tony ignored his outstretched hand and slowly walked past the man before stopping. "Roads, what is this I hear about you not letting homicide in to view the crime scene?"

Tony watched as Roads looked at him, somewhat perplexed. A younger male in uniform behind Roads snickered. *Yeah. No one liked Roads.*

"How could I prevent you? You just got here!"

Tony glanced at Bentley, who managed to pull off a very convincing unreadable face. Looking back at the confused Roads, Tony folded his arms.

"My aide has been here for nearly half an hour and wasn't allowed inside."

Tony felt the strands of pleasure curling through him as Roads' eyes grew wider and he glanced from Tony to Bentley. It was a petty delight, but Tony still enjoyed it.

Tilting his head slightly, Tony addressed the younger man in uniform. "Could you get us some gloves, please?"

The uniform nodded, obviously straining not to laugh as he walked away. Without waiting, Tony nodded to Bentley and followed him, leaving Roads alone in the front hall.

As they walked down the small hallway, Bentley moved up next to Tony. "Thank you for not making me look helpless."

Tony eyed her skeptically. "What do you mean?"

She shrugged, "You didn't make it look like I was tattling on him, or anything like that. I guess he'll probably see it that way, but the other officers won't, so thanks."

Tony nodded as they reached the door to the victim's apartment. He hated how cops let their egos get in the way; and if he had to be the one to take them down a few notches, that was fine with him.

The young uniform was smiling and holding out two pairs of disposable gloves at the apartment's open door. They both thanked him as they entered the crime scene.

As soon as he crossed the threshold, the loud chanting pounded through Tony's head. The sensation was similar to when he held his breath underwater. This time, however, it wasn't as overpowering. It was almost like he had subconsciously prepared for it because he didn't so much as falter when he heard it. Tony walked straight through the doorway without drawing attention to himself. Once over the threshold, there was an almost audible pop, and the chanting ceased. He really wanted to poke at the whole occurrence, but right now, he had to concentrate on the crime scene so he filed it away to mull over later.

As expected, Tony found most of the cops milling around in the front room, which served as every room except the bedroom and bathroom. Looking around, there were no signs of a struggle, similar to the other crime scenes. Tony turned to Bentley when it occurred to him she might not know what she was about to walk into. He did not want her walking into the scene cold turkey.

"What do you know about these murders, Bentley?"

She showed no emotion on her face as she answered, "Rumor suggests they were almost like crucifixions."

Tony nodded, "Close enough."

He turned and started wading through the crowd, heading toward the door everyone was standing away from. Walking into the room, Tony could tell the forensic team had already been there. He was not happy to be called onto the scene so late. The only window in the room he saw was open with fingerprint powder sprinkled in places. But the smell remained very strong.

From behind him, Tony heard Bentley gag. The foul odor was something she would just have to ignore and try to make herself numb to.

Without turning to look at her, Tony spoke to the young cop. "Are you going to be able to stay, Bentley?"

There was a pause before she answered and Tony sensed she was rallying herself.

"Yes, sir."

Taking her word, Tony moved further into the tiny room. The bed was facing the door on the opposite wall. The foot of the bed was only about two feet from the door and the window was above the bed. There was a small closet on the same wall as the door, and a bedside table, but that was it. Tony noted that there were no touches to suggest the woman's personality who lived there. Off-white mini-blinds covered most of the window. A digital alarm clock and a book were placed on the small table. If the cover were any indication, it seemed to be an explicit romance novel. The bed had one pillow, which was covered in the same cream color as the sheets and comforter. The bed was neatly made; and Tony assumed Jessica Abrams was an undeniably tidy woman.

The body was hung on the far wall. The messiness of it was made even more obvious by being located in such meager, but tidy surroundings. Like the other two victims, the wrists and ankles were tied and slit. The front of the head was scalped and a bloody mess, with matted, blond hair sticking to her back. There was a hole in the chest above her heart. Tony was willing to bet, once again, that the heart was missing. There were no other markings that Tony could see. Moving closer, until he was only inches from the body he studied what he could see of the back, but there was nothing.

The Demon Culeen, or whatever it was, did not leave any calling card this time. That bothered Tony, since it made the first death stick out more in his mind. Tony glanced at the walls, but found no symbols.

"Why the bedrooms?"

Bentley looked at him from across the room where she was writing in her notebook. "Sorry, what, sir?"

Tony turned to her. "I asked, why the bedrooms? In the first murder, the victim was found in the living room, but the last three have all been in the bedrooms. Why? The bedrooms, at least two of them, are so small, wouldn't it be easier to hang the victim in the front room?"

It felt good to say his thoughts out loud. After working with Rick for so long, Tony was used to bouncing ideas around, and hoped Bentley could do the same.

"I'm betting it's personal, sir. That's why it was done in the home. As for the bedroom… That's more personal, more private. And probably fewer witnesses."

Tony watched the young cop for a moment. She had a good point, but if the Culeen, or the people who thought they were Culeen, could conceal what they really looked like, why would they need more privacy? Maybe they couldn't fully hide. Just because people saw Girl Scouts didn't mean they couldn't see Girl Scouts carving up a victim.

He knew right then: that was it. *The killers could change their appearances, but not disappear completely.*

"Very true, but why not the bedroom for the first victim?" Then it dawned on him as he began removing his gloves. He added, "Unless there was something wrong with the first victim's bedroom."

Tony wanted to go back and revisit the first crime scene. It was nagging at him now, and he knew there was something there, something very important that they missed the first time. He maneuvered his way back to the outer hall, but stopped and turned before heading down the stairs, knowing before he turned around that Bentley was right behind him. She was obviously startled when he suddenly addressed her.

"Bentley, go back to the station and dig up as much as you possibly can on our three dead victims, and I mean *everything.*"

She looked at him a moment. "Not Will Nylan?"

Tony shook his head; he wasn't sure what she might find on him.

"No, just concentrate on the other three. If we can't find anything, we can study his case. He survived, which suggests he might have been a hasty target, or maybe not part of the original plan."

Bentley nodded. Satisfied she would do what he asked, Tony headed out to the first crime scene.

After thirty minutes, Tony had driven across town and returned to the original scene. Traffic began to snarl up early and he was not looking forward to the drive back. The odds were not in favor of it clearing up soon.

When he got to the house, he parked in the driveway. As he sat there, took a deep breath, feeling unsure and cautious about all the strange things that happened during his first visit. When he stepped out of the car this time, however, there were no flashes from high school. Tony was relieved, but it reminded him that he couldn't help Chris. Maybe if he had known about her damn secret life, he could have helped her somehow. He was a cop. She should have come to him for help. It really aggravated him when people didn't trust him to help in times of trouble.

Feeling a fresh wave of anger flowing over him, he stomped up the steps to the door. People were dying and he was still getting the runaround. Cursing everyone in general, Tony unlocked the front door. About halfway to the bedroom, Tony realized he hadn't heard any chanting when he walked through the door.

Why could he hear the chanting sometimes, but not at others? He couldn't think of a good answer off the top of his head. He intended to bring it up to Chris, if he ever saw her again. A pain stabbed his chest, but he wouldn't kid himself. He had no guarantees she would keep appearing.

Running his hand through his hair, Tony entered the bedroom. He was sure there were already pictures of the room somewhere on file, but he always preferred to see things in person. Too often, things could be overlooked in a picture. Tony walked into what he assumed was the master bedroom.

A pale, simple, wooden headboard stood against the middle of the wall on Tony's left, with a small end table. Only a lamp and an alarm clock were placed on it. The walls, like those in the rest of the house, were a pale, generic off-white. He saw a large window on the wall across from him. It was on the right half of the wall, but occupied a good part of that half. The white blinds were closed. Tony noted they weren't mini-blinds but full-sized ones. Directly to the right of the window, on the adjoining wall, was an open closet, which apparently had no door. Further over, on the same wall, was the master bath.

As Tony looked around, he couldn't see why the murder didn't take place in there. Growling his frustration, he turned to leave the room. That was when he saw it.

In a thin line across the door was red-and-white powder. Now that he saw it, he noticed it bordered the entire room. Tony reached into his inner coat pocket and took out a small evidence bag. Using his pen, he scooped some of the powder into the bag and sealed it. He planned to take it straight to the lab. Hopefully, there would be something crucial to the case about this powder. Giving the room a more thorough once-over did not reveal anything else. He tried not to put too much hope on the mystery powder as he headed back to the station.

It was six before Tony got back to the station, so he expected to be reamed for not having his report in by five. It was not something he looked forward to, but he didn't have any control over the traffic, especially on Mariners' game nights. Then he had to stop by the lab to drop off the bag of powder. He barely set foot into the station when he heard Binns's booming voice.

"Hollownton! Get your late…" Before the captain could finish his sentence, his cell phone started ringing.

Tony rolled his shoulders in preparation before walking back to the captain's office. Along the way, he received a number of sympathetic looks from the other cops at various desks. When Tony got to the doorway, he saw a very nervous Bentley sitting in the further of two chairs. As Tony sat down, Binns snapped his phone shut and bore his eyes into Tony.

"Tell me you have a lead, Hollownton. The higher-ups are not taking this ever increasing death toll well; and frankly, neither am I!"

Tony waited a beat before speaking. "Are you saying you want an oral report now?"

"Yes, give me your report and catch Bentley up. Then go out there and write it all down before doing anything else."

Tony nodded, feeling glad he kept thinking about how he would report it all day. "Sir, as you know, we currently have a total of four victims, one of whom survived. This suggests he was probably not part of the original plan. Although there are two victims of each sex, I have no reason to believe it is a pattern. From my interview with Will, I learned there is the murderer, a female, and two strong male accomplices."

Tony took a deep breath. *Here comes the tap dancing.*

"The woman believes she is a mythical creature. She is, most likely, part of a cult that contends they are not human, and call themselves *Culeen.* The drawing on the first victim's back is similar to a calling card.

"I sent a sketch artist over to Will's hospital room earlier today to get some idea of the three suspects; and they should be on my desk now. I believe, sir, from what I've heard, this 'Culeen cult' might be following the woman. They target only the people they believe are helping a rival cult, which is called the *Nym*."

The captain continued to watch him closely. "What's your next move?"

Tony sighed. "I'm going to the hospital to speak with Brad's co-workers; then to the diner where victim four worked. I sent Bentley back here to dig up more information on our vics and to see if there were other connections we may have missed. I want to know if there is some common thread that made this woman choose them, but I haven't had time yet to speak with her."

Binns glared at Tony for a second before turning his attention to Bentley. Squirming in her seat, she struggled to keep eye contact with the captain, scoring her points in Tony's book. Not many people could keep eye contact with Binns, especially when he was mad.

She cleared her throat before speaking. "Sir, I haven't had much time to look up the information on the victims. The only common factor I found when making calls and looking up their interviews is the three dead victims all routinely spent time at The Rain in downtown Seattle."

As soon as she finished speaking, her shoulders rounded in, and she broke eye contact with Binns before staring at his desk. There were a few moments of silence before the captain spoke.

"Fine, I want daily reports now. You said you're headed to the hospital?"

Tony nodded, but had no idea where this was going.

"Good, I'll call the wife and tell her to expect you. Will is on her floor and she can alert the staff you're going to question him." With that, Binns picked up a pen in front of him and returned to the paperwork scattered across his desk.

Tony took that as their cue to leave and got up. Bentley, looking slightly confused, practically leapt up behind him. Once they were at Tony's desk, he sat down without taking his coat off and started his report. From the corner of his eye, Tony watched Bentley gingerly sitting down at Rick's desk. It was plain she felt uncomfortable using his desk, but Tony knew the odds were pretty high that Binns insisted she do so. Tony wasn't sure how he felt about that, but he already had enough on his plate to deal with.

It took Tony less time to do the report than he expected. As he sent it off, he looked across the desk.

What could he do with Bentley? Being assigned an aide to begin with irritated him. He felt no urge to become a mentor to any young officer. He knew it had something to do with Rick's recent behavior; and Binns was nervous about Tony working solo on, what was fast becoming, a complicated, serial killer case. But Tony sensed he might be stuck with Bentley even after the case was over. Not to mention her involvement in the case itself. Tony could hardly get information out of the Nym as it was now. With Bentley along, the small drizzle of information he managed to glean would, no doubt, dry up completely. He had to find a way to exclude her from the gist of the investigation.

Running his hand through his hair, Tony checked his watch. It was not quite seven o'clock. He noticed the blinking light on his desk phone, but didn't hear it ringing. That meant he had to be really out of it, or he'd have noticed it earlier. Sighing, he picked up the receiver and listened to the message.

Viggo's voice came through the earpiece, but there was no joking or levity in her tone. "Hollownton, you need to get down here as fast as you can. There's something about this second vic you need to know. Give me a call no matter the time because I can only hold this 'til tomorrow morning, but that's it."

Tony felt his blood pumping faster, and that was definitely not good. Part of him really did not want to know what she found. Somehow he sensed in his gut that it was going to change things in a bad way. As he put the phone back on the cradle, he turned to Bentley; but it took a second or two for her to notice and look away from the computer screen.

"Bentley, when you find a good stopping point, go ahead and clock out."

She looked at him for a beat, "Sir?"

Tony stood up and pushed in his chair. "Go home, Bentley."

There was another beat as she looked up at him. "With all due respect, sir, if you are not going home, then I shouldn't either."

Tony wasn't sure which to address first: her incessant use of the term "sir," which he hated, or her actual statement. He took the safe path and decided on neither.

"Do what you want then. I want all you can dig up first thing in the morning." Without waiting for her comment, Tony walked out of the station and headed toward his car.

Once he shut the car door, he pulled out his cell phone and dialed Viggo's number.

She answered on the second ring. "Hello? Viggo here."

Tony noted the solemn tone in her voice. "It's Hollownton." He heard the shuffling of papers in the background.

"Hollownton, I'm still at work; can you make it down here right now?"

She sounded a little desperate, spiking Tony's worry even more.

"Yeah, I'm on my way."

She didn't even answer him, but hung up the phone. Tony dreaded what she was about to tell him.

Tony barely entered the morgue when he saw Viggo hastily walking down the hall toward him. She was being trailed by a kid of about twenty. The kid seemed nearly Tony's height and built like a thinner football player. His black hair was short. It looked like a spiked style that grew out a little. Unlike Viggo, the kid's lab coat was completely unbuttoned. It looked like Tony wasn't the only one who got stuck being a trainer. Maybe that was why Viggo was in such a bad mood.

She stopped and turned to walk beside Tony as they reached each other, forcing the kid out of the way before walking behind them.

"Room four, Detective. This is the new summer intern, Donald, who, for some reason, prefers to go by 'Nald.' Don't ask me why because I don't have the faintest idea."

Despite his feelings of dread about what Viggo had to show him, Tony chuckled and turned his head toward the kid as they walked.

"Nice to meet you."

The kid, Nald, simply nodded. Apparently, one day spent with Viggo convinced the kid not open his mouth. Tony glanced at Viggo as she opened the door to the room that held his second victim.

"Scared him into silence did you?"

Viggo snorted and the kid shut the door as she snapped on a pair of gloves.

"No, I just can't hear the words, 'dude' or 'nah' anymore."

Tony glanced at the kid who looked a little sheepish. *Poor kid, being stuck with Viggo on a bad day.* Tony wanted to say something to comfort the kid, but decided it wasn't wise, not with Viggo's current mood.

"So your body," Viggo started, waving the kid over as he slipped on a pair of gloves.

Tony folded his arms over his chest.

"She's real young, though you already knew that. Initial tests are telling us she was pregnant. I'm not sure how far along yet, but I'll have all those details for you in the morning."

There was a pause, and if Tony hadn't been familiar with her speech pattern, he would have missed it. He wished he realized earlier that Viggo was pregnant. This case had to be hell for her. He wanted to console her, but knew he couldn't.

"From the size of the hole, I'd say she was no further along than early second trimester." Viggo stuck her hand in the wound. "As you can see, the fetus was removed. There is no way that it survived. The uterus and flesh around it are more torn up than your first victim."

Tony flexed the muscles in his folded arms to keep his emotions in check. He tried to distance himself.

"Here, it's shredded and ripped, not precisely like the last one, or even like the rest of her wounds. The amount of blood loss suggests she was most likely still alive at this point. I'm willing to bet this was the first wound she endured after being bound to the wall."

As she moved up to the chest, Tony glanced at the kid. He wasn't doing as well as Viggo or Tony. His tan skin turned pale and he appeared to be trying as hard as he could not to look at the victim's empty belly.

"The chest wound is identical to your first one." She reached into the hole. "It's about an inch wider."

Tony uncrossed his arms and took out his notepad before writing everything down.

"Other than that, it's the same, one rib missing and all. I think the killers are using medical equipment of some kind. That's the only thing I can imagine. There are no markings on the head, pubic area, or back. There are still rope burns on the wrists and ankles, which indicate she struggled much harder than the guy did. Her nails are freshly painted. I would put down money that she painted them shortly before her killers arrived. Time of death was about three-thirty am. I'm kinda surprised no one noticed the smell sooner."

She snapped off her gloves and checked her watch. Throwing the gloves away, she turned to the kid. "Donald, it's almost six-thirty. Go on home for the day, and I'll see you at eight am."

The kid nodded as he removed his gloves. He was grabbing the doorknob when he turned back to her. "My stuff is still in your office; could you unlock it for me?"

Viggo snorted, "Oh yeah, duh." She rolled her eyes at her own absent-mindedness.

Tony made a mental note of that. He knew that Viggo never locked her office during the day. It made him wonder if there were something else going on beyond the victim's pregnancy. Viggo motioned for Tony to follow her as she left the room behind the kid.

Once she had the door unlocked, the kid slipped inside. Tony followed him with Viggo bringing up the rear. The kid, *Donald…* why was Tony having so much trouble with his name? …put his lab coat on the door hook before pulling on a black hoodie. Next came a yellow baseball cap with a school mascot on it. To Tony, it looked like a devil. As he was yanking a black and yellow backpack off the floor, next to the open door, Tony heard Viggo behind him.

"Oh my gosh, what the hell is that on your hat?"

Both Tony and the kid started laughing at the startled inquiry.

"It's my college's mascot. The Arizona State Sun Devils," Donald replied.

Tony found it ironic, but didn't comment. Donald was smirking at Viggo. His head was tilted down slightly and his hands gripped each of the straps across his chest. Tony could tell the kid had a comment, which he was trying hard to hold back.

Viggo snorted, "A devil in the morgue. That's all we need."

Donald just shook his head and walked out of the office, closing the door behind him. Sighing, Viggo sat down at her desk. Tony followed suit and took the chair across from her. As soon as he sat down, he hoped he wouldn't be there long.

"Viggo, this has got to be the least comfortable chair I ever sat in."

She gave him a mischievous smile. "I know, it discourages people from spending too much time in my office. My chair, on the other hand, is fantastic."

Her smile fell and she touched her glasses, in a nervous gesture. Tony was waiting for her to drop the bomb. The one she didn't want the intern to hear.

"As much as I love talking to you, Hollownton, this is more important. This," she slid a file across the desk in front of him, but didn't take her fingers off it, "will bump your third body to top priority. As well as all your blood work."

Tony did not want to take the file.

"There was a fingerprint and blood found on the outside of the stomach wound that didn't belong to your victim." She released the file and Tony wondered why this was bad news. "It belongs to a Rick Nelson. A Detective Rick Nelson, assigned to Homicide in King County."

Tony's blood ran cold. His partner? His partner was one of the killers? It didn't fit; Will absolutely would have identified Rick as one of his attackers.

"Are you sure?"

She nodded, "I had the tech run it three times. It is, without a doubt, Rick's. I'm so sorry, Hollownton. I just thought you'd want to know before everyone else."

Tony nodded as he stood, grasping the folder. "Thank you, Viggo."

She gave him a weak smile as he moved to the door.

"I can only hold this until morning, Anthony. Come tomorrow, this will be the worst kept secret in the department. So do whatever you have to tonight."

Tony nodded as he continued out the door. He didn't know if there was anything he could do. Before he was even out of the morgue, Tony called the captain and requested that Rick be picked up. Tony had a sneaking suspicion, however, that the officers they sent would not find him.

"Why, exactly, am I having a detective picked up?" Binns asked him.

Tony sighed into the phone. This was going to suck. Even if Rick were involved, years of friendship felt like a dead weight in Tony's stomach.

"Viggo found evidence of Rick's blood and skin on the second victim."

A lot of loud cursing erupted from the phone. "All right I'll take care of it. You better find out what's going on here soon, Hollownton, or I'll have to give in to the pressure I'm due to receive and yank you off this case. As it is, you'll have to deal with IA, and we both know how beloved Internal Affairs is."

Tony grunted into the phone for his answer before he and Binns hung up.

Sighing, Tony turned out of the morgue driveway and toward the hospital. This case just kept getting worse.

Pulling into the hospital lot, Tony shoved his thoughts of Rick as far back into his mind as possible. He needed desperately to concentrate on the case clues; but thinking about what was happening to Rick kept pulling him into a spiral of anger, confusion, and sadness. He needed to focus on something else. He needed new thoughts that would put his mind in a better place for the interviews he was about to conduct.

It took him a minute or two, but he thought of one. As he opened the glass door, he received the perfect train of thought to refresh his frazzled brain.

The captain was married to a nurse. How in the world had that happened? Nurses were friendly and helped people. What could a nurse possibly see in Binns? Tony flashed his badge to the first nurse he passed on his way to the elevator.

Exiting on the second floor, Tony walked purposefully up to the nurses' station. He had a sneaking suspicion the woman he saw there was Mrs. Binns, He wasn't sure how he knew that, but he was almost positive.

She was an Indian woman in her mid to late forties. Her inky black hair was pulled into a tight braid that went down her back as far as Tony could see. She had large, dark brown eyes and emitted an overwhelming vibe of authority. She wore large gold hoops in her ears, a thick layer of bangles on each wrist, and at least, six rings that Tony could see. Judging by her appearance, Tony had her pegged as more of an administrator than an average registered nurse.

When Tony stood directly in front of her, she finally looked up at him. The movement of her head reflected a sparkle that caught Tony's eye. When he looked right at it, he noticed she had a small stud in her left nostril.

"Yes?" was all she said as she looked up at Tony.

Tony played his hunch and didn't pull out his badge. "Your husband told me I should see you first about speaking to some of the night staff."

The woman seemed to appraise Tony for a moment, and when she answered him, she had a slight accent. "Yes, and that would make you Detective Fineman?" She quirked an eyebrow at Tony.

Tony sighed and pulled out his badge again. "No, Hollownton." He laid the badge down in front of her on the counter.

She didn't do more than glance at it before returning her gaze to Tony. "Yes, I know, but one can't be too careful." Her bangles jangled together as she stretched out her hand. "Lalita Binns. It's nice to meet you Detective Anthony Hollownton."

Tony nodded as he took Mrs. Binns's hand. "You too, Mrs. Binns."

She let go of the firm handshake and wrinkled her nose. "Eek! Please don't call me that! Mrs. Binns is Alfy's mother, a woman I wish to be associated with as little as possible. Seeing as how the old bat won't die, I prefer that people call me Lalita."

Tony just blinked a moment at the strange woman in front of him. *How could she end up married to the captain?*

His thought was interrupted by more jangling as Lalita made a dismissive gesture and reached for the phone. "But you're not here for me; you're here to talk to Melissa." With that, she entered some numbers on the phone, and in a matter of seconds, her voice came over a loud speaker. "Paging Doctor Melissa Horn."

It took almost ten minutes for the doctor to appear. As she stepped off the elevator, Lalita pointed her out to Tony. He thanked the captain's wife before turning to face the doctor. She appeared to be a little older than Tony, and about two inches shorter. Her honey-blond hair was tied back in a low ponytail, but a good number of strands escaped, framing her slightly tanned face. The doctor had pale eyes and a naturally smiling face.

When she reached Tony, she lifted her hand from her side and gave him an apologetic smile. "Hi Detective. I'm so sorry to have kept you waiting. I was on the other side of the hospital. I know this is your second trip here to speak to my colleagues and me, so I'm extra sorry to have caused you such an inconvenience when you're working on such a time-sensitive case." She paused and continued to smile as she shook Tony's hand.

Tony wasn't sure how to take this doctor. He wasn't used to a Nym being so upfront, apologetic, and helpful.

Doctor Horn blinked at him a few times before continuing. "Well, then, I haven't eaten yet; so if it's all right with you, could we conduct this interview down in the cafeteria?" She continued to look at him and smile.

Tony just nodded; unable to remember the last time he ate.

Neither of them said anything as they made their way down to the cafeteria. Not until they were actually standing near the food court did Doctor Horn turn to Tony and speak.

"I'll meet you in one of the side booths over there. They are mostly empty this time of day." She motioned vaguely to the seating on their right. "Oh, and don't eat any of the chowder from the fast food chain. It does not get switched out all day. It's probably been sitting there since late this morning." Doctor Horn grimaced before making her way over toward the salad bar.

Tony watched her for a moment, then walked over to the pre-made refrigerated sandwiches. After grabbing a roast beef, he picked out some chips and a bottle of pop before paying and searching for the doctor. She was sitting in a corner booth, furthest from the other people, and poking some lettuce with a fork when

Tony spotted her. As he sat down across from her, she smiled up at him.

"So what questions do you have for me, Detective?"

Tony took a swig of pop before pulling out his notepad. The doctor's eyes didn't even flicker as the notepad came into view. She was acting so different than the other Nym Tony met.

"You sure you're Nym?"

Doctor Horn almost choked on the lettuce and laughed at his question. "Yes, I am. Half anyway, my father is very human, which makes me a very weak Nym. I take your question to mean I act differently than everyone else you've come across?"

When Tony only nodded, she smiled again.

"Oh, well, I just figure if Will trusts you, than you must be fine. Will is a smart guy and I have faith in his judgment. It's that simple; he trusts you so I trust you." She took a sip from her juice. "But you wanted information about Brad. I've been thinking about it all shift, since Paul told me you would be coming by.

"I met Brad about two years ago, when he transferred from another hospital and was seeing Marianna. By the time I met him, he already knew she was a Nym. Marianna told him that I was Nym as well, which was actually quite rude of her. But that doesn't matter anymore. I don't know Marianna's last name. I don't really know her, period. She and Brad broke up about three months after he transferred. The Nym community is large enough not to know everyone, but small enough to allow you to find anyone. Since I didn't know her, and had no particular reason to search her out, I have no idea where she could be now.

"Brad made friends very easily, but did not have a lot of close friends. He went down to The Rain a lot with the boys. Oh, I mean Tracey and Stacey; they are the two nurses you'll want to talk to. They're also twins, so we mostly just call them 'the boys.' Anyway, the three of them liked to go to The Rain, at least twice a month. The Rain is a biggest thing for the younger Nym. I think it's because there is such a mix of people, from Goth to Prep, that tend to hang out there.

"Let's see, Tuesdays and Sundays were his days off. He never missed church; and belonged to the Second Presbyterian Church uptown. I know his folks are in Oregon. Um, that's all I could get on my own, but I figured any questions you might ask could possibly jog my memory."

Doctor Horn took a few bites here and there as she spoke, but after she finished talking, she started to eat in earnest. Tony allowed her a few minutes free of questions so she could concentrate on eating her lunch. He considered the information and made some notes to possibly track down this Marianna. Then he resigned himself to making a visit to The Rain. It was not something he looked forward to, but then Tony was never a big fan of clubs in general, he enjoyed having his personal space.

"Could you describe Marianna for me?"

"Oh, sure; she had black hair, oh, but it was dyed. She was about five-two and a little bit on the round side. Very pale blue eyes. She was quite striking, actually, almost ethereal."

Tony knew that description wouldn't get him very far. It sounded like any number of women on the street. He was not sure what more information he could ask from the doctor, but felt reluctant to let anyone so willing to be so helpful go.

"Was there anything strange or odd that you can remember over the past few weeks with Brad?"

Doctor Horn raised her eyebrows at Tony. "I assume you mean other than the obvious. No, not really. No telling signs that Brad was getting into something he shouldn't have, or that anything was following him. There was nothing out of the ordinary that I noticed. But you will have to ask the boys; they would know better than I."

Tony nodded as he took another sip of his drink. "And how would I go about tracking them down?"

She waved her hand in a dismissive gesture before grabbing her now empty salad container. "Don't worry about it. They know to expect you. Just stay put and I'll grab them. Knowing how they are, I expect they're probably off flirting with other members on the nursing staff. They are young, but they have a healthy respect for authority, and I'm sure they'll come straight down."

She didn't wait for Tony to respond before getting up with her trash and leaving.

When Tony looked at his watch for the second time after Doctor Horn left, it was quarter to eight. He debated whether or not to get up and hunt for the two nurses himself. After all, he still had to check out George's Place tonight. Grabbing his garbage and half empty soda bottle, Tony was startled by the two young men who slid into the seat across from him. They both had scrawny builds and were around six feet tall. They each held one of those iced coffee drinks Starbuck sells in grocery stores. Tony was pretty sure they couldn't be older than twenty-five, and looked almost identical. The only differences he could see were the one on the inside of the booth had a more pointed nose than his brother, and his hair was a lighter blond.

"Detective Hollownton?" asked the one on the inside of the booth.

Tony nodded and took out his notepad. He patiently waited for one of them to speak. They were both teeming with so much energy, Tony wanted to drop their age down a few years. The one on the inside seemed to crack first, making a noise similar to a cat coughing up a hairball. Tony assumed it was a nervous habit. He thought that would break their silence, but neither of them made a sound. They just sipped their drinks and stared at the table.

"Okay, so let's start with you telling me about Brad's social life. Who were his friends? What about his favorite hangouts? Were there a lot of girls? Did anything strange happen recently?"

Both twins stared off for several seconds, obviously thinking. At least, that's what Tony assumed they were doing. The one on the outside seemed to float back first.

"I didn't really pay attention to any girls who might have been hanging around. The three of us would go to The Rain every other week. The day varied, depending on our schedules. Brad wasn't much of a socializer. I mean, he had friends, but not a lot of people he would hang out with, if you know what I mean. As far as I know, it was work, church, and going to The Rain with us. That was all he ever did. There wasn't anything funny going on, that I knew of. I mean, the report of the Culeen nest did not start circulating until Saturday. Brad was already dead at that point. But this isn't the way they normally do things. Culeen usually aren't so obvious."

They didn't know about the Demon Culeen, Tony realized. Apparently, that part was not circulating with the rest of the story, which he found odd.

"He was getting a little bit of extra attention at The Rain two weeks ago," the other twin stated. "We went on Friday night. There were a lot of people there. But there was this one lady, in her late thirties maybe, who kept sending over drinks for Brad. She was… I don't know… there was something off about her. Brad just kept sending them back each time they came. He was polite at first, but after three or four, Brad simply tipped the waitress not to bring anymore over. That was all that happened though." He stopped talking and shrugged.

Before Tony could respond to that, the outside twin jumped in. "How come I don't remember that?"

The first one shrugged again. "You were off dancing with some guy the whole night. Why should you remember?"

Tony intervened before the conversation got utterly derailed. "What did she look like?"

"Um, medium brown hair. It was wavy like movie stars from the forties. It was almost as if she was trying to be like Jessica Rabbit, you know, similar dress, less makeup though. She wore tall heels. She clearly thought very highly of herself and wasn't too pleased that Brad didn't."

"Did she give a name or any distinguishing information?"

Tony had a sneaking suspicion she might have been the Demon Culeen Will mentioned. The only problem was how she managed to go out in public without the Nym noticing what she really was. This bar might have turned out to be his first solid lead.

The nurse shook his head. "No, she just sent the drinks." Tony nodded, jotting down the last of his notes before slipping the pad back into his pocket.

"Thank you. You two have been very helpful."

The one sitting on the outside straightened. "We have? Cool!"

Grabbing his trash, Tony inclined his head toward both of them as he got up and left. His watch told him it was eight-fifteen. He hoped Will was still awake. He wanted to get Will's description of the Demon Culeen and see if it matched the woman from the club.

Mrs. Binns smiled and waved cheerfully, making her bangles jingle when Tony passed. He couldn't help smiling back. *How could someone so friendly be married to the captain?*

As Tony approached Will's door, he heard Tiffany's voice from inside the room. He paused in the doorway, almost feeling bad for interrupting. Then, with a sigh, he knocked on the mostly open door. Both of them looked up, and watched Tony as he entered and stood at the foot of the bed with his hands in his pockets.

"I have some more questions, Will."

Will's hand drifted to cover Tiffany's, where it sat on the bed. "All right, shoot."

"The…woman who attacked you. Would you describe her as looking similar to Jessica Rabbit?"

Will lifted one eyebrow. "Maybe, if I were a teenager. Her hair wasn't red, but I guess she was similar. Older though, maybe forty."

Tony sighed and took his hand out of his pocket and ran it through his hair. "Do you ever go to a club called The Rain?"

Curiosity brightened Will's face. "Yeah, sure. But not in the last year or so. Why?"

Tony just shook his head. There went the club as her hunting grounds theory. Tony thanked Will and said good night to the couple.

How did she find Will?

If the other vics were from the club, Will should have been too. Unless she attacked him just because he worked for the police. It wasn't perfect, but Tony could see her possibly trying to take out anyone she thought might threaten her mission. If that were true, she might start going after him. Was that why Chris thought he might be in trouble? Did she know that all along? That thought occupied Tony's mind on the drive to George's Place.

George's Place was just north of SeaTac Airport. Though it was right off the freeway, there were no signs for it. Travelers usually stumbled upon it during the day and on weekends. High school and college kids took it over in the afternoons. At dusk, though, a whole different crowd frequented George's Place.

It was the favored place of one of Washington and Oregon's largest biker gangs, the Ghosts. Their involvement in illegal activity could never be proven, but they always seemed to be around when illegal things happened. Tony really hoped this case didn't involve the Ghosts. He didn't need it getting any more complicated.

He pulled into the gravel lot about nine. It looked like any other diner across America except the twenty or so motorcycles parked out front. Crunching across the gravel, Tony prepared for the added challenge of having to question a motorcycle gang along with the staff.

When the bell above the door jingled, every person in the diner turned and stared at Tony. It was not a comfortable feeling. To his right, all the bikers were spread out, taking up half of the diner. To his left was the other half of the lunch counter and a dozen booths, only four of which were occupied. Directly in front of him was a hostess platform, which held the cheap, beat-up menus, and a green “Please Seat Yourself” sign. Beyond that was a small hallway leading to the bathrooms and the kitchen.

A large man in his fifties stepped out of the swinging door that led to the kitchen. He was six-two and beefy, like an athlete that started to soften a decade ago.

He had a thick mop of black curly hair, and folded his meaty arms over his pristine, full-length apron before demanding, "What do you want?"

Even though he had a sneaking suspicion it wouldn't help, Tony pulled out his badge. "Detective Anthony Hollownton, Homicide. I have some questions pertaining to an ongoing investigation."

There were a few grunts and grumbles from the bikers, along with whispers from the other patrons, as well as the three waitresses who stood huddled at Tony's left.

"Yeah, sure. Get out of my place," scoffed the man in the apron as he motioned with his chin toward the door.

Tony felt his temper flaring in his stomach. *This was absurd!* It was a horrible and long day; this was his last stop; and he didn't need more issues.

"Not a chance. I came down here to play nice where everyone is more comfortable. But if you prefer to be difficult, that's fine. I can have a small army of cops down here in no time, and we can all go down to the station together."

Part of Tony knew threatening this particular crowd was probably not the best move, but he was pissed and in no mood for anything other than full cooperation.

One of the bikers, a short bald man in his thirties, slid off his bar stool. "Try it!"

Tony felt the tension and animosity in the room rising higher. He wasn't sure who to keep his eyes on. Half the room was a potential threat, and his effort could go sideways, fast.

George unfolded his arms and took two menacing steps toward Tony.

"Oh, please, George! Knock it off! Nothing good is going to come from all that blustering."

George stopped about a yard from Tony, and turned to the woman talking. She was a short, redheaded woman in her sixties who was getting out of one of the booths. She was only five feet tall, at most, but must have had some authority because even the bikers went still.

"And you, Robin, sit your tiny self down before I beat you!"

Tony watched in shock as the biker sat back down on his stool. The woman nodded. Reaching into her back pocket, she dropped some bills on the table, and took her time walking to the front door. When she was next to Tony, she turned back to George.

"You are going to help this cop with whatever he needs. You hear me? May I remind you that you have four girls at home. You have just as much vested into this capture as the rest of us. Or would you like me to explain to them that although you could have helped, you chose not to?"

George glared at the woman, surprising Tony. Most people would not even think of challenging a man of George's size, but this woman was standing there, with her arms crossed, chastising him like a child. Finally, George growled, and to Tony's surprise, looked away.

"Fine, he can set up in the far corner. That way, the Jespers will have a harder time hearing everything."

That got Tony's attention. *Was this a Nym hangout? Was that why they were so against outsiders?*

The woman nodded her head in approval before heading out the door. Tony turned toward her and said, "I'll need to question you as well."

The woman snorted and looked over her shoulder. "I know plenty of information you would like to get your hands on. But none of it will help you with your current case." She smiled before jutting her chin toward their silent audience. "They'll all help you though." Then she walked out the door.

Tony knew there was nothing he could do to stop her. After a few moments of silence, he wondered if the diner's patrons would do as the older woman commanded them.

"Hey, sis, get me two more beers. There is no way I am talking to a cop this sober," a blond biker shouted as he pounded the table in front of him.

Several other bikers cheered their agreement. The youngest-looking waitress rolled her eyes before walking across the restaurant to the bikers. The hair from her choppy bob fell over her face as she walked.

When it seemed the diner at large would ignore him, Tony walked to the far corner booth and slid across the dark red vinyl, putting his back to the wall. After about five minutes, one of the waitresses walked up to his booth. She was no taller than the older woman, and looked Hawaiian. Her black hair was chopped close to her head, and her nametag read "Estella."

"What can I getcha?" When Tony just looked at her, she shrugged. "What? You're gonna be here a while. Might as well have something. Coffee?"

That was absolutely the last thing he wanted. But he knew that was probably what he would get if he didn't suggest anything else. "Apple juice, please."

Estella gave him a curious look before leaving to retrieve his juice. Tony watched as the third waitress, a young Latina, walked over and stood next to Estella as she was pouring his juice. He couldn't hear what was being said, and wished he actually possessed the supernatural hearing these people kept talking about.

His waitress came back and set the full glass down in front of him. Before he could say anything, she pulled a small bag of potato chips out from her apron pocket and sat across from him.

"Sorry, but since you're delaying my smoke break, I am just gonna eat something." Then she popped a chip into her mouth.

Tony pulled out his notepad. "Can I get your basic information please?"

"Sure, Estella Hong, age twenty-four, born and raised on Oahu. Been in Washington two years. Worked here one."

Tony nodded. "What can you tell me about Jessica Abrams? Anything could be important, even if it doesn't seem like it would."

Estella bobbed her head a few times. "Not much to tell really. She worked here longer than me. But she was only part-time. She was studying at the U for Psych or something. She pretty much just studied and worked. Jessica was pretty shy. Lidia and I only got her to go out with us in the last month. Mostly, she just kept to herself, with her nose in a book." She tipped the bag over her mouth.

Tony ran a hand through his hair and almost held his breath. "Where did you go out?"

Crinkling the now empty bag, she gave him a look indicating that was a silly question. "The Rain. Where else? They have some of the best drinks around and it is mostly our people, ya know."

"Were the three of you there two Fridays ago?"

She looked at him suspiciously. "Yeah."

"Did anything out of the ordinary happen?" Estella shook her head. When Tony continued to watch her, she shrugged. "It's not like we go there to hook up. We just go to drink and unwind."

Tony sighed. "Okay, if that's all you can think of, I'll talk to one of the other waitresses." As she got up, he pulled out one of his cards and slid it across the table. She looked down at it a moment before sliding it into her apron pocket.

While waiting for the next waitress, Tony tried to think of a game plan. *Was the Demon Culeen hunting for victims based on that one night at the club? Or was she still going there and trolling for them?* There was no way he could track down and question every person who went there that night. The best he could hope for was to ask the club for any security footage going that far back. Maybe, just maybe, the Demon Culeen would be visible on the tape. He hoped there wasn't a caveat like, *does not show up on camera* type thing. Tony shook his head. He had no proof the killer wasn't human. All he had was other people's say so, which just wasn't enough for him to jump to that conclusion.

He looked up from his notepad as the Latina waitress slid into the booth. They went through the same song and dance he did with Estella. This was Lidia. She painted the same shy picture of Jessica, and also stated nothing odd happened at the club. After Lidia left, Tony interviewed the last waitress and all the regulars, including the bikers. While the bikers were somewhat hostile, they did talk to him. But none of them gave Tony any new information. All they did was paint a more vivid picture of the shy, academically driven girl.

By ten-thirty the only person Tony had left to interview was George. The larger man sat across from him in the booth, his arms crossed.

"Is there anything you can tell me about Jessica that the others haven't already?"

It wasn't the most tactful way to put it, but Tony was exhausted and the other man kept glaring at him from the kitchen for the last two hours.

George continued to glare, but leaned forward. "What? Like if she didn't work for me, she might still be alive? Or how worthless the Nym community is since we still haven't caught the being that is responsible? You know, most people think you are going to figure it all out first, and then get yourself killed in the process. They say finding your rotting carcass is how we will discover who is really responsible." George leaned back again.

Surprisingly, Tony wasn't mad. He knew George was baiting him, but he also knew the other man was pissed at the situation and needed to lash out at someone. Instead of engaging his anger, Tony laid several of his cards as well as some bills on the table.

"I am coming in tomorrow to talk to your day shift crew. Please tell them to expect me. Call me if you or anyone else can think of anything useful." Tony made sure to keep eye contact until he was done.

He didn't wait for a response, but just headed out to his car. Maybe he was crazy, but he could almost feel the collective sigh of relief coming from the diner's patrons at seeing him go.

It would be close to midnight by the time he could crawl into bed. After such a long day, he was immensely grateful to finally be at the end of it.

Chapter 10

Tony heard thunder crashing all around outside. He knew immediately where he was in this dream, and recognized his parents' house as soon as he saw it. He was standing in the middle of his old bedroom, which was decorated just as he remembered. When he moved out, it was converted to a guest room.

The walls were still their flawlessly pure white. There were posters from Mariners games going back more than two decades. His bed was a mess of blue blankets and sheets. Several baseball bats leaned against the closet door; and his soccer equipment lay in a bag in front of the bats. At the foot of the bed was his movie collection that filled five bookshelves and spilled onto the light, wooden desk next to it. Tony shook his head and smiled. He was such a movie buff in high school. He scanned through some of the titles, wondering what he possibly could have been thinking.

He heard something hit the window. Turning, he pushed back the pale blue curtain. It was hard to see in the dark, but out on the lawn, he spotted a teenage Christina waving up at him, and beaming. This scene was familiar, but he couldn't put his finger on why. It wasn't his imagination as much as a memory. He was sure of that.

She came to visit a handful of times in high school, mostly during the last two years when they became close. The girl looking up at him was definitely the girl he remembered from high school. Her hair was dyed several shades darker than her natural red and she wore it in a long braid that often whipped around her neck. She was a little more than twenty pounds overweight.

She was always cute, but he never told her. Most of their years in high school, she tried to be tough and intimidating, and not the type of person Tony tell they were adorable. The tough image was always ruined when she grinned like she did now; and just too innocent-looking.

He waved back and headed out the bedroom door, quietly sneaking past his parents' room as he did so often during the last half of high school. Letting his feet guide him, Tony floated along, assuming this was just a memory evoked by seeing Christina again. Part of him felt sad because he knew the girl he was sneaking out to see would be dead in ten years; and there wasn't a thing he could do about it.

He stepped outside and closed the door without making a sound. Christina joined him and together, they began walking down the street in silence. Once they were far enough from his house, Christina stopped mid-stride.

Tony turned to her. “What’s wrong?”

She grinned at him; and the next thing he knew, she was hugging him. He smiled and his arms went around her, feeling just as he remembered it. Her hugs were always warm and welcoming.

Then he heard her speak into his ear and his memory fell into place, showing him the actual night. Dread filled him and he screamed inside his head.

“Oh, Two-Tone, it’s so good to see you! I’m glad I got to before college starts up. It’s too bad Cheryl’s already in boot camp.”

He heard the words escape his mouth without his brain’s permission. “I missed you too. Why did you agree to volunteer at that children’s camp most of the summer anyway? It doesn’t matter. Come on; some people I know are getting together down at the park, and I said I might stop by.”

She just smiled at him and let go, completely trusting his judgment. Tony yelled at his younger self to go anywhere else, except that stupid party. That party was one of, if not *the* reason why he never saw or talked to Christina again. When Cheryl returned from boot camp, she hunted him down relentlessly gave him a black eye for taking Chris to the party, which pretty much ended his friendship with her. How could he have been so stupid?

They were coming up on the park and Tony tried to force himself to keep walking past it. No matter how hard he tried to change things, they continued to play out just as they did before. Some of the guys saw them coming and waved them over. One of them started talking to him. He reacted just the same as he did that night, no matter what happened, so instead of paying attention to anyone in particular, Tony watched the rest of the group.

Christina was a master at pretending to be comfortable in situations she didn't like. But Tony knew her well enough to sense she wanted out of there. Her back was completely straight and one arm was clasping the other.

Why didn't he notice that?

Why didn't he notice that guy across from him leering at her?

Why did he walk away from her?

He heard himself laugh and turn down a beer. That guy was getting closer. Christina noticed it, but why didn't he? The guy was heading straight for her now and there wasn't anything he could do about it. Tony felt his body move, following the guy he was talking to before he began to scream her name in his head and everything went black.

Chapter 11

"Shut up, Tony, just shut up!"

He knew he wasn't dreaming anymore. He could feel a hand over his mouth as he woke. His heart began beating fast again, and he started struggling.

"Damn it, Tony! Calm down."

Tony instantly recognized that voice. He opened his eyes, and found he was still in his bedroom, but it was dark outside. Then he recognized the figure he was struggling against and ceased his resistance. Although he couldn't actually see her, something told him it was Cheryl.

"Finally! Geez! That was some nightmare. Don't freak out; I'm going to turn the light on." She removed her hand from his mouth and switched on the lamp.

Tony was startled at first, then his brain tried to explain what he saw. Part of him screamed that he had to be dreaming. This couldn't exist in real life. None of it could. His heart was racing as he looked at the Nym in front of him.

She was in her other form, and must have been in a hurry to reach him. Her skin was the same pale, translucent white Christina's was. Her hair was still black, but so were her eyes, although slightly bigger. Her wings were completely black as well, and she looked eerie, like some avenging creature straight out of a nightmare.

Tony struggled to reconcile his mind. It was all true. Supernatural species actually existed and were running around killing each other and humans. His reality shattered. But he wrestled the panic it into the furthest corner of his brain. He could lose his mind about it later. Right now, he needed to solve the case; and more urgently, figure out how and why Cheryl managed to get into his bedroom. She looked tired and hesitant, as if waiting to restrain him. When he didn't move, she cocked her head to the side.

"You're not reacting like most people would at seeing a Nym. Am I not the first then? Someone must have told you a great deal for your reaction to be so nonchalant."

Tony sat up. "I've been seeing Chrisa in my dreams lately. She explained some things, although I did not fully believe her until right this second. Trust me, inside, I am freaking the hell out, but I have much more pressing matters at hand."

She straightened, her eyes narrowing. "That is a very level-headed way of thinking. Suspiciously so. You have been seeing Chris, huh?"

He noticed the razor sharpness in her voice and spoke quickly. "The real Chris. She's thinner and wearing lingerie. Which, I must say, creeped me out the first couple of times I saw her. No, wait. I still have a problem with it."

Cheryl's mouth twitched as her body relaxed. "I half expected her to find a way to get to you." She shook her head solemnly. "We have to leave, so pack light. I need to take you somewhere safer than here. We need to hurry too."

Tony opened his mouth to ask what she was talking about, but she held up her hand. "Tony, we don't have time. Get your stuff together and I'll explain later."

Not sure what was going on, but positive arguing wouldn't help right then, Tony did as Cheryl said.

Fifteen minutes later, he was walking down the street with Cheryl. She ducked into the darkened doorway of a small shop. Tony followed her, and when they were only several inches apart, he could hear her cursing.

"What? What is it?"

She glared at him. "Will you keep quiet?! They'll hear you."

Since she was whispering, he followed suit.

"What are you talking about?"

She glared at him again and Tony rolled his eyes.

"Don't say anything else, okay? They might recognize your voice. The Culeen are everywhere. They must have been planning to take you tonight."

Tony felt as if his heart would stop and his blood ran cold. They were after him? Cheryl waved her hand as is if she were dismissing the question he dared not say out loud.

"We can't leave by sky because there is a swarm coming. They'll see us on the ground. Even if I were strong zap us to where we're going, they are close enough now to sense the magic."

Tony's brain began to overload, this was just too much to swallow. He closed his eyes and took a deep breath. There was a loud noise that cut sharply through his head, nearly piercing right through his brain. It sounded like soprano hitting a glass-shattering high note. Tony doubled over as the sound persisted. He was holding his head in his hands when the noise unexpectedly cut itself off. The ensuing silence made him collapse to the ground, still holding his head. He felt hands shaking his shoulders.

"Tony? Tony, are you all right? Talk to me! What is it?"

The pain finally subsided, and keeping his eyes closed, he got back up. Cheryl retreated slightly, trying to give him as much room as possible in the tiny doorway.

"There was this, this… sound. I couldn't hear it except in my head. It was so high-pitched, it hurt my ears. It was like a laser burning through my head."

Hearing Cheryl's intake of breath, he opened his eyes again and resisted the urge to rub his forehead. When he looked at Cheryl, her mouth was wide open and she was staring at him in shock.

"No, Tony; there's no way you could have heard that."

He grunted at her. "Oh? I beg to differ."

He could almost see all the composure draining from her body.

"Tony, are you sure that's what you heard? I mean, no words or anything?"

He was really getting aggravated with her now. "Yes, I'm sure that my head was being drilled by a high-pitched noise, Cheryl!"

She shuddered slightly. "There is much more to this than Chris let on." She took a deep breath as if trying to compose herself and turned to walk out onto the sidewalk.

Tony felt his hand shooting out before it grabbed her arm, pulling her back. It was much harder than he intended and it swung her back hard enough to hit the door to the shop. He let go, but stood in place so she couldn't leave the doorway.

"Explain now." It came out as a growl.

"Tony?" She seemed more surprised than anything else.

Tony took a few deep breaths. Cheryl was a friend and a woman; and Tony made it a rule not to hit either of those, but his patience was thinning fast. Cheryl seemed to regain some of her composure.

"Tony, that noise was me. I was sending a signal out to the nearest Nym-friendly cabbie to come and pick us up. Look behind you."

Tony turned his head slightly, and sure enough, there was a cab parked and waiting. He turned back to her.

"But to the cabbie it was simply words. That high pitch is what the magic behind the call actually sounds like. No one should have been able to hear it, but another Nym. And even then, only if he were standing between me and one of the cabbies. There is NO way you should have heard that! Let alone, have it inflict physical pain. This is bigger than I thought! What was Chris thinking in handling you by herself?"

Tony stiffened. "She was probably doing what she thought was best."

Cheryl rolled her eyes and snorted before pushing past him and opening the backdoor to the cab. When she noticed Tony was not with her, she swung her body back into the small entryway.

"Get into the cab. We don't have time for you to pout, or whatever the hell you're doing."

Tony crossed his arms over his chest. "No, I'm so far beyond tired of this. I want to know what is going on before I go anywhere else." He could feel the tension stretching much too thin between them. "I am WAY past my tolerance for this! Especially this Nym concept of 'we decide what you get to know' crap."

Several seconds went by as the two of them stared each other down. Then, Cheryl stalked toward him, her anger crackling through her. The rubber band of tension was beginning to fray. Her voice came out low, like a steel blade under a thin layer of silk. Not overt, but the threat was evident.

"I could make you."

Tony's sense of control snapped at the same moment as the tension. "No!"

It was the most threatening thing Tony ever heard said to him, and many times more threatening than he could ever be. He only became more shocked when Cheryl flew backwards and hit the cab. Instead of falling to the ground, she landed hard on the side of the back seat.

Forgetting his anger, Tony ran to her. He was astonished when he got there before she had a chance to fall out of the cab. With one glance, Tony realized she was unconscious and his training overrode his panic. Throwing in his bag, he slid Cheryl across the seat, and got into the cab, slamming the door. They started moving immediately.

"The hospital," he commanded the driver without even looking up.

"No way, man! I was told safe house and we're going to the safe house."

Tony looked closer at the man. "Look, I'm a cop…"

The driver held up a hand. "I don't care what you are. The safe house is where you're going."

Tony couldn't believe the stubborn arrogance of this man. "This woman needs immediate medical attention."

The driver snorted. "I've seen 'em heal worse things than that without any help. So just shut up." The last part came out more as a sharp bark.

Tony looked down at Cheryl, whose head and shoulders lay in his lap. If he couldn't get anywhere with the driver, maybe the people at the safe house be able to help.

"Besides, you're the one that did it to her, so why should you care if she's okay?"

Tony opened his mouth to protest, but the driver's laughing cut him off.

"I take that to mean you didn't know you were doing it. You should pay more attention to your emotions, before they get outta hand."

Tony closed his mouth. *How did this guy know all this?*

Before he could ask, the driver spoke again. "Here we are." The cab slowed to a stop in front of a long driveway.

It was a huge property, full of large trees with no house in sight. The other side of the street was exclusively trees. The only place in the area where trees grew so dense was national forest on the peninsula. The rich paid tens of millions of dollars to buy the property on the edge of the park. Reality hit him as the car stopped. The forest was a good hour's drive from where he lived, and they hadn't even driven ten minutes.

The cabbie turned and smiled. "I'll help you out."

The driver's door popped open and he exited the cab. Tony followed suit as the cabbie came around the car.

The man was the tallest person Tony ever saw, at least seven feet tall. He was also extremely muscular with tan skin, and black hair from what Tony could see under the man's hat. The headlights from the cab were not bright enough for him to make out anything else.

"Here, let me get her."

Tony stepped out of the bigger man's path. The cabbie opened the door all the way, folding his upper body inside. After a second or two, he reemerged with Cheryl in his arms and Tony's bag dangling from one wrist. He turned, shutting the door with his hip, and began walking toward one of the thicker trees. Tony jogged after him, trying to match the larger man's stride. He caught up just as the cabbie placed Cheryl in a sitting position, against the tree.

"Wait, I don't know where to find this safe house you keep mentioning. How am I supposed to help her?"

The cabbie stood up and turned to smile at Tony. "I keep telling you, she's going to be fine. Just stay put and someone will be along to get you here real soon." The man chuckled to himself before walking back to the cab. He was about halfway there when he turned around and started back. "Oh, and by the way, you left this in the cab."

Tony looked down at the man's outstretched hand holding Tony's notepad. He took it, grateful the other man noticed; otherwise, Tony would have lost most of his case information. He dropped it into his outer right pocket, intending to move it to its normal spot later.

"Thank you; how much do I owe you?"

The cabbie's laugh surprised him. It wasn't a reaction Tony expected. It was pleasant, slightly musical, and unlike any other laugh Tony ever heard.

"You don't owe me anything."

For a moment, it looked as if he intended to add something, but changed his mind at the last second. Striding back to his cab, he held his hand up in a wave. "Good luck."

Tony squatted down beside Cheryl to check on her when the cabbie's words made him look up just in time to see the cab turning around on the narrow road and returning the way it came. It was almost impossible to see her with the headlights gone. The trees were close enough together that beams of moonlight were few and far between.

"Now would be a good time to gain consciousness, Cheryl," Tony said under his breath in the general direction of her body.

"Who goes there?"

Tony jumped and his hand automatically went to his gun at the sound of the female French accent. When he was scanning the area around them, he thought about how cliché the question was.

"I know you're here. I heard you speak."

The tone she used made Tony shiver. She definitely possessed the voice of a predator. When his scanning was to no avail, he tried to hear her location.

"Stay where you are! I'm a cop and I'm armed," he warned her.

He hoped she wouldn't call his bluff, and would obey his order by staying where she was, but she had too much of an advantage.

There was a rustling in front of him on his left. Shifting, he aimed his gun at about stomach level; that way, no matter the height, he'd be sure to hit something.

"Anthony Hollownton? Is that you? Where's Cheryl?"

That was absolutely the last thing Tony expected to hear. Next, there was a click before a large flashlight came on, shining directly at him. Before he could protest, the light dimmed, and the rustling moved closer.

"OH, NO! What happened to her? Were you guys attacked? Are you okay? How did you get here so fast? How did you get here, period? We weren't expecting you to be all the way out here. Hold this."

The flashlight was shoved at Tony. He exhaled the breath he was holding and holstered his gun before taking the flashlight.

"Shine it at her chest."

Tony did as he was told; if it could help Cheryl, he wouldn't ask any questions. The woman put both her hands high on Cheryl's chest. After a few seconds, Tony felt a strange tingling before he saw Cheryl's eyes open.

"Get that out of my face!"

Tony quickly moved his arm. After the light was moved, Tony managed to get a good look at the woman with the French accent.

She had curly black hair, the front tried back with the ends touching her shoulder blades. He could see, even in the dark, her skin tone was tanner, indicating she probably came by the accent honestly. She held a gun in her right hand, and Tony could see a sword sheath peeking out behind her right side. When she took the light from him, he could no longer see the woman very well.

"Cheryl, what are you doing our here alone? How did you get here so quickly? I was under the impression it would be at least another hour?"

Cheryl slowly sat up, propping her back against the tree. "I have no idea. The last thing I remember is arguing in front of the cab."

Both women stared at Tony.

He shrugged. "Don't look at me. I haven't got a clue what's going on. The cabbie refused to take us to the hospital."

Cheryl blinked at him twice before turning her head toward the French woman. "What time is it?"

The other woman moved the light to illuminate a gold pocketwatch that appeared from somewhere, and replaced the gun she held. "It is... forty minutes after two. When did you leave his apartment?"

Cheryl became very still. "Two, or two-fifteen."

The other woman snapped the watch shut and her hand disappeared. "That is impossible."

The two women continued to stare at each other.

"I know."

Tony shifted his feet to maintain his balance. "Where is 'here' by the way?"

The French woman answered, "On the peninsula."

Cheryl started to get up. "Let's take the conversation inside, you know, just in case."

Tony and the other woman stood up and moved out of Cheryl's way so she had more room to push herself up. She was obviously putting in extra effort, but appeared fully capable of doing it on her own.

"Good call, if I'm not back soon, Wyatt Earp is going to come out here looking for me. You okay to walk on your own?"

Cheryl just nodded her reply as they started moving.

Tony couldn't help himself. "I'm sorry; who is waiting for you?"

The woman looked over her shoulder at Tony, since she had taken up the lead. "My partner, Mick. I just prefer to call him Wyatt Earp because he was one of the original cowboys. He often brags about his sharp shooting."

Tony didn't say anything but let the woman's words sink in. He assumed that meant he was the only non-Nym present, which was not the most comforting thought. Meeting someone old enough to have been an original cowboy was a different ballgame. It was one thing to hear the Nym had long life spans, and quite another to be introduced to a living example. How many of the Nym he encountered were that old? Or older?

After ten minutes of silence, they reached a large cabin that seemed to appear out of nowhere. It was a rambler, built to look like a regular cabin. The exterior was covered in half logs that may or may not have been fake. Tony couldn't tell. There was a covered front porch with two rocking chairs and a large porch swing. Nothing about the place screamed safe house except its location. Tony could make out a tall man standing on the porch with his hands on his hips, watching them approach.

Although light came through the windows of the cabin behind him, Tony couldn't get a good look at the man whom he assumed was Mick. When they got close enough, Tony's suspicion was confirmed. An ancient gun holster hugged Mick's hips, cradling two equally old-looking guns. Tony wasn't sure how the man could keep them in good working condition for more than one hundred years, but he was reluctant to ask. Anyone with the kind of obsession the French woman described was bound to get fanatical when asked about his particular subject of mastery. Tony was not in the mood for that brand of crazy.

Mick also had a modern-looking shoulder holster, totaling four guns on the man, from what Tony could see. Mick was about six feet, with sandy blond, severely short hair, and a stocky build. Tony could definitely see the man as a ranch hand.

"I see you picked up some stragglers, Porthos." Mick's voice was not quite as deep as Tony would have thought.

"Yeah, they were out by the tree next to the road." Porthos didn't hide her skepticism at how quickly they arrived.

Why did that name ring a bell? And in a national forest, filled with trees, why did Mick nod when she said 'the tree near the road' since the whole place was filled with trees? *What was with these people?* Tony was beginning to dislike all the Nym just on principle alone.

"How'd ya get here?"

The question was directed at Cheryl. As a human, Tony obviously wouldn't know about something so complicated as a car ride. Maybe it was from the lack of sleep, but Tony was becoming seriously irritated now. Cheryl just shrugged her response as the three of them drudged up the stairs and onto the porch. Mick raised an eyebrow, but didn't say anything.

Tony scanned the inside of the cabin as he stepped through the front door. They were in a large living room. On the wall to his left was a good-sized fireplace with a flat screen TV hanging above the mantel. CNN was on, but muted, without captions. All the furniture he could see was over-sized black leather. There was a couch, a loveseat, two chairs, and a recliner with the footrest in the up position. All were in a semi-circle facing the TV.

Further back on the same wall was a dark hallway, which Tony assumed led to the bedrooms. To Tony's right was a light-colored, wooden dining table with eight chairs neatly arranged around it. Beyond the table was an open doorway that Tony could tell was a full bathroom. Straight across the room was a black-and-stainless steel, fully equipped kitchen.

Tony could see a lot of money went into this place. Too much to only occasionally use it. It made him wonder how often citizens in the Nym community had to go into hiding.

He heard Mick shutting the door behind them before sliding several deadbolts. Then he heard chanting. He knew where it was coming from this time, and he turned to watch Mick drawing symbols in the air over the door. Tony felt his skin crawling. This chanting was not harmful or negative, but it also didn't have the positive effect of Chris's either. When Mick finished, Tony heard the same popping noise as before.

He ran both hands through his hair. "I hate that. I don't care how many times I'm around that damn chanting, it bothers me every time."

All three Nym stopped walking toward the leather furniture.

Cheryl rubbed her eyes. "What do you mean ‘every time’? How many times have you heard it?"

They all seemed a little too interested in his answer.

"Half a dozen maybe, this week."

The three of them exchanged glances.

"When? Where were you?"

Tony detected a frantic undercurrent to her words. Shrugging, he stuck his hands in his pockets. "Various places and people."

Cheryl jumped on that answer. "Who?"

Tony hesitated. He didn't know these other people, and was not sure he completely trusted Cheryl either.

"You KNOW who."

Cheryl blinked her confusion at him. "Why was she chanting? What could have possibly happened?"

Before Tony could respond, Porthos broke in and addressed both Cheryl and Tony.

"The caseworker? She's dead. I know that. Many people were very upset over it. Her husband nearly lost his mind. Mick and I had to help subdue him. How could she be involved?"

Cheryl turned her head toward the other two Nym, but continued to watch Tony as she answered. "She's been visiting him in his dreams. Trying to help him that way since she failed to do it in life."

Mick expelled a shocked curse and Porthos crossed herself. Tony had no idea what was going on. Porthos reached into her pants pocket and held something inside the pocket in her right fist. The other hand went up to her chest, surrounding, what Tony assumed, was probably a crucifix hidden under the garment.

"Why has she not crossed over? She needs to cross over. The longer she waits the slimmer her chances become."

Cheryl gave a heavy sigh, "I have no idea."

Porthos crossed herself again, and Tony felt panic rising in his chest. He ripped his hands from his pockets and made a silencing motion.

"What the hell are you talking about?"

Mick snorted, "Nicely put." Though it was meant as a joke, his heart didn't seem to be in it.

Porthos turned and looked Tony straight in the eye. "The dead can visit us for a month, tops, after they die. They are allotted that time to say goodbye and such. Then, God willing, they cross over and go to Heaven, Hell, or Purgatory, in rare cases. They cannot visit us while in the process of crossing over. It's for our benefit as well as theirs. Not until the mourning process is finished, or about eighteen months.

"For some reason or another, after eighteen months, most of us have reached the acceptance stage. Being visited in our dreams by our dead loved ones is more of a comfort than a detriment to the healing process. She has been dead what? Nine months? No less. She could only be visiting you if she had not crossed over yet. If she does not cross soon, she will be stuck here eternally, if she is not already."

Tony was more agnostic than anything else, but Chris was a devout Catholic. He was shocked and slightly horrified she would deliberately choose to trap herself on the earth as a ghost. Next time he saw her, if he ever saw her again, he intended to make her promise to cross over... if indeed, it was still possible.

Mick folded his arms over his chest and cleared his throat. "That is one theory anyway."

Porthos glared at him. Mick ignored her; all his attention was on Tony. "Look, we Nym, as a general rule, live a very long time. Long enough to cling to all sorts of outdated ideas. Don't get me wrong. I am very impressed that she can visit you. My understandin' is that it takes quite an amount of power to accomplish. But I don't think she's puttin' her soul or whatever in any danger. That's just superstition. You get a lot of that with Nym."

There was silence for several minutes before Cheryl turned to Tony.

"Regardless of that, she is visiting for a reason. So I need to know what's going on with you, Tony. Chris jumped on your case so fast, and there was only high clearance information, so she didn't share anything. Just made me promise to step in when certain things happened. She predicted the Culeen coming after you. I still don't know how she knew that."

Tony waited a second. “What do you mean ‘after’ me?”

Cheryl seemed to debate explaining before she opened her mouth. “I’ve been following you for the last two weeks. Checking to make sure things were okay, at first. Then, in the last couple days, I noticed I was not the only one following you. Two Culeen-entranced humans were picking up your trail at the station in the morning, then leaving when you went home for the night. I stopped following you after Saturday, and I started following them. They were talking about taking you this morning, and ‘taking you out’ was how they put it. They could not figure out what ‘she’ wanted with you. They were careful not to go back to the lair, so I don’t know who ‘she’ is, but I would assume it’s the colony’s queen.”

Tony could not have been more shocked. He was followed by three different people and never noticed. He had a pretty good idea who the “she” Cheryl was talking about was. But he wasn’t sure whether or not he should share that information. He decided to take a page from the Nym playbook, and pushed all the shocked, scared, angry, sad feelings aside.

“I was assigned to a murder case, then everything went haywire.”

Mick folded his arms over his chest. “How so?”

Tony mimicked the other man. “I’m not at liberty to share information on an ongoing investigation.” Both Porthos and Cheryl started to get angry, but Mick gave a sharp laugh.

“You must have been hanging around the Nym lately! Fair enough. I would appreciate though if you could tell us exactly how you got here tonight.”

The two women did not look happy, but neither said anything.

They all continued to stand there as Tony filled them in on everything that happened from Cheryl waking him up, and on. Tony felt there was no need to share his dream with anyone. No one spoke the entire time. When he finished, Mick gestured for everyone to sit down. They all moved and sat in separate seats. Tony took the chair on the left side of the semi-circle, and Cheryl sat next to him, leaning forward on the loveseat. Across from them, Mick sat in the recliner, after he pushed the footrest down, and Porthos sat next to him in the other chair.

Cheryl put her head in her hands. “That still doesn’t explain how we got here so fast.”

Tony nodded. “I don’t have a clue.”

Telling the story jogged Tony’s memory of his notepad in his outer coat pocket. Not wanting to lose it, he grabbed it and opened his trench coat to slide it into its usual spot. As he slipped it in, he hit resistance halfway through. Confused, he took the pad all the way out and reached into his pocket. The shock must have been blatant on his face because Cheryl raised her head and looked worried.

“What, Tony?”

So everyone could see it, Tony pulled his pad out of his pocket, and sat there for a second, his mouth dropping open as he viewed a pad in each hand, they were identical.

Mick let out a string of curse words.

Cheryl’s hand hovered above the pad in his right hand. “This is the one the driver handed to you, right?”

Tony just nodded. Cheryl snatched the pad from his hand and flipped it open to a random page. After less than a second, her eyes went wide, she gasped, and dropped the pad, which hit the floor close to her feet. She instantly curled her legs away from it, and pulled them up onto the couch.

“What?” Mick asked.

“What is it?” Both Tony and Porthos spoke at the same time.

For a moment, Tony wasn’t sure Cheryl would answer. Very softly, she replied, “It’s all Elderspeak.”

Porthos vigorously crossed herself several times, and spoke what Tony felt pretty sure was Latin. She reached into her pocket again. This time, she pulled the item all the way out. It was a very old, wooden rosary. She began clacking the beads together in prayer while looking at the notepad on the floor. Mick erupted with a very long and creative stream of curses.

Tony could feel his panic rising, caused by the others' reactions. He really didn't want to touch the pad again, but that little voice in his head told him he was holding it the whole time; so it couldn't have been that big of a deal. Bending down, he grabbed the pad off the floor, and leaned back as he flipped it open to the first page. It was almost anti-climactic. All he saw were swirly symbols, which he didn't even recognize as a language. He looked up at the group.

"I don't get it."

Cheryl's eyes kept glancing at the pad, so Tony closed it and put it in the right side inner coat pocket. All three of them visibly relaxed.

"Tony, that is the language of the Elders, both light and dark. Very few of us know how to decipher it. Many who have tried, resulted in a bad end, either suffering death or insanity. That book could contain spells to help you, or spells that will make you wish you were dead. Nym, by order of our ruling council, are not allowed to learn the language. The Culeen can't either. We aren't even supposed to look at it."

That was why they freaked out. Tony could understand that; although he wasn't sure he wanted to know what an Elder was.

"Four thousand years ago, the Nym and the Culeen were, for most intents and purposes, the only supernatural beings that we knew of. History has it that one day, those seventeen men and women walked into the Nym High Council chambers and announced themselves. They called themselves the Elders and told the council they were a very old, but dying race. They claimed the world was becoming too small for them to hide any more. At first, the council thought they were just humans until they started displaying their power. It was more advanced than anything the council could fathom, several times over. Their magic trumps ours and the Culeen's every time. There are rumors that they are the original species from which we and the Culeen were descended, but no one knows for sure."

A long silence ensued. Tony really didn't like knowing that there was a third, and more powerful species out there. Two supernatural species were hard enough for him to handle. Now there was another, which the other two were both afraid of.

Tony rubbed at his face. "So how do I find someone who can read it? And, can anyone tell me why the cabbie gave it to me?"

Cheryl stiffened and gave Tony a worried expression.

"Tony, the cabbie was probably an Elder, whether good or bad, I don't know, but an Elder nonetheless. As for finding someone to read it for you, there's only two beings I know of that can read Elderspeak." She looked at the other Nym.

Tony waited, but no one said anything. "And that would be...?"

Mick slowly leaned back in his chair. "A caseworker by the name of Christina Mirin."

Tony let out a very loud curse. "No way! No way she is the only one who can read this! That is just un-freakin'-believable. There has to be someone else."

Porthos continued counting on her rosary, "There is only one other person in the United States that I know of, and he resides in Boston. I do not think you have the time to seek his services."

Tony was furious at pretty much the entire world. The whole universe had just turned upside-down and fallen into his lap. Now, he was expected to deal with everything in it while lying about the case he was working on. Things were just a little too fantastic; and somehow, he knew they weren't going to get any better.

"So how in the world did she learn this all-but-forgotten language?"

Everyone looked at Cheryl. She and Chris had been friends for almost a year before Tony met them, which made Cheryl the reigning expert.

She shrugged. "I don't know. She never told me how she learned it. She already seemed to have a good grasp on it by the time I met her. Since she is part human, I guess it gave her a loophole. I don't have the faintest idea who taught it to her. It's not like Elderspeak is a language you can just pick up on your own."

Tony jumped as his phone began to vibrate. The three Nym looked at him, concerned, until he pulled the lit phone from his pocket. To his surprise, the captain's number was flashing on the screen. This did not bode well.

"Hello Captain?"

"Nelson's disappeared, I've had men out hunting him down for five hours. Both he and his wife are missing."

Tony jumped up as his heart rate sped up. "What about the baby?"

There was a pause that conveyed the captain's annoyance at being interrupted. "She was at her maternal grandmother's house. I have men watching her house, Nelson's townhouse, and his sister's place in Shoreline, just in case either of them show up. It's not looking good for him, Hollownton. Even if they find him, and he is declared innocent of all charges, he is still off the force. Find out whatever he was into, Hollownton, and do it fast. I can only keep Internal Affairs off your back for much longer. So get things done!"

The captain hung up before Tony had a chance to reply. He couldn't help but wonder if his involvement in the supernatural world got Rick into whatever trouble he was in now. A wave of guilt began pushing through him. Those around him were dying, injured, or in trouble, and Tony felt somehow, it was all his fault.

As he slid his phone back into his pocket, he noticed the three Nym watching him. But instead of addressing the questions he knew they had, he asked one of his own. "How am I getting to work tomorrow?"

Cheryl folded her arms, "You're not."

Tony snorted. "Yeah, right! Try and stop me." He wasn't sure if there was anything he could do to prevent her, but with lives at stake, he sure as hell intended to try.

Strangely enough, Cheryl caved. "Fine, but I'm following you every step of the way. We'll take one of the SUVs parked out back and I'll drop you off so you can pick up your own car. But I still have questions about what's happening, Tony."

Tony looked his old friend in the eyes. “Tell you what: I’ll have answers for you when I have a grasp on what’s going on.”

He could tell she hated his answer, she was practically fuming.

Mick snorted. “Leave the human alone. He needs sleep and he has a damn good point. If we’re gonna keep secrets from him, then he has every right to keep secrets from us.” The other man stood up and waved his hand to Tony to follow. “Come on, grab your bag and I’ll show you to a room you can crash in for a few hours.”

Tony lay awake in the foreign bed, knowing he needed to talk to Chris badly, but he didn't have any way to guarantee he could reach her. Clutching the small notepad, he hoped that having it on him might mean he could bring it with him into a dream.

He was completely wired. Knowing sleep was his best bet failed to sedate him. On the contrary; it just made his anxiety worse. Tony flopped onto his stomach and cursed a few times. He could get maybe three more hours of sleep if he passed out now. Somehow, he didn't think that was going to happen. Thoughts of the day continued to flash in his head. He needed to concentrate on the case, but the case was tangled up with the Nym; and for some ridiculous reason, the Nym all knew him. Right down to that one little, blond boy.

Tony wasn't sure how long he lay there staring at the wall, but after a while, he felt sleep tugging at him and he was more than willing to succumb. He was careful to make sure his final thoughts before he tumbled into the unconscious abyss were of Chris, hoping maybe, just maybe, that would get her attention.

Chapter 12

Tony found himself in the same bedroom again. For a split second, he held his breath. Did it work? Had he gotten Chris's attention? Then he took a better look around. Although the room was set up the same as the room he and his dream wife shared, this room was different. The bed was all black. The sheets, the pillows, and the bed frame were all the color of ink.

He felt slightly glad he appeared next to the bed, instead of upon it. The rest of the room was as uninviting and cold as a spider web. It felt as if once you entered the room, you were trapped; but he didn't feel any panic, which worried him. Clasping his hands behind his back, Tony walked over to the window. He felt a funny tug, but he couldn't quite put his finger on what it was. Once he got to the window, he gasped.

Where was he?

The window had no glass, although there was a barrier of some sort. The view outside the window almost looked like a desert. The ground was perfectly flat as far as Tony could see. It was that clay red color you only saw in the Southwest. There were no plants or animals anywhere. The sky was an unnerving reddish-purple, and almost murky. There were thin, pale blue clouds overlapping each other and moving more swiftly than Tony knew clouds could. This wasn’t coming from his imagination. He didn't dream of crap like this. His dreams tended to be based on reality. This was certainly not reality.

Was this where they kept Chris? As soon as that thought crossed his mind, Tony dismissed it. The entire place seemed desolate and covered in a thin layer of slightly lesser evil. Chris wouldn't stay there.

Just then, Tony heard a sharp gasp behind him. Spinning around, he saw a figure standing behind him, rubbing her arms and looking around with an expression of both worry and fright. It was Chris.

"Chris?" Tony started moving toward her with his arms out.

She instinctively took a step back, which stopped Tony dead in his tracks. Chris never backed away from him before. He dropped his arms. It took her a moment to really see him, and her expression hurt Tony. Her wariness and fright were because of… him.

"Chris, I would never hurt you. What's wrong? Where are we?" Tony desperately wanted to wipe the panicked look off her face. All the other important things he intended to discuss with her were instantly replaced by his irresistible urge to comfort his friend.

Her expression didn't change. "What do you want? I already told you years ago I would not help you. Even if you resurrect and killed me again. I will do everything in my power to stop you, you sadistic prick." As she spoke, her voice and posture grew stronger, but her eyes stayed the same. She was far beyond scared.

Tony couldn't have been more shocked if Chris had actually stabbed him. *What was she talking about?* He never laid a hand on her during their entire friendship, and he wasn't about to start now. *What was going on?* He was positive the woman was Chris and not just from a dream. He knew the difference by now. *Kill her again? Can the dead die twice?* There was only one way that could've popped into his head. *Resurrection!* How could he resurrect Chris? *Was that possible?* That thought turned his blood cold.

"What the hell are you talking about, Christina? What's going on? What are you stopping me from doing? I'M NOT DOING ANYTHING!" Tony began to feel the fingers of panic. He knew it was happening, but he couldn't stop it. For some reason, Chris hated him now, and was frightened of him, but he had no idea why.

She seemed to be getting defiantly angrier. Her shoulders clicked back and her eyes narrowed. "You're not funny, so don't try to be. We've been through this before. Playing innocent only works once and I won't fall for it again." With the last word, she whipped her head to the side to show Tony the long burns that looked like deep scratches down the back of her neck.

Tony expelled several curse words, but refrained from reaching out to touch the hideous marks. Now that he really looked more closely at her, he noticed a variety of scars all over her body. He didn't remember her having those before. What happened in the day or so since he last saw her?

"Geez, Chris! What the hell happened?"

She whipped her head back and actually looked surprised.

"What?" She was staring at him and still holding her hair. She seemed to be really studying him, like a professional art collector, authenticating a rare painting.

"I'm asking you, what's going on. Why are you so scared of me? Last time I saw you, you looked fine." Tony's overwhelming worry and panic were hard for him to conceal. What could've happened to his friend?

Without a word, she lunged at him. Tony didn't have time to move away, but she wasn't trying to hurt him. Her fingers burrowed through his hair and her palms slid against his temples. He was surprised by the gesture, but remained completely still. Then he saw a pale green light coming from her hands. He watched her expression go from concentration to astonishment.

She released him so fast, her hands flew out. She was backing away too rapidly, and fell onto the bed. Without a stop, she scuttled away until the bed was between them. When she was standing again, Tony watched her right hand automatically go to her cross, which usually hung around her neck. The silver keepsake was absent, however. He had never seen her without it. Her hand shook a little before simply flattening at the base of her neck. When he looked at her face, he could tell she was back to being frightened.

"Who are you?"

Tony didn't understand the question. "You know who I am."

She was shaking her head a little too quickly. "No, I don't. You're not the Anthony Hollownton I know. You feel like the Anthony Hollownton that died years ago, only to be replaced by the monster I know now."

Tony felt the world tilt. "What?"

She was shaking a little. Her eyes darted all over the room, as though she were looking for something. "How old are you?"

Did she sound even slightly optimistic? Or was he imagining it? Tony ran his hand through his hair, deciding to go along with her until she calmed down.

"Twenty-nine. It's May. I'm working on the case where I learned you were Nym and the whole world has been turned on its head." He wasn't sure Chris would reply.

She just kept staring at him.

"How are you here? You're not capable of time travel. I would know if you were. Who did you make a deal with to get here?" Chris demanded, speeding up her words as she spoke.

Tony sensed her frightened panic now replaced the anger that he glimpsed there a moment before. He wasn't sure what to address first. She believed him, which was good; but time travel? Either she was crazy, or things just rose to a whole new level of bad.

"What do you mean?" He decided to be cautious.

"You're thirty-seven years old, according to where I'm from. Tell me what you were doing before you slept. Maybe that will give me a clue as to how you got here. Or whether he brought you here to fool me."

She seemed to believe him, but didn't move any closer. He couldn't really blame her, but it still hurt. What did she see that made her so afraid? Then it clicked. Chris was afraid of *him,* or him as he would be at age thirty-seven.

He told her about Cheryl and the safe house, saying he was thinking of her as he fell asleep. When he finished his explanation, Chris was sitting on the far edge of the bed and staring across the room.

Her hands were folded over her chest and resting on her shoulders. She appeared so bleak and shut off, it hurt Tony. But he stayed where he was, trying to move as little as possible. The last thing he wanted was to find out what would happen if she were pushed.

After a minute or so, Chris gave a pained chuckle. "Ironic."

When she didn't say anything else, but continued to stare, Tony shuffled his feet.

"What's ironic?"

She looked up at him, with a defeated expression, but Tony detected a small aspect of peace in it.

"You summoned me. But since I was dead at the time, you couldn't summon 'the me' from your present. I exist in the future, and you have resurrected and killed me several times."

Tony felt bile rising in his throat. "What did you just say? Why would I do that?"

The idea was beyond sick, and something his mind just couldn't wrap around actually doing. She gave him the saddest smile he ever saw; and a sharp pain spiked through Tony's body and broke his heart.

"That's a long and terrible story," Chris replied. "If you are whom you claim to be, then you can change it. Make the outcome different. Then none of this will have to happen. Or things could get worse. Things can always get worse. You taught me that."

Her eyes glassed over slightly with her last sentence. She looked vacant for a second, like the lights were on, but no one was home. The expression gave Tony the creeps.

"How could this happen? I would never hurt you, Chris. You're telling me that I did this to you?" His gesture encompassed all of her.

She gave him that smile again, making his chest ache.

"Things change, Hollownton. People change with the times. At first, you think you're doing the right thing, but in the end, you're not. You become the incarnation of your decisions. Tell me what happened last time you saw me." She almost sounded wistful, like she was struggling to stay in the present, but could only make it halfway there.

That scared Tony more than anything else. Tony sighed, but still didn't move any closer. His friend appeared to be nothing more than a shell. Almost as if her personality was carved right out of her. She couldn't even call him by his first name anymore. Tony wondered if she even remembered his nickname.

In a quiet voice, he told her about their last meeting. She listened intently, the hollow quality and sorrow never left her eyes. What did he do to her?

She sat there staring at him for quite some time. At first, it was unnerving to Tony, seeing those blank, yet tragic eyes. Then Tony realized she was thinking. Trying to remember the events he just related to her. Finally, she shook her head, as if trying to clear it.

"I think I vaguely remember that. Parts of it anyway. It was the last time I saw you for quite a while. I want to say a year, but I am not certain. It was so long ago. I remember coming back, though, and finding you changed. Soon, you were consumed by other influences that would alter you completely." There was a pause and she seemed to get angry.

"And me and my stupidity! They never warned me when I took your case of the consequences. My blind affection for you stopped me from seeing the changes until they were irreversible. I should never have died the first time! I should have… I don't know." She rubbed her hollow face.

Her personality kept washing in and out like the tide. Perhaps, she couldn't maintain her solidity for too long. Tony wanted to hug her so bad, he ached; but he knew this Chris would be even less receptive than the old Chris.

"What can I do to change things?" Tony inquired.

It was the only thing he could think of saying to help his friend, and everyone else. She looked up at him again and he watched the gears in her head slowly begin to turn. It was unnoticeable at first. Then, as if she flooded back into herself, and right before his eyes, she turned to steel. Her back straightened, along with her arms, and her chin lifted up. At that moment, Tony realized she had not been looking at him in the eyes. But she did now. Her cold, green eyes bore into his.

"I'm going to tell you how to summon your Chris, the dead one. Specifically, the one from your time. I'll just have to pray I'm making the right choice. I'm giving you temporary power over me. Do you understand? It's one thing to have power over the land of the living; and quite another to have power over the land of the dead. Your 'me' could be quite pissed at you, but you can't tell me where you received the information! Do you understand?! To know what future is in store for me would kill me right then. Not literally, but you know what I mean."

In her last sentence, Tony glimpsed some hope. It was only a small show of her former personality. He hadn't totally beaten it out of her. A wave of relief washed over him, and he almost missed her staring at him, and waiting.

"Okay, I'm ready now; show me," he said, folding his arms over his chest.

She watched him for a second somewhat warily, as if his posture made her nervous. Afraid she might fade out again, Tony uncrossed his arms and jammed them into the pockets of his sweats. She relaxed slightly. He barely noticed it.

"As you're falling asleep, picture me as you last saw me, in our last meeting. Repeat this three times, 'Christina I summon thee from the land between. I call on thee to visit me within the land of dreams.' Do you have it?" She looked at him expectantly.

Tony felt a tad creeped out, but he repeated it. Something about it, however, didn't feel right. Probably the whole "summoning the dead" thing.

"I don't need to call her by her last name?"

Older Chris gave him that heart-wrenching smile again. "No, if you have a personal connection to the person or they do to you, then no last name is necessary."

Tony shuffled his feet again. Part of him didn't want to leave this woman that was once his friend. He also didn't want to return her to the hell that his future self confined her in. She quieted his thoughts by straightening her lingerie.

"Can I help you with your questions? I assume you were calling me because you had more questions. I might not remember much, but if you need help badly enough to have called me, I would like to try." She wasn't even looking at him, but watching the closed door as if she expected it to do something fascinating.

Tony felt like a jerk. "Why would you help me, knowing what I could become? And what I've done to you?"

She fidgeted, but didn't change her gaze. "Believe me, it's hard. But I have to remember you were not always like that; and by helping you… maybe I'll be helping us all. I'm just praying you are whom you say you are. And that this isn't another one of your tricks."

Tony couldn't fathom the leap of faith she was investing in him at that moment. "I promise you, I'm telling the truth." It was all he could give her, but no real assurance. There was nothing he could do to truly convince her who he was.

She looked at him closer then. Despair filled her face before she turned away again. "I've heard that before. But you feel different, you've never been able to fool me that way before."

She sounded so hopeless, Tony wanted to wrap her in a bear hug, almost more than he wanted to breathe.

"The second notebook I mentioned. It contained Elderspeak. I was told you were one of the few who could read it."

Wrapping her arms around her own waist, as if trying to comfort herself, or perhaps, just trying to hold herself together, Tony wasn't sure.

"I did. I bartered with a Demon Culeen to burn it from my brain. That, and several other things, after Hollownton resurrected me the second time. He was so furious when I ruined his chances for that information, it took two days for him to kill me again. That was the first time I endured a death by torture. I was naïve at the time and thought that would make it final."

The older Chris snorted, but it was so faint, Tony barely heard it. He didn't want to know what she bartered for, or what the man she called Hollownton could have done.

Her eyes started to glass over again, but this time, she scrunched them closed as if to resist it. "What's your next question?"

Tony could barely even remember his previous question. He scoured his mind for just one, even though it was a feeble excuse to prolong the woman's stay. "Who can I trust to help me with this case? I'm hunting down a Demon Culeen." He doubted she remembered the specifics, but anything would do.

She stared at the door for a while. "I think there is no one, really. I would have said me, but I'm already dead. No one knows enough this late in the game to be of any real use." There was a pause as she swallowed. "I'm assuming William was already attached."

Tony nodded, then realized she wasn't really looking him. "Yes."

"I remember that, I remember you telling me, about William... about the baby." She seemed to get lost for a minute or two before coming back. "No, no one. I think you are on your own this time, Anthony."

Tony could have cried when he saw the effort it took for her to say his name. The way she said it made it sound so foreign, like it never even crossed her lips. It made Tony realize just how much affection Chris put into his name every time she said it, even when she was mad at him. Tony's chest hurt like an open wound for this woman. He couldn't imagine how she wound up like this. She seemed almost broken. Shaking slightly, she stood up.

"I promise you, Chris, I won't let this happen to you," Tony told her softly.

She gave him that sad smile again. "I need to go. I can't sleep very long anymore. My body will be waking up soon."

She spoke to his shoulder. He could hear it in her voice, she didn't believe him, as if even a tiny bit of hope would crush her. Without another word, the older Chris walked out the door.

Tony collapsed on the bed after the door closed behind Chris and felt hot tears dripping down his face. How could he ever hurt his friend? He vowed that if he ever stumbled across a spell that could resurrect the dead, he would burn it and any other copy in existence. He could not let the future repeat itself.

Chapter 13

Tony woke with a start and reached for his gun, but found nothing: no gun, and no table. Blinking back the panic, he remembered where he was. Turning to his left, he glanced at the digital clock in the far corner of the room. It was six am. He had an hour before he had to get up. Groaning, he rolled out of the bed and went about getting ready for the day, but his thoughts were consumed by the visit from the older, and very broken Chris.

When he finally made his way to the kitchen, the only other person he saw was Mick, who grunted a greeting over his coffee mug. Mick instantly returned to the newspaper spread out before him on the island in the middle of the kitchen. After some raiding of the fridge, Tony moved to sit diagonally from the other man with a bottle of apple juice and a bowl of generic corn cereal.

Mick looked at him over his paper, and raised an eyebrow. “No coffee?"

Tony took a swig of juice before answering. "No, I don't like the stuff."

The other man snorted loudly. "Weren't you born here?"

Tony nodded, "Yep."

Mick shook his head and returned to the paper.

Tony was beginning to respect the other man, and wanted an objective opinion about the dream he had. He wasn't too sure how Cheryl would take it. "Is it possible to call someone into a dream from another time period?"

Setting down his cup, Mick looked up at Tony, with a thoughtful expression. Both hands went to the ancient gun holsters, rubbing the leather in a habitual gesture. "I suppose so, but I have no idea how. Could get kinda mucky, I think, messin’ with the whole linear time thing. Couldn't make a habit of it. Be interestin’ to see where your current path ends up, since the future's always changin’. Probably addictive though. Nope, I see no reason why it couldn't be done. You do it?"

Despite his rapid fire of thoughts, Mick’s words were slow in pace. Tony hesitated before nodding.

Mick nodded back. "I take it you got bad news."

Tony just nodded again.

Mick gnawed on the toothpick Tony didn't notice before. "Well, good news is: you can change it; bad news is: you might not know how." Mick finished with a shrug.

Tony hesitated before asking his next question. Resurrection was simply not a pleasant topic. Certainly, not one to be discussed with anyone religious. Mick didn't strike Tony as a terribly religious person, so he thought maybe now was the best time to ask.

"What about bringing people back from the dead?"

Mick leaned back on his stool, crossing his arms, and giving Tony his full attention. "And where exactly did that come from? Your dream again, I suppose," Mick drawled, raising both eyebrows.

Tony cursed in his mind. Perhaps this wasn't the best time after all. "Yeah, someone mentioned it."

The toothpick reversed its position once, then twice, as Mick watched Tony for a few seconds before leaning over his paper again.

"It's not worth it. No matter who you might be thinkin' 'bout bringin' back. It uses major bad mojo and they don't always come back quite right. It takes a lot of skill, in the first place. We're not talkin' zombies either, those are easy once you got the right cocktail. No; bringin' back the dead means you got access to the soul. It has to be snatched up before it crosses over and the body's gotta be in workin' condition. General rule is, they don't last long though. We always die untimely deaths. You know 'em when you see 'em. Their eyes look dead most of the time. I was told once that was a defense mechanism. Real ones are pretty rare. Shoot, I didn't believe in 'em 'til Porthos and I had to put a group of 'em down 'bout seventy years ago. They didn't even try to resist us. Every single one wanted to die. Hell on Earth, if you ask me."

Mick physically seemed to shake the memories out of his head and blinked a few times before draining his mug.

"They were all human though. Yer friend, the caseworker, isn't. Things would just work different on her. If you care 'bout her at all, you won't think 'bout doin' it." Mick gave Tony a meaningful look before getting up for another cup of coffee. Tony felt the need to defend himself, probably because the future Tony was capable of doing it, and multiple times.

"I wouldn't. It sounds so wrong. I was just wondering if it could actually be done."

Mick nodded, but didn't say anything else. They sat in silence until the two women joined them and began organizing the schedule of who would follow Tony, and when. Tony really wanted to protest the need for a babysitter, but he knew he would lose any arguments. Normally, even that would not deter him from trying, but lately, he thought maybe he should just keep his mouth shut.

Tony heard his phone ringing from where his jacket lay on the back of the couch. He managed to grab it right before it went to voicemail, but didn't recognize the number.

"Hello? Anthony Hollownton."

"Hi, this is Max Kim, May's uncle. I hear you're looking for me."

Tony couldn't help wondering how word could have gotten to the man so fast.

"Yes, I need to interview you about...." *What was the best way to put it?*

"I figured as much. You got a time or place in mind?" The man on the other end sounded weary and tired, as if the call was draining his energy.

Tony did a rapid fire check list of when he could fit the interview in. He had to go to the department, the morgue, George's, and The Rain. That was only as long as no other deaths were reported last night.

"How about The Rain at seven pm?" He thought it wouldn't be too crowded on a Wednesday night, although he had no experience with clubs.

Tony could almost hear Max flipping through his own schedule.

"Yeah, I should be able to make that."

Then, there was a strained silence, and Tony cleared his throat. "Okay, I'll see you at seven. And I am so sorry for your loss."

There was another silence before Max hung up.

No sooner did Tony put the phone back, than it started to ring again, flashing another number he didn't recognize.

"Hello? Anthony Hollownton."

"Are you watching the news?" It was Will. He sounded worried.

"No, what channel?"

"Five."

Tony picked up the remote from the table and flipped to the station Will told him. As he clicked up the volume, the three Nym became silent as the dead. On the television, the peroxide-blond, overly made-up reporter displayed a well practiced frown. Her eyes gave away her true worry.

"That's right, folks. I, for one, could never have thought of such a thing. We're being told, however, the best detectives from the King County Police Department are moving on this as fast as they can."

The camera angles switched, and the reporter turned with it. "For those of you just joining us, the story of the hour is quickly becoming the story of the year. The murders that recently hit the Seattle area are now being considered a serial murder case. Although we have been reporting the murders as we get information on them, little was actually known until this morning."

There were several curses from behind Tony before Mick came over to stand next to him, thumbing his gun belt.

Will's solemn voice came through the phone. "Oh, just wait; tell everyone it gets worse."

Tony snorted, *just what he needed*. "Will says it gets worse."

Mick mumbled something Tony couldn't hear.

"A reliable source told Channel Five this morning that one of the main reasons these crimes have not been solved was because one of the detectives assigned to the case, a Detective Rick Nelson…"

A photo of Rick appeared on the split screen next to the reporter, "may actually be involved with the crimes. When called for comment, the department did not respond, but at seven am this morning, a press conference was held by Police Chief Reynolds. He stated that there is indeed a manhunt in progress to find

Detective Nelson who has mysteriously disappeared, along with his wife Amanda Nelson."

A family photo replaced the one of Rick in uniform. "If any of you viewers should see the detective, or his wife, the police say not to approach him or her, but immediately call nine-one-one."

Tony didn't realize he was cursing until Will interrupted him.

"Just wait."

Tony glanced at the phone, "No way!"

Will gave a half-hearted chuckle. "Oh, yeah."

The reporter switched angles again, this time the camera zoomed in for a close-up.

"Our source also told us something the police will not confirm."

Both Tony and Mick cursed. Porthos and Cheryl moved closer and stood on Tony's other side. Porthos had her right hand on the hilt of the sword at her hip, and her other hand in her pocket. Tony had no doubt she was fidgeting with her rosary.

"These seemingly unrelated murders are actually all connected. The victims are part of a secret society known only as the Nym. Our source unfortunately didn't have anymore information regarding this secret society, but we will keep you, the viewer, informed as the story unfolds. More on this story, and any new updates after the break."

The camera faded to a toilet paper commercial, and Tony clicked it off. There were curses and prayers being volleyed around as the three Nym struggled with the public announcement and being “outed.” Tony stared at the phone and a jolting shock ran through his system.

Who could have leaked that to the media? It could only hinder the case.

"Did you see the press conference?" Tony asked Will. Glancing at the clock, Tony assumed it must have been a short one, considering it was only twelve minutes after seven.

"Yeah, I did. The chief gave them next to nothing. He refused to answer any questions and seemed royally pissed off to discover there was a leak somewhere. Especially, since only a few people knew about this case."

Tony heaved a weary sigh. Even he would have put himself at the top of that list. He felt pretty sure that others would also. *That was just great.*

"All right, thanks, Will. Call me if they report anything new, okay?"

"Yeah, sure. Who are you with anyway?" Will attempted to mask the tone of protective curiosity from his voice.

Tony heard it, nonetheless. Apparently, Will was taking his promise to Chris very seriously.

"Cheryl and two others at the safe house."

"Which safe house?"

"The one on the peninsula," Tony replied, wondering how many there were.

"That would mean you're with Porthos and Mick. They bicker like alley cats, but they're really very good."

Tony snorted. "Do you all know each other?"

Will laughed. "I only know of them by reputation. It's important to know the safe house guards. They'd have no idea who I am." Tony could almost hear Will smiling. "Talk to you later, Tony."

"Yeah, later, Will."

Tony hung up the phone just as Porthos flipped hers open and pressed a speed dial. After a few seconds, someone on the other end picked up. "Donald, are you all right?"

The name clicked in Tony's head. *That kid at the morgue... No way!*

"What do you mean, 'you were sleeping'? Don't you have to be at work by eight?"

Tony couldn't hear the other side of the conversation.

Mick leaned in to whisper to Tony. "Donald's her baby brother. She's more protective of him than a cougar with her cubs. Always worryin' 'bout him for somethin'." Mick snorted. "Shoot, the boy is seventy-five years old. He can take care of himself. I'd already been livin' out on my own for sixty years at his age. She was swashbucklin' with the Musketeers, and pretendin' to be a man half the time, so you'd think she'd realize that. The kid knows he's fine on his own. She should accept it too." Mick straightened his back.

Tony wasn't sure what to react to first: that seventy-five was still considered a “kid,” or that Porthos was at least three hundred years old! *How long could Nym breed for anyway?* A three-hundred-year difference between siblings seemed a bit much to Tony.

"What do you mean, you have no idea what I'm talking about? Don't you watch the news? Turn that monstrosity you call a television on to Channel Five."

There was a pause as if she was interrupted.

"I do not care if the anchor for Channel Seven is hotter; go to Channel Five. Call me back after you hear the story." Porthos rolled her eyes at the phone. "You'll know which story." Then she hung up, but didn't put the phone away.

She looked at the group. "My little brother currently interns at the morgue. He'll be able to tell us what, exactly, they found on the bodies."

Tony couldn't help scoffing. "No, he won't. His boss was pretty careful to leave him out of the incriminating parts. I know, and I'm sure as hell not going to share." Tony looked Porthos dead in the eye. "And if you tell your brother to snoop, I'll have Viggo dump him so fast, he'll get whiplash."

Okay, so he was pissed. His case was no one else's business and he planned to go with Chris's advice and keep everyone out of the loop. They were all still staring at him when Porthos's phone rang. As she flipped it open, even Tony could hear the swearing coming from the other end.

"Do you know anything helpful?" Porthos asked while putting her brother on speaker phone.

"Cha, nah. Viggo kept it all hush-hush, ya know. I got to help with the autopsy, but none of the actual tests. She was pretty freaked out about it though. She called this detective guy Hollownton, and she was pretty agitated 'til he got there. He was a little wonky though."

Everyone’s eyes looked up from the phone to Tony.

Porthos was the first to comment. "How so?"

"Oh, ya know. He wasn’t like others. Not one of us, but not a run-of-the-mill human either."

The Nym all looked at Tony in examnation.

"And what do you think he is, little brother? A sensitive? A medium?" She glanced at Tony from the corners of her eyes. "Or something darker?"

Cheryl stiffened from Porthos's other side, obviously, not appreciating her last question.

"Nah, man, nothing like that. It was like he knew. You know, like he knew what killed the lady. I don't know… could be a witch maybe."

Tony saw all three sets of shoulders drop as they collectively exhaled at once. However, why the seventy-five-year-old intern's opinion mattered so much was beyond him.

"All right, well, keep your eyes out for anything off at work this week. Things could get bad quickly."

There was a sigh at the other end of the phone. "I'll be fine, Antoinette. I can take care of myself. But, yeah, I'll let you know if anything twitchy happens. Get it? Morgue? Twitchy?"

Porthos made a disgusted noise and hung up the phone. She was muttering what sounded like French. *Was Antoinette her first name? And Porthos simply a nickname?* Tony felt odd calling someone he barely knew by her nickname.

Cheryl folded her arms. "Right, well on that note, let's get Tony to work. It's an hour's drive and having him show up late would look suspicious."

Heading for the door, Cheryl just assumed everyone else would follow her, and they did. Porthos stopped at the base of the steps that led up to the porch. Tony followed suit, which, in turn, made Mick stop. He scanned the area with his hands on the butts of the two newer guns.

"What? What is it?" Tony looked between the two Nym.

Mick finally looked at him curiously. No one spoke until Cheryl's voice wafted from around the corner where he assumed a vehicle would be.

"She's not on first shift, Tony. Porthos is staying put, so hurry it up."

Mick let his hands fall back to his sides as he laughed at Tony. "Shoot, son! You had me goin' there for a second."

With that, he headed toward the sound of Cheryl's voice. Tony glanced at Porthos, who was trying not to smile, before following the other two Nym.

Tony rode for about fifteen minutes in silence as Cheryl drove an all-terrain vehicle Tony never heard of. He was in the passenger seat. Mick had plucked a worn cowboy hat and a pair of black shades from where they were perched on the dashboard, and put them on. Now, he appeared to be dozing in the middle row of seats. At least, that's what Tony thought until Mick spoke and Tony detected no traces of grogginess in his voice.

"So, uh, how is it you two are acquainted?" Mick asked with a small smile on his face.

Cheryl answered before Tony could open his mouth. "What makes you think we know each other?"

He chuckled behind them. "Shoot, honey, you don't fool me. You don't pull strings to get safe house duty for a stranger when you ain't even a caseworker. Plus, you both interact like people who've known each other a long time. We got forty-five more minutes to kill. Might as well satisfy my curiosity."

Tony could hear the amusement threaded through Mick's voice.

Cheryl shifted in her seat. "We went to high school together."

There was a howling laugh from the backseat. "That there's priceless. I didn't know you were so young. I figured you for a deuce; and here you aren't even half a century! How'd you meet? That small of a high school?"

Tony watched as Cheryl's eyes and lips thinned.

Being unsure why, he decided to answer instead. "We worked on the same play together in theatre our first year."

More laughter from the backseat.

Tony figured it was time to change the subject. "So… is Porthos her real name? Or is it Antoinette?"

That was followed by silence in the backseat. Tony felt the other man's mood dropping.

"No, it's Antoinette. But don't call her that. She goes by her husband's name. You know, like from the Three Musketeers. He was famous in their day, but he was human. He died fightin' for a cause both of them believed in. After that, she would only go by his name. I'm told she was much lighter and prone to less worry when her husband was still alive. It was before I was born though, so I don't know for sure. Like most Nym that marry humans, she watches over her descendants. You know, the ones that have so much human in them, there's no way to tell they carry Nym genes. It's kind of a sad story, so she rarely discusses it. I wouldn't recommend bringin' it up." Mick folded his arms and leaned back against the seat.

Tony again shifted topics, but wanted to avoid sharing anything about the case. "How long have you two been partners?"

Mick seemed to think about that for a few moments. "Since tommy guns were the in thing. So I don't know… 'bout eighty years maybe. I love to irritate her, and despite my age, I'm one o' the best there is. So it's been a mutually beneficial relationship. We're due to switch up here soon though. Command doesn't let partners stay together longer than a century. They claim it keeps us from gettin' complacent."

Tony sensed, although Mick did a good job of hiding it, that he would miss his partner. Since he kept striking out with his choice of conversation topics, Tony opted to keep his mouth shut and the car fell into silence again. He didn't particularly like being left with his own thoughts though, since they continued to center on his dead friend.

"Is that how you all met the caseworker then?" Mick inquired.

Figuring Cheryl would not answer, Tony replied. "Yeah, that's how I met Chris anyway. Cheryl knew her from before."

There was a thoughtful silence.

"You know, it's all over--what she did. Took a while, but people put two and two together. Then there were other stories circulatin' 'bout her. Don't know if there's much truth to 'em though."

Tony longed for Mick to indulge his curiosity, but Cheryl beat him to the punch.

"What stories?" Her voice managed to mix worry with curiosity.

"Oh, the most prominent one was 'bout her when she was a kid. I'll spare the gory details, although she not only escapes a Culeen den, but also saves a cousin from the den at like, only eight years old. Seems a tad too Herculean to me."

"She was twelve," Cheryl corrected him. Her tone was so solemn.

Tony knew there were important details being omitted. That thought was only confirmed by the string of curse words that he heard being expelled from the backseat.

"I heard several versions." Mick was leaning forward now so he could see Cheryl's face.

Her expression was angry, but blank, as if she were hearing the story in her head.

"Magic was never Chris's forte."

There were more curses as Mick leaned back against the seat. Part of Tony wanted to ask about the story, but another part, and the more prominent one, knew nothing positive would come from knowing.

The rest of the ride was silent. They hit some traffic upon re-entering King County.

Tony had a thought. "You can't follow me the whole day."

The answer came from the back seat. "Why not?"

He wasn't sure how to put it. "I've been assigned a new, young detective-in-training to work with. Would you care to explain to her why two strangers won't let me go anywhere alone?"

Tony hoped that would be enough of a reason. He tried not to suggest he really didn't want them around while he was doing his job, or at least, trying to do his job.

Cheryl turned off the freeway, only to get on again, but in the other direction. "Then you're going to need your car."

Tony was surprised. "You're not going to argue about it with me?" He was anticipating some kind of protest.

She shrugged. "It makes sense; plus, I've tailed you for a while, and it's not like I can't do it now."

He wasn't sure if that was really a comforting thought, but he kept his mouth shut. Having gotten what he wanted, he decided he shouldn't argue.

It took ten minutes to get to his apartment building. Cheryl was careful to park out back in case the Culeen were still watching Tony, they wouldn't notice he had help. That was the way she put it anyway.

Tony walked through the lobby of his building, nodding at the security guard as he passed. When he reached the tenant parking lot, he scanned the area. He didn't expect the Culeen following him to jump out and yell "BOO!" but he hoped maybe, just maybe, he'd catch a glimpse of one of them. Of course, he didn't.

His entire ride to work was consumed by his thoughts of Chris. If the last dream were true, at some time in the future, he would become a monster and torture her for years. Tony couldn't believe he could do a thing like that. He also didn't believe he would call an older version of his friend to him through time. He couldn't believe it, despite the nagging voice in his head, which kept insisting he knew it wasn't a lie.

What could he possibly do to make it up to her? Track down her husband? And tell him what?

He decided to summon her tonight and tell her to leave. He blamed himself for her misfortune, yet he had no idea how he could have prevented it.

Everything around him seemed to be going down the toilet, and there was nothing he could do to stop it. After parking his car at the precinct, he directed his anger at the killer responsible for all of this. If Tony could take her down, things could be all right, or at least, they might suck less.

At quarter to nine, Tony walked into the precinct and saw Bentley was already at Rick's old desk, which someone had thankfully, cleared. She was squinting at the computer screen and pulling on her brown hair, one strand at a time. Tony figured it was an absent-minded gesture, and she probably didn't even realize she was doing it.

Tony also noted the captain's office door was shut and the blinds were all closed, which was not a good sign. He strode across the room and pulled out his chair.

She looked up, her hand rising. When she saw who it was, she dropped her hand. "Good morning, sir."

Tony started wondering just how young she was. "Good morning, Bentley. All right, so what have you got?" Tony tried his hardest to make his voice sound authoritative and encouraging. He found himself momentarily grateful that he coached soccer for four years. At least, he knew how to adopt a teaching demeanor.

Bentley sat up as straight as she could, and clicked the mouse. She gave a brief overview of each victim, but said she hadn't come across any new information, or any that Tony did not already have. There was nothing to add or subtract from his nightclub theory.

Tony nodded when she was finished. "That was good."

Bentley smiled; and it seemed so innocent. If it were any other situation, Tony figured she might have even preened.

"You ready to go interrogate some people?"

Tony watched the excitement growing in her eyes. She was trying rather hard to keep her emotions to a minimum. Tony didn't want to tell her she was failing at it. His new trainee, or whatever she was, seemed like the kind of person whose emotions were always written on her face. It wasn't necessarily a bad thing, unless you were a cop.

Curiosity about his new aide gnawed at him as he wound his car through the traffic and down to George's, but before he could ask anything, she beat him to it.

"So where are we going?"

Tony mentally kicked himself for not telling her earlier. "We're going George's Place to interview the day staff. Then we'll swing by the morgue and hope our third victim is done. Later tonight, there's an interview at The Rain with victim number two's boyfriend. Then The Rain interviews sometime in between that. I want to ask if they have any security footage from that night. If they do, I want you to sit down and look for our prospective murderer. Can you handle all that on your first day?"

He didn't intend to let her hear all of the interviews. He could barely get any information as it was. He knew he had to keep Bentley out of the loop if he wanted to continue getting any information at all. Luckily, if there were any security footage, it would keep her preoccupied. She tried to give him a stoic face, but was not very successful. Tony swallowed his smile.

"Yes, sir."

Tony spent the rest of the ride thinking about ways to tap dance around his new trainee. He actually wanted to get to know her, and wasn't as anti-social as he seemed, but at the moment, his main job was keeping her uninformed.

George's Place at ten am was a lot different than its nighttime counterpart. It looked the same, of course, but the energy was worlds apart. Now it seemed more family-friendly. The contrast was a little disturbing. As they walked in, Tony scanned the diner; there were no bikes outside and no bikers inside. It was mostly filled with families and people just passing through.

A woman came toward them from the kitchen. She was holding one of those large, leather planners that had all sorts of things built into it. Tony had not seen one of those in years. She was almost a little too intense for Tony, who was barely functioning on so little sleep. Even Bentley seemed slightly taken aback.

The woman walking toward them was about five-eight with dyed, medium blond hair and a thousand-watt smile. She appeared to be one of those genuinely happy people that Chris disliked so much. Tony reined in his thoughts; now was not the time to think about his friend.

The woman, who was dressed in business casual, stopped a few feet in front of Tony and Bentley. "Good morning! Two for breakfast?" Even her voice was perky.

Normally, it wouldn't have bothered him so much, but today, it really got on his nerves.

"I don't know if your boss told you about me, but I'm Detective Anthony Hollownton."

Her smile vanished and her eyes widened just a touch. "Oh, all right. If you'll follow me please."

The woman glanced at Bentley, but said anything about there being two of them. She struck Tony as very professional.

Why was she working here? She showed them to the same table he occupied the previous night.

About halfway to the table, Bentley leaned in and asked, "Is it just me, or are we getting death glares from the kitchen?"

Tony glanced over at the hatch, and sure enough, two men were standing in the window, watching them. The older, and shorter of the two was downright glaring. Tony did his best to ignore them as he slid into the booth. Bentley plopped down beside him, trying to take up as little room as possible, which was hard. She was about six feet tall and not a stick-figure, but she did manage to give Tony some space.

The cheery woman sat down across from them, looking at Tony expectantly. "Can I get you anything? You can start with me since I'm the manager, but it would be so rude of me not to offer you both something first. After all, this is a restaurant." She smiled at both of them again.

Bentley looked as if she wanted something, but thought better of it and kept her mouth shut.

Tony tried to hide his smile before turning back to the manager. "No, thank you, we're fine." Tony pulled out his notepad, careful to make sure that it was the right one.

The woman put her planner on the table and folded her hands on top of it. "Very well then. My name is Patricia Kelly. I grew up in Golden, Colorado and graduated Colorado State with my MBA five years ago. Worked in the hotel industry through college and the two years after. Three years ago, I moved out here. I just needed a change of scene. Within two months, I had this job; and I'm quite happy with it. Slower pace, decent pay. I met..." Her smile dimmed by a few hundred watts. "...I met Jessica when she started last year. Sweet girl, real quiet, but she could get very animated when talking about her family. She came from a large family, and had..." Patricia began counting on her fingers.

Bentley glanced over at Tony, who didn't acknowledge the look. Just because they already had this information didn't mean they weren't interested in hearing what Patricia had to say.

"...I think it was five siblings. I'm never sure because the family as a whole uses names interchangeably. They live in Black Diamond; well, her parents and three younger siblings do. I'm not sure about the other two siblings. They seemed quite the close family. Also, she had a thing with one of her neighbors. His name was... oh… I know this, he brought her flowers here once..." Patricia tapped her fingertips against her chin and looked up at the wall behind Tony while she scoured her memory.

Tony didn't want to rush her, but this was new information. Maybe even something that could help them. Most likely, it wouldn't, but it was worth a shot.

"I know it was a D name; Dylan, Damon, Dean... uh, something like that. He lived in her building." She waved her hand in frustration for not remembering the name.

Tony intervened. "That's fine, Ms. Kelly. That's actually very helpful, thank you."

Patricia flashed him another blinding smile. "You're welcome; and who shall I send over next?" She blinked at him expectantly.

Tony handed her one of his cards, which she took with a nod as she stood up.

"How about one of the cooks? Then I can speak to the other one; and beyond that, is up to you."

The manager nodded again before grabbing her planner and walking purposefully toward the kitchen. When she was out of earshot, Tony leaned into Bentley.

She spoke as he opened his mouth. "She scares me."

Tony snorted. He was starting to like Bentley.

Shaking his head, he changed the subject. "Go run a check and find me that neighbor; we need to talk to him right after we leave the morgue."

Bentley was trying to absorb all the information she could. Tony could see it in her face.

"Yes, sir." She all but launched herself from the booth before regaining control and striding for the door.

Tony smiled at her enthusiasm. Just as he hoped would happen, the older cook emerged from the kitchen and made his way toward the booth. Tony wasn't sure what tipped him off, but he just knew the man was Nym. He didn't actually look it though. The man was maybe five-three, and appeared to be in his early thirties with thinning hair. The man's face was almost childlike, which didn't match the, *I am not someone you want to mess with* Nym attitude.

The other man slid into the booth, burying his hands into the front pockets of his full-length apron. He stared at Tony coldly, running his tongue back and forth between two molars on the left side of his mouth. Tony couldn't resist the urge to snap the man out of his feelings of superiority.

"You're a Nym, aren't you?" Tony said it as a statement of fact, instead of a question.

The other man's back shot straight up and his eyes widened. "How'd you know that?"

Tony shrugged. "Talent. Name?"

The other man's eyes narrowed for a second as if he were trying to see right through Tony. "Napoleon," he spat out.

Tony didn't even bother to write it down. "Real name?"

The other man's lip twitched. "Reed White."

Tony noted that. "All right; you know why I'm here, so what can you tell me?"

The other man shrugged and opened his mouth, but didn't get the chance to speak, or at least not that Tony heard.

A tall, thin, African-American, college guy stepped in with a curvy Latina clinging to his arm. "What up, everyone? Don't worry! Milo is here so you can start the party." The kid had a voice that projected all over the place.

Reed rolled his eyes as various employees happily greeted the two kids.

The mood was so different from the mood at night. Tony had trouble reconciling the two. The diner was like its own tiny community. The only exception was the man sitting in front of him, who was now turning his back to Tony.

"I didn't know her. The only times I spoke to her was saying things like 'order up.' I don't know anything about her. She was quiet, talked a bit with two waitress on the night shift, and to Trisha. That's mainly because Trisha likes to be on good terms with everyone."

Though Reed said the last part with a flat tone, Tony could tell the other man liked his boss.

Tony sighed, "Fair enough."

Reed watched Tony for a second before sliding out of the booth.

Tony interviewed the entire staff. There was the other cook, a man in his twenties with dark blond hair so long in the front, he kept swiping it away from his glasses. Tony thought the hair was winning.

Next, was the bookkeeper who only came in twice a week. She was in her mid-thirties with curly brown hair.

Then came the three waitresses: a brunette with a Texas accent, an African-American woman, also originally from the South, and a Puerto Rican woman who was obviously the lead waitress.

Tony wanted to know how George managed to hire staff from all over. His cop senses told him there was something amiss. You just didn't see so much variety in a Seattle diner.

Three regulars were sent over to Tony as well: an older man who stood about five-one and was in his seventies with a cigarette box nestled in his front shirt pocket; then Milo, and his fiancée, Lottie.

Bentley came back in when Tony was questioning the Texan woman. After the next interview, Tony sent Bentley back out to call the morgue continuously until she reached Viggo. He said to tell Viggo they were coming in.

Tony learned from the lead waitress that the only Nym on the shift were Reed, herself, and the older customer Tony interviewed, who was actually more than five hundred years old.

So when Bentley returned the second time, Tony let her stay until the last interview. He didn't get anything new from them; at least, no new information that was pertinent to the case. It was almost a waste of time. But he did get the name of a potential boyfriend. That could turn out to be good. Tony thanked the perky manager as they left. As soon as they returned to his car, Tony turned to Bentley.

"Okay, tell me you got something on the mystery boyfriend."

Bentley nodded as she took out a small notebook. "There was a Derek Lowman, two floors above her. Twenty-five, medium build, works as a crane operator in Seattle. When I called his work, they said he hadn't been in since early last week. His boss said that if we found him, we could tell him he's fired. So that just leaves his apartment since he has no siblings and his parents died two years ago. We're going to have trouble tracking him down."

Tony turned onto the freeway. "Why do you say that?"

Bentley shrugged. "I remember only finding three neighbors on that floor when I did the interviews, and all of them were female. I know he's not one of the people I spoke to when I called the building yesterday afternoon. So I'm guessing he's hiding somewhere, or he's dead."

Tony was surprised by the young officer's thoroughness. There were a few seconds of silence. Tony did not want her asking him about the case. If she were as smart as he was beginning to think, she would notice he wasn't giving her all the information.

"So Bentley, we have twenty minutes to kill. Tell me about yourself."

That seemed to catch her off guard, and Tony could sense from her body language it was not a subject she wished to discuss.

"Um… okay, I'm local. I grew up south of Everett. I'm an only child. I went to Western and earned a BA in Lit. Then I became a cop and I intend to make detective next year." She was looking straight ahead and pulling at her hair again.

That only confirmed Tony's theory that it was a subconscious gesture. She seemed so uncomfortable talking about herself, he almost laughed.

"Where exactly south of Everett?" Tony grew up just outside of Bothell in an unincorporated part of north King County.

Her hand moved faster. *Was she uncomfortable with the question?* Or that he knew the area?

"Okay, how about, what high school did you go to?" Tony was a bit of a jock and got to know all the schools in that area.

"North Snohomish High."

Now he knew why she was so antsy about it. North Snohomish catered to the upper-middle class families. The school was known for all its snooty, spoiled, rich kids. Not exactly anyone you chose to be associated with. Tony laughed. He should know, since he graduated from there as well.

She stiffened a little at his reaction.

"Let me guess, you're from north of the school, right? My parents live on eighth, but I use to tell people they lived in Bothell."

She relaxed and released a small laugh. "Yeah, we were only two streets up, but I'm sure you know how it is."

Tony nodded. North of the school ranged from middle class to lower-middle class. The kids that lived south of the school were the ones that gave it such a stuck-up reputation.

"Yeah, you were probably a few years behind me."

The rest of the ride to the morgue was spent with small talk about high school and the ridiculous things that happened with all the rich kids.

When Tony pulled into the lot, he suddenly remembered he asked Bentley to call Viggo.

"Did you get hold of Viggo?"

Bentley nodded, but pursed her lips. "Yes, but she seemed really upset about the third body. She just finished the last of the tests when I got her on the phone. She sounded worn out, you know, really tired."

Tony didn't blame Viggo. She was the one who found Rick's prints at the crime scene. He couldn't imagine the flack she must've been getting. She was probably being hounded by reporters.

"Did you tell her we were coming?"

Bentley nodded. "Yeah, and she said we better not have another damn body for her."

Tony nodded and got out of the car. Taking a deep breath, he prepared himself for the stressed-out Viggo he expected to encounter.

Striding down the hall, Tony peered into each room for Viggo, with Bentley trailing after him. Viggo didn't answer her office phone when he dialed it, so now, he had to search her out. They found her in her office. *Why didn't she answer her phone?*

Tony knocked on the door as he opened it. When Viggo looked up, Tony could see circles under her eyes. She was obviously swamped. Viggo waved her hand at Tony and Bentley to come in before shutting the door behind them. As they did, Tony looked around, but didn't see the intern anywhere. He wondered where the kid had gone.

When they sat down, Tony spoke. "I tried to call you, but got no answer."

Viggo snorted. "Yeah, that's because I unplugged it half an hour ago. I couldn't stand any more media calls, or calls from your and my bosses, who are all breathing down my neck for progress reports. I even told the kid to shadow someone else because he was getting on my nerves. You've been appointed as a trainer too, I see."

Viggo turned to Bentley. "You're an unlucky girl. This is not the best case to cut your teeth on. Either that, or you must've done something to piss someone off."

She stared at the Bentley for a beat before Tony intervened.

"Okay, so tell me about the third body, Viggo." He just wanted to get on to the next place. It felt like there were too many interviews, but not enough time to fit them all in.

Viggo didn't look at Tony right away, but instead, bent down to grab something off the floor. When she sat back up, she was holding a file in her right hand. She tossed it a little too violently at Tony. He had to slam his palm down on it to keep it from flying off the table and skittering across the floor. That would not have been a good addition to his day.

Viggo spared one more glance at Bentley. "Here's hoping you're not squeamish, girly." Then she turned her full attention back to Tony. "We have the same basic markings as your last two victims. The wrists, ankles, scalp, and heart. There is one major difference though; and it changes your killer's MO a bit. Tests revealed she had sexual relations within an hour of her death. Not only is that completely new, but it means the torture went on for a much shorter time period. Your killer is becoming more proficient.

"I'll have DNA for you in another few hours. There were two different DNA samples this time. The bed partner, and some left on the scalp. I would put money on the scalp DNA being Rick's; I don't know why, but I've just got a feeling. I haven't mentioned it to anyone else though. It's just something to think about until the results are back."

As she stopped for a breath, Tony's phone went off. Looking down, he swore; it was the captain. This could not, in any way, be good.

Grimacing, Tony stood up and answered the call. "Yes, sir?"

"Write this down." Binns sounded pissed.

Tony felt his blood run cold; there must have been another murder. Hastily, he yanked out his pad and pen.

"Five-two-three-seven-eight West Walker North in Edmonds. Get over there now and solve the damn case, Hollownton. You have until five on Friday before I yank it from you. You hear me, Detective?!" The captain seemed to be growing even angrier.

Tony felt himself stiffen. "Yes, sir."

Then he heard the dial tone. As he slid the phone back into his pocket, Tony looked over at Viggo.

She read his face and started cursing. "I don't need any more of your butchered bodies, Hollownton."

Tony could tell she had much more to say, but held her tongue in front of Bentley. Bentley was slowly standing up, as if not sure quite what she should do.

Tony looked her in the eyes. "Grab the file we need to head north."

Without another word, he exited the morgue, making a mental note to read the file, and come back for more details from Viggo. Sex definitely changed things. Tony didn't know enough about the killer as it was, without her changing things on him.

Edmonds was fifteen minutes north of Seattle, and firmly in Snohomish County. That put this murder out of his territory. Tony was definitely not in the mood to deal with that kind of mess.

Trying to spend the entire silent car ride organizing his thoughts, his mind was whipping around, a mile a minute, making it hard for him to concentrate on anything. Hearing Binns's new deadline was not helpful. Tony tried desperately to untangle all his thoughts of Cheryl, Chris, and the safe house from his mind. At the very least, he wanted to shove them into the back of his mind. He wasn't entirely successful, but managed to ignore them long enough to pay more attention to the case.

When they reached the development of townhouses, Tony started cursing. There were both Snohomish and King County patrol vehicles lining the "Spring Valley Development" streets. He had to circle twice before leaving the tiny development and finding a place to park on the main road. Not the best start.

Bentley seemed to pick up on that as well because she strove to keep in step with him as they passed the main entrance, which featured a manmade waterfall under the name of the development.

"We're in Snohomish, aren't we?" Bentley commented.

Tony just nodded.

"Damn it. I hate Edmonds PD. Dicks pull me over every time, without fail, when I come to visit my cousin, the dickwads..."

The last word was under her breath, and Tony could tell it was a substitute for something a little stronger. Since they were reaching the first group of people, she carefully toned it down.

It wasn't hard to figure out which of the cookie cutter townhomes housed their victim. The sheer volume of mingling cops on the slightly larger than postage stamp-sized lawn was a dead giveaway.

As Tony and Bentley walked up, he noticed the cops were predominantly from Edmonds. They were standing on the lawn and turned to watch Tony and Bentley advancing in near silence.

One younger cop in uniform finally approached them when they set foot on the next lawn over. Tony didn't stop. It was his homicide, and he intended to display dominance. The young uniform dropped his hands to his belt, while paying a little too much attention to Bentley. That told Tony the kid was fairly new to the job, or at least, Tony hoped the uniform was.

"Can I help you guys?" asked the uniform as his fingers played with his belt.

Tony pulled out his badge and briskly walked past the other man. "Detective Anthony Hollownton, King County Homicide, and Officer Bentley." Tony didn't stop walking as he spoke.

Bentley tried to stay only one step behind him. Tony knew she was trying to flaunt as much confidence as Tony did in their right to be there. Without stopping to talk to anyone else, they went up the two steps and through the front door, which was cracked open. As soon as he stepped inside, Tony knew why. He heard Bentley gagging behind him. The smell of blood was so strong in the air, Tony wondered if this was truly one of his vics. There was never enough blood at the other scenes to warrant a smell so strong. Just then, a tech of some kind walked up to them and handed them both surgical masks and gloves. As Tony thanked the small woman, he recognized her as one of King County's nameless techs.

A few seconds later, two men in their mid to late thirties walked into the dining room, which was attached to the entryway where Tony and Bentley stood. Tony knew by the way the two men carried themselves and their clothing that he was looking at his Snohomish counterparts.

The two men stopped in front of him and his suspicion was confirmed.

"I'm Johnson and this is Trevor, we're from Snohomish Homicide. Can we see your IDs? Just to be sure you are who you claim to be."

As he yanked out his badge again, Tony couldn't help the pessimistic thoughts rolling around in his head. *Just what he needed, pissy homicide detectives.*

The two men scrutinized both his and Bentley's IDs longer than was necessary before nodding their approval. The taller one, who first addressed them, gestured toward the back of the house, which was around the corner from the dining room table.

"Body was found by the guy's female roommate this morning. She just came home from her boyfriend's house to clean up before her first class this morning. You want to see the body first? Or question the girl?"

Tony wanted to do both, but if Bentley was still having stomach trouble and gagging in the doorway, it could only get worse when they looked at the body. The surgical masks helped a lot, but couldn't keep everything out.

"Bentley will question the girl while I check out the body." He could see Bentley giving him a curious look from the corner of his eye, but she didn't say anything.

Johnson nodded. "Fair enough; Trevor can take her upstairs; and I'll show you the body."

With that, Trevor moved to the staircase at the far left corner of the entry. He gestured for Bentley to go first, and she hesitated for a split second before raising her chin and jogging up the stairs. That caught Trevor off guard and he hustled to catch up with her. Tony turned back to Detective Johnson.

When the man saw that he had Tony's attention, he spoke without moving any closer to the crime scene. "Look, I would have never invited you to this scene. I just want to be clear here, people above my boss pulled strings to bring you out here; especially after we found the tape."

Tony interrupted the other man, holding up his hand. "What are you talking about? What tape?" Tony had a bad feeling regarding the answer.

Johnson looked somewhat confused for a second before motioning for Tony to follow him. He spoke over his shoulder. "We have to go past the body to get to the TV. You'll probably want to see the tape first."

Tony could feel his dread building; this could not be good. As they turned the corner, Tony's body ceased all movement. The man was up on the wall like the others. There were the same wounds, or so Tony assumed. The body was covered in blood as well as the wall, the floor, and parts of the ceiling. The wounds were much more brutal this time. The scalp was torn, and there were tufts of hair sticking to the blood on the wall. The chest wound showed the ribs this time, which had somehow been snapped back and were protruding from the chest. The ankles were slit so deeply that the man's feet were almost dangling from his legs. The same deep cuts were done at the wrists.

Tony barely registered Johnson speaking from the other side of the body.

"His eyes and tongue were removed as well, pre-mortem."

It was hard, but Tony managed to rip his gaze away from the body to look at Johnson. That sinking feeling grew stronger as he fought the urge to gag.

"How do you know that?"

Johnson's expression was grim as he motioned again for Tony to follow him through a doorway into what looked like a living room. Tony followed the other man, being careful to avoid the overwhelming amount of blood on the floor. When they reached the living room, Johnson stopped and stood at the back of a cream-colored couch that was directly across from a forty-plus-inch TV. A remote was balanced on the back of the couch, and Johnson picked it up.

"This was sitting on the dining room table with a note that said, 'Watch me.' Your techs already have the note." Johnson clicked the remote. Within two seconds, a very attractive brunette appeared on the screen. Tony knew she was his killer, and it wasn't just because she looked so similar to Jessica Rabbit. Her voice also would have been a sexy purr if not for the thread of insanity, which she did nothing to hide.

"Hello there, Detectives. You mean nothing to me except to help me get what I want. I want King County Homicide Detective Anthony Hollownton." She smiled as she pronounced every syllable in his name.

This was not good.

"Since I'm sure Anthony will see this tape, I left it for him as a present… eventually. I'm just going to ignore the rest of you." She actually shifted her gaze to the right, which was unnerving since she was looking right where Tony stood.

"Anthony," she scolded with a purr. "I had a party planned for you today. But you didn't show up. That is terribly rude of you. The Culeen I sent to fetch you were very put out. So put out, in fact, that I had to kill them." She paused for a second, still smiling. Tony could hear his heart thumping in his ears.

"So I just had to make do."

The camera swung away to show the barely sedated victim, still alive, but tied to the wall.

"The resemblance is quite striking, isn't it?"

The camera zoomed in. She was right. The man was barely twenty, but he did look strikingly similar to Tony. Not enough for them to be mistaken as blood relatives, but still close. The camera swung back to the woman's smiling face.

"Now, you see I found someone to take all my frustration out on. Isn't that nice? I'll be getting back to you soon, Tony." She blew a kiss to the camera before the screen went black.

Tony couldn't breathe. Someone had died expressly because of his actions. This man was ruthlessly tortured because of him. Panic crashed over him in huge waves. Without thinking, Tony beelined straight out the front door.

Once outside, Tony ripped off his mask and forced himself to breathe. He could think of nothing more than to leave the townhouse. The horror and guilt suffocated him like a heavy, wool blanket. It became intolerable. This man had been tortured and killed because of Tony. It nearly overwhelmed him.

Walking to the edge of the lawn, he jammed his hands into his outer coat pockets and stared down the street. Tony was trying desperately to register the events going on around him. It was one thing for people to be killed by a supposed Demon Culeen crazy lady; but it was completely different when people were being killed because of *him*.

Chris was abducted or whatever because of him. Plus, there was no way he could forget about the dream he had the night before. Every time he thought about the possibility of what happened to Chris, and imagined himself doing that to her, Tony's stomach churned. He couldn't even fathom having those events taking place. Why she agreed to help him in the end remained a riddle to Tony and he still wondered about it.

A nagging feeling that whatever happened to Rick might be partially Tony's fault bothered him as well.

Now, a totally innocent guy that probably did nothing wrong was dead because of him. Tony wanted to yell at the sky. If a big, omnipotent being were really up there, Tony wanted to know why the guy was sleeping on the job. Having no one to place the blame on only made Tony feel worse. His thought-swamped mind was temporarily distracted by Detective Johnson, who was standing next to him.

"Look, I don't want to have to report that you seem unfit for duty. We all know the pressure you're getting over this one. I know, if places were reversed, I'd want to catch the psycho myself. So I'm giving you a warning. Snap out of it! If the wrong people see you crack like that, you'll be ripped off this case and stripped of your badge faster than an egg can boil. I'm going to pretend I didn't see it, this one time, but you have to do a better job of hiding it, okay?"

Tony knew Johnson was just concerned about him and he should have been grateful to the guy for trying to help him out, but his anger needed someone to blame. He wanted to shove the guy and tell him to go to hell. Tony wasn't sure how much longer he could restrain himself, so he just nodded at the other cop instead.

Using all of his will power, Tony made his mind blank, and then thought of nothing but the body. Not why the man died, or who the man was; just the facts and clues that could help him catch the killer. Vacating all facial expressions, Tony turned around and strode purposefully toward the body.

It was almost two by the time Tony and Bentley finally left the crime scene. After questioning the roommate, Bentley showed a fair amount of initiative by interviewing all of the neighbors before meeting up with Tony again. Bentley walked in as they watched the video for the second time. She stood there silently, listening to Tony and Johnson discuss the tape and the body. By the time they left, she seemed a little bit paler and her eyes appeared darker. The innocence in them had flown.

They remained silent for a good fifteen minutes. What exactly she was thinking, Tony didn't know and wasn't about to ask her. He had enough to deal with already on his mind.

"I'm swinging by the station. I want you to write down and organize all the information you've gotten from the roommate and the neighbors. When I get back, I want a full report on it."

Tony watched her bristle from the corner of his eye. He knew why she was pissed. She was deliberately being left out of everything. The irony of the situation was not lost on Tony, but he wasn't about to do anything to fix it. That was probably why the rest of the trip to the precinct was brimming with tension.

At his desk, Tony wrote a edited update report for Binns, and sent it attached to an email. He was picking up his phone to call Viggo when it rang. Tony had the distinct feeling it would not be good news.

"Get in here." That was all the captain growled before hanging up.

Tony knew Binns hadn't had time to read the report, which made him less eager to enter the other man's office. He feared that whatever the captain wanted to say to him was not something he wanted to hear. Once inside the captain's small office, Tony shut the door behind him and took a seat. Binns was obviously pissed, but for once, it didn't seem to be because of Tony. Maybe in Tony's general direction, but not at Tony directly. That made him worry more than before. It meant something else must have happened. Just what he needed.

Binns shifted in his chair and seemed to be trying to find the right words as he stared past Tony. "I don't think you've been compromised. You're a good enough cop to not get yourself into trouble. But this video has really painted us into a corner. With the murderer targeting you specifically, I'm getting a lot of pressure to take you off the case. On the plus side, we now know what the murderer looks like; and her photograph is going out to every cop in the tri-state area. We also sent it up to border patrol, just in case she gets any ideas. The bad news is: they're bumping you from the case."

Tony clenched his fists and started to protest, but Binns talked over him.

"Look, it is over my head now. Eight am tomorrow, you will be briefing some feds on this case. Then IA wants a word with you. The feds can choose to keep you on or not. It sounds like now that you are a target, they might just put you under watch until they can catch her."

Tony did not want another set of babysitters and he certainly did not want to be kicked off the case.

Binns interrupted his thoughts again. "You have the rest of the day. Use it wisely… compile your paperwork or something. You understand me, Detective?"

Tony understood clearly. His captain just told him he had a limited amount of time to do everything he could to solve thess crimes. Once he nodded his understanding, Binns waved him away dismissively.

Without so much as a pause when he passed his desk, Tony said, "Bentley, we're leaving."

Bentley blinked a couple times before scrambling after him. She didn't catch up until they were out of the building.

"Sir, I thought I was staying behind?"

Thoughts swirled through Tony's mind. They needed a game plan.

"That was before we were ordered to hand our case off to the feds. Now that we have been told to do so." He checked his watch. "I have sixteen-and-a-half hours before I, at least, am off the case. I want to get as much done as possible in what little time we have left. So we'll head out to The Rain to question the staff and see their security system. I am also meeting the boyfriend of victim three there at seven, so I'll be stuck there a while. Will you call ahead of our arrival and tell them to call in the staff who was on duty from the Friday before last?"

Bentley nodded vigorously as she pulled out her phone. "Yes, sir."

"Good. And if they don't have security footage, or after you're finished watching it, I want you to take my car and retrace victim five's steps last night. Surely, the murderer did not come across victim five as accidentally as she would like us to believe. Did you get enough information from the roommate to do that?"

There was a pause. "I think so, sir."

Taking a deep breath, Tony squeezed the steering wheel. He always preferred to have a game plan. If Bentley could retrace their victim's steps, perhaps he could shrink his search area of abandoned warehouses in which the Culeen might be taking up residence. He would be losing the case in the morning, but if he were really lucky, he might know exactly where to find the murderer before then. That still left him wondering how he could bring her in. There had to be some way to do it.

Bentley interrupted his thoughts, sounding excited. "They said they can get all the staff there, but one guy. A part-time bartender who only comes in to cover for people, or when they get as crowded as they were last Friday. They haven't been able to reach him for almost a week. Get this: his name is Derek Lowman. Fifty bucks says you can guess his address."

Tony's adrenaline spiked. That was not a coincidence. Could Derek have been feeding the Demon Culeen her victims? If he had access to the Nym community through Jessica, then he would know who the Nym were as soon as they entered the club.

But why kill Jessica? If she were their best bet to finding the others, wouldn't they want to keep her around? He had to be missing something. Tony tried not to get his hopes too high. Something could always go wrong. He still had to figure out how to bring in the Demon Culeen; but how to arrest something like that was beyond Tony.

The ringing of his phone from his pocket stole his attention. Before he had time to dig around and grab it, the ringing stopped. He hoped whoever it was could wait another fifteen minutes.

A different ring started. Bentley jumped before pulling her own phone out of a pocket.

"This is Bentley."

She was silent a few moments before moving her phone away from her face and tapping the screen.

"Okay, you're on speaker phone."

Viggo's voice filled the car. "Hollownton?"

"Yeah, I'm here. Just driving."

There was a heavy sigh. "So, I think we have a problem."

A new sense of dread snuck into Tony's system again. "What would that problem be?"

"That other DNA on your fourth victim. Yes, Rick's DNA was there. But there is something odd about it. There is another person's DNA around it. I know this sounds crazy, but it is almost like someone took Rick's fingerprint and planted it there; except they also left some of their own inadvertently. The other DNA is the same as what is all over her body. So I assume the person she slept with was the one who planted the prints.

"I went back to victim two and reexamined the print; and I can't believe I didn't notice it before! The print is too perfect, and there is nothing on the surrounding area. Like someone washed the area before placing the print there. I'm trying to figure out how the print could be so complete, and from the angle it is, while cutting out the baby. I can't think of anything.

"So whoever this woman is, Rick might not be working with her, like we first thought. She might have abducted him and Amanda and just used his prints to get us to chase our tails. Which, can I just say, royally pisses me off!"

The silence in the car was so thick, it could not have been cut with a knife. Tony almost couldn't believe it. *Rick might be innocent?* Then why was he acting so strange at the second crime scene? There was so much Tony still didn't know and there was not enough time to figure it all out. He didn't like it, but Rick had to wait. He had to catch the murderer first.

"That is good to hear, Viggo. Are they giving you the fifth vic?"

There was a snort. "No, some inter-county nonsense. But they are going to let me see their ME's report when he finishes." She didn't try to hide her frustrated disgust.

"You might not like this, but I think that could be good for us. Can you concentrate on trying to clear Rick? If what you think is true, both he and I would be extremely grateful."

"Done." The phone line went dead.

Bentley slid her phone back into her pocket. Tony could tell she wanted to say something, but was struggling with it.

"Spill it, Bentley."

She shifted in her seat. "This does not seem to add up to me. There is a killer, who might be the head of a cult. She abducted one of the officers on her case, but not the one who lives alone. She takes the one with a wife and takes the wife too. Then, she uses his prints in an attempt to throw us off the trail. She is only killing people she thinks are involved in a rival cult."

Tony waited, but there wasn't anything else. "What part does not add up?"

Sighing, Bentley folded her arms. "Why now? Why Seattle? I mean, if there had been a cult like this in the area, we would have known about it. Let alone two cults. So they obviously moved here. Why start killing now? Why move to kill?"

Tony did not have any answers for her, at least, not any he could give her. He certainly couldn't tell her the truth. "Maybe there was someone here she wanted to kill and she is using the other cult as an excuse?"

She seemed to think about that. "Yeah, that makes sense. But why Rick? If she did indeed take him and his wife?"

"That, I don't know. Maybe she picked Rick because she figured she could use Amanda as leverage to get him to do what she wanted."

"Yeah, I guess." She did not seem sold on the idea.

There was no further talking as they drove to The Rain. Both of them had too much to think about.

The Rain looked like a nondescript warehouse. The windows were blacked out, and the brick had not been cleaned in a while. The only indicator of it being a nightclub was the pale blue neon sign, which was currently turned off, above the door. When Tony knocked, the steel door seemed to echo.

A tall woman with a crown of light brown curls and black-rimmed glasses appeared in the doorway a minute later. "Badges?"

Both Tony and Bentley flashed their IDs. The woman looked at them for a long time. When she was satisfied, she nodded and moved over so they could come inside.

The inside of the club reminded Tony of the Chipotle, where Rick loved to eat. There were steel sheets and beams throughout, and the tables, chairs, and bar all appeared to be made of steel. Scattered amongst the tables closest to them were about a dozen blurry-eyed employees.

Tony turned to the woman who let them in. "Are you the manager?"

She nodded and stuck out her hand. "Chloe Gatesburg, General Manager. Though I am off Thursdays and Fridays, so I do not know how much help I can be."

Tony nodded. "Do you have security footage that Bentley can watch from that night?"

Chloe reached out to shake Bentley's hand. "Yes, absolutely. I figured you would want to see it, so I queued it up for you. If you will follow me."

With that, she proceeded to walk Bentley toward the opposite end of the building.

Taking a deep breath, Tony looked out at the dozen employees. "Thank you for coming in early to talk to us. Let's make this easy. How many of you have seen a picture of the woman we are looking for?"

All but three hands went up.

"How many of you could have possibly come into contact with her last Friday?"

A table of four near the back were the only ones with their hands down, but one man spoke from his seat.

"We work the kitchen. We don't really see a lot of customers, period."

Tony nodded. "Okay, I want to start with the server she kept handing drinks to."

Two women stood up, then looked at each other, both confused.

The one on the right, a blond in a leather jacket, spoke first. "I served the table with that nurse that was killed."

The one on the left had a shaved head. "He didn't ask about the murdered guy. He asked if there was someone at one of your tables she was sending drinks to. I had one of those."

Adrenaline rushed through Tony. *Could this be the next victim? Could he know whom she was targeting next?* "Okay, I'll talk to your first." He pointed to the blond. "While I am doing that, can you pull up the information for me on that table? I want that man's name."

The bald woman looked down at a man sitting across from her.

He looked at Tony. "Sy Owens, I am one of the assistant managers. I can get that for you."

Tony nodded. "Good. Let me know when you have it. I'm going to set up in one of those booths."

He motioned to the only row of booths on the other side of the room. If he had to be here a while, he didn't want to sit on one of those metal chairs. As Tony moved, the assistant manager and the bald server headed toward the row of computers behind the bar.

The blond waitress seemed fidgety. Not in the sense that she was trying to hide her guilt, but she did not seem like the type that could sit still for very long. When Tony pulled out his notepad, she seemed to fidget more.

"Can I get your name first please? Then tell me all you remember about that woman buying drinks."

She nodded, flicking her nails off each other. "Cindy Craig. I've been a server here for about four months. I am also a full-time student at PLU. Um, at first, I really didn't notice her sitting at the bar. I don't know when she came in, or anything like that. I just remember a new table of three guys sat down. Two of them were twins. They had one round before one of the twins got up and started dancing. He didn't come back for like, two hours. I only know that because it was after my break. It wasn't long after he left, maybe ten or fifteen minutes, that I felt someone at the bar grabbing my arm as I walked past. When I turned, I saw the woman whose photo was on the news."

Tony interrupted her. "Would you describe her exactly as you remember her, please?"

"Oh, sure, she had pale brown hair that was rather full, like she spent a lot of time on it. She was wearing a slinky, red dress, which didn't made a lot of sense. She was way overdressed. Her makeup was a little on the heavy side. But when I got a better look at her later, I realized it was tattooed on her face. She had purple eye shadow, thick eyeliner, and really bright red lips. She was maybe forty. She kept trying really hard to appear slinky and sexy. She made me uncomfortable.

"Anyway, she grabbed my arm and waited until I was looking at her face before she spoke. She said, 'Be a doll and give this to the yummy young man over there.' I remember the words because I thought it was a strange way to talk. I nodded and took the glass from her. She let go of my arm and I headed to their table. When I set down the drink, and told the guy who it was from, he smiled politely and told me to tell the lady, ‘No, thank you.’ So I returned the drink to her and repeated the message. She frowned, but did not say anything.

"About ten minutes later, she tried again, saying the same thing, but with a different drink. The guy was a little less polite and firmer in his refusal. That time, she scowled, but still didn't say anything. A half hour passed and I figured she just gave up. But she didn't. She tried a third time: same words, different drink. This time, I knew he was going to say no. So when I got to the table, I apologized first. The guy looked rather annoyed at me. His friend made a comment about it being ridiculous. The guy pulled out a twenty and handed it to me, asking that I not bring any more drinks from her over. She became livid when I told her that, like she was going to hit something. She tried to get me to bring him two more drinks, but I flat-out refused. She stopped when Derek, the bartender, told her to lay off."

That made Tony pause in his notes. *Was that where the two of them met? Or was this just a phase in their plan?* "Did he sound like he knew her?"

Cindy blinked at him a few times. "No, not really. I mean, he seemed to be talking to her later that night, but it wasn't like they were friends."

"Did you notice when she left?"

Nodding, Cindy stopped fidgeting. "Yes, Derek and Mike had just made the announcement for last call. She left within five minutes after that."

"Have you seen her before or since?"

She shook her head.

Tony pulled a business card out of his pocket. "If you remember anything else, or see her again, give me a call."

Cindy nodded and took the card before sliding out of the booth.

Within ten seconds, the other server slid into the booth, pushing a sheet of paper toward him. Her blue eyes were bright with excitement. "Here, Sy was able to pull up the cards. I circled his. I remember because it was this bright green and it stuck in my memory."

Tony looked at the sheet. *Spencer Eldridge*, not the most unique name, but it should be enough.

He looked at the woman across from him. "Would you give me just a moment to make a phone call, and come back in about three minutes?"

She nearly leapt out of the booth. "Oh, yeah, absolutely." Then she headed across the room.

His heart was racing as he pulled out his phone.

The captain picked up after the first ring. "This better be good."

"I have a strong lead on who our next victim might be."

There was silence on the other end for a beat. "How strong?"

"She tried to buy drinks for two men at the bar. The first was our first victim. The second was a Spencer Eldridge. I bet if we run a search, we can find him and send patrols over to watch him." Tony could hear typing in the background, then silence. He held his breath as they waited for the search results.

"Jackpot, Hollownton. There is only one in King County. If it is the same guy, I will send a car to watch the place. Do you want to be there when they ID him as a possible vic?"

"No, I'll send Bentley there to talk to him. She is watching the security footage as we speak. Tell the plain clothes not to talk to him until she gets there. We carpooled, so if you could send plain clothes to pick her up, that would be helpful."

"All right, I hope you're correct on this. I would love to tell the feds we caught her before they could get here." Without another word, Binns hung up.

Tony slid his phone back into his coat pocket. The server noticed and returned. When she slid back into the booth, she smiled at him.

"Cindy told me what you're looking for, so I'll just dive right in. My name is Fanny Lewis. I have been here a year, as of next week. My description isn't going to be much different from Cindy's. The woman was a brunette trying to look like Jessica Rabbit. That sticks out in a club like this. It's not like Comic-Con is going on, or anything like that. That's what made me notice her when she came in around ten o'clock. I was grateful when she sat at the bar. Then, after she was here a while, I don't know how long, she reached out to me, as if to grab my arm, but I moved beyond her reach. She let her arm drop when I looked at her. She told me she wanted to buy a drink for one of my tables. So I obliged and brought the drink to him.

"He was sitting with three women. Maybe six feet tall with shaggy, black hair. He was wearing a red plaid shirt, with a kinda lean build. The first drink was a cocktail of some kind. He turned it down, saying he only drank light beer. I brought it back to her, and relayed his response. She smiled, and about fifteen minutes later, she got my attention by waving before she sent a bottle of light beer over. He accepted that one. When he got it, he made eye contact with her, and inclined his head before taking a swig.

"But that was the entire exchange. She never spoke to him or sent over another drink and he never went over to her. That in itself seemed strange."

Tony watched her for a moment. *Why would the Demon Culeen send over a drink, but not follow up?* Then a thought pinged in his head. "Did she order the drink before you brought it over? Or did she already have it in front of her when she told you to give it to Spencer?" He was willing to bet there was a drug in that drink.

"It was already in front of her."

Excitement zipped through Tony. She was either drugging her victims, or her accomplices. That was something they could work with. Drugs could be traced.

"Okay, thank you for your help." Tony gave her his card.

Fanny hesitated a moment before leaving the booth. As soon as she did, Tony pulled out his phone and called Viggo. He was surprised when she picked up. He expected her to be in the lab.

"I haven't exonerated him yet, Hollownton."

"Did you do tox screens on the victims?"

"Yeah, and before you ask, they all had an anomaly in their blood. It was some organic compound we couldn't identify. But researching it was put on the back burner. Why?"

"I think our murderer was drugging the victims, which was how she made them so compliant."

He could hear her taking deep breath. "Okay, I'll have the techs look into it."

"Thanks, Viggo."

"Uh-huh." Then there was a click.

Tony put his phone back and slid out of the booth. He wanted to talk to Bentley before the other officers got there. He headed down the hallway where Bentley and Chloe went when they first arrived. The walls were all black, but the bright bulbs in the ceiling produced enough light for Tony to see where each door led as he passed it. At the end of the hall, and to the right of the exit, Tony found Bentley and Chloe sitting in high-backed, leather chairs staring at a computer screen. Trying to be as unobtrusive as possible, Tony cleared his throat to get their attention. Both women jumped.

He looked at the manager. "Could we have a few minutes alone please?"

Clicking the mouse to pause the video, Chloe practically flew from her chair. "Oh, sure, of course." She skirted past Tony and closed the door on her way out.

Bentley watched him closely and he could tell she was trying to ferret out what he was going to say.

"We have a change of plans again."

Bentley shifted uneasily.

"One of the waitresses served another young man our murderer sent drinks to. Only this one took it."

Bentley's eyes widened. "Please tell me this is a possible victim. One that is still alive and one we can track."

Tony smiled. "Bingo!"

Jumping up from her seat, Bentley grabbed her jacket off the back of the chair. "You want me to go there and talk to him, and confirm it was him on the tapes?"

"Yes; did you see her sending drinks yet? The waitress said she didn't get here until ten."

Bentley nodded. "Not yet; we just saw her sit down and start talking with Derek. But I can fast forward it and see if I get a glimpse of our mystery guy. Chloe told me she would copy the recording and give us a USB. So I figure I can get a look at our guy, then head out, and she can give you the copy. Should I call for a ride?"

Tony was really starting to like Bentley. Once she was in her element, she was an entirely different person.

"No, I have plain clothes coming to get you, but be prepared. The waitress never saw the bartender open the beer."

She cut him off. "You think she's drugging them? It would explain why they were so cooperative in their own deaths. I'll call and see if we can get a tech to take a blood sample just to test him. It is a long shot but it could still be in his system. Don't worry, in case they are watching the house, we'll be discreet about it."

Nervous energy started working its way through Tony's system. They were close; he could feel it. "Before you leave, would you write me a copy of your notes on victim five? I want to trace his steps just to cover all our bases."

There was a moment of hesitation, where he wasn't sure if she would say yes, but eventually, she nodded slowly. "Are you sure you want to do that alone?"

Tony couldn't explain the whole Culeen nest thing, so he thought fast. "We only have tonight before we're off the case. I want to do everything I can before that happens. Besides, you were going to check it out by yourself originally."

She just watched him for what seemed like a minute. "Yeah, but the murderer is not targeting me. Just promise me you will call for backup before anything happens."

Tony sighed. "I promise."

"Fine," she said, leaning over the desk. "Then leave me alone so I can get out of here."

"Yes, ma'am."

She snorted, but didn't look up.

When Tony walked out of the office, he could see Chloe down the hall.

As he passed her, he paused. "Thanks, if you could make me a copy, that would be great."

Chloe nodded as she pushed off the wall and returned to the office.

Tony looked out at the club. The staff was mingling around. Some seemed to be setting up for their shifts, while others were chatting. But there was a lull as they noticed Tony.

He pointed to the assistant manager that helped him earlier. "Okay, I'll talk to you next. Then you can go back to your regular plans."

It was just after seven by the time Tony left The Rain. None of the interviews he did after talking to Bentley provided any clues. No one else interacted with the murderer. When he was interviewing the other bartender, Bentley's ride arrived. She came out and handed him a report of what victim five's day looked like.

Max had shown up early so Tony spoke to him as soon as the other man arrived. He did not want to make the grieving man stay longer than needed. He had no new information for Tony except one thing. They had been on a date two Fridays ago. They went to a movie then got a drink at The Rain. Tony hurt for the guy. Getting that drink had altered Max's life forever.

Tony didn't have to retrace the victim five's steps to know where the Culeen found him. He worked in a warehouse in Everett, in an area that was full of them. It would be an easy place to gain a tail, and almost seemed too easy after everything else.

The murderer slipped up when she plucked her latest victim from her own backyard; and now they would get her.

Tony knew his babysitters wouldn't appreciate going into a Culeen's nest unprepared, so when he got to his car, he turned around and leaned on the hood, hoping they would get the hint. They did, but it took a few minutes. Mick came strolling from an alley beside the club, and Cheryl emerged from across the street.

"What's goin' on, Detective?" Mick asked, burying his hands in his pockets.

Tony waited until Cheryl was close enough to hear him before answering. "I know where the nest is."

Both Nym went deathly still.

"How?" Cheryl's voice was so quiet, it was barely a whisper.

"That's a really long story that I don't have time to go over right now. Let's just say I am pretty sure our latest victim was chosen because he works in the warehouse district in Everett."

The Nym exchanged glances.

"Did anyone check that far north?" Mick asked suspiciously.

Cheryl shook her head. "Not that I know of. It seems too far out of their usual hunting range." She looked at Tony. "You're going there now?"

He nodded.

"I'm calling for backup. If you're going to be making arrests, I would like to clear as much supernatural stuff as possible."

Tony really hated hearing that response. Part of him wanted to refuse, and tell them that the police could take care of the situation. But he knew he was only fooling himself.

Even if he could convince the department that he wasn't crazy, and their murderer was a Demon Culeen, he still wasn't sure how they could go about arresting her without evidence from the Nym. He was about to lie on a big scale, and the thought made him sick, even though he knew there wasn't any real choice.

"Fine; call your backup on the way there, but I have to appear alone if we are going to draw them out."

Cheryl looked like she was going to argue, but Mick beat her to it.

"Not the best way to protect you, but yeah, I see the merit. Give me your gun."

Tony just looked at the other man. He wasn't about to give up his weapon.

Mick sighed. "I'm gonna give it back to you. I may not be great with magic, but there are some spells I had to learn to survive. One of which is how to give an everyday weapon a temporary magical boost, so it can do damage to a Culeen the same way it would to a human. It only lasts ‘bout two to three hours, but unless all hell breaks loose, you won't need more time than that." Mick held out his hand.

Tony eyed the other man's hand and debated for several seconds before handing over his gun. Worst case scenario: it wouldn't work and he would get killed. As soon as that thought entered his mind, Tony banished it. Thoughts like that could also get him killed.

He heard soft chanting and felt the air thicken around him. It wasn't oppressive or comforting; but felt more like the humidity in the air skyrocketed. The air became increasingly warmer and Tony felt his body start to sweat. Then came the pop, and the air chilled. It was drastically cold by comparison.

Mick handed him back the gun. "You okay there? You look like you've been sweatin’ and it’s maybe sixty degrees out here."

"He has a strange, adverse reaction to magic. I don't know why," Cheryl chimed in.

Tony pretended not to hear their exchange; and instead, placed his gun back in the holster before pulling out Bentley's notes. He rattled off the address so the Nym would know he was changing the subject. Mick obliged by repeating it back to him. Tony inclined his head before getting into his car. He didn't want to stand around talking. As it was, he expected to hit rush hour traffic, and would be lucky to arrive in Everett before seven-thirty. He did not want to give the Culeen the advantage of night.

He wasn’t lucky. There was an accident outside Lynnwood that narrowed the freeway down to one lane. It was after eight o’clock when Tony pulled into the parking lot where the victim worked. His nerves were shot.

All the lights were off in the building in front of him, and there were no other cars in the parking lot. He lost Mick and Cheryl three blocks ago when they veered off to the left.

Presumably, that was so the Culeen wouldn't see them coming, or they were meeting their backup. Tony didn't know which. He took several deep breaths before getting out of the car. He had no idea how to prepare to encounter the stuff of nightmares, which he only recently believed were real.

Pushing all thoughts from his mind, Tony pulled out his gun and hung his arm against his jacket, so the gun wouldn't be so visible. His heart was racing and adrenaline rushed through his system. Taking one more deep breath, he started moving toward the warehouse, which stood to the left of where he parked. Tony was willing to bet money that if he wandered around long enough, they would find him if he didn't find them first.

Concentrating on his surroundings, from what he could see in the sparse lights scattered around the property, he strained to hear any indication that he wasn't alone. There was a sudden bang on his left.

Tony turned, lifting his gun, but quickly lowered it when he saw two workers closing an industrial-sized trash container. He struggled to regulate his rapid breathing. His heart beat so fast, it was all he could hear.

"Looking for us, are you?"

Tony spun around in a crouch to see the voice he heard behind him. A man, maybe thirty years old, with a thin build and greasy hair, smiled at Tony from where he stood leaning against the building.

"Hello, Detective. She'll be so glad you came to see us." With that, the man moved off the wall and began walking away with his back to Tony.

Tony was breathing so hard, he feared he might pass out. He stood watching trying to decide if he really wanted to follow the other man. Before he could make a decision, he saw movement above him. He looked up to the roof of the closest building. Mick was crouched in a shadow, watching Tony. When Mick knew Tony could see him, he gave Tony a thumbs-up before easing out of sight.

A wave of relief that Tony didn't expect washed over him. There may not have been any other cops there, but at least, he wasn't alone. That made all the difference. Tony flexed his arms to relax his tense muscles before following the greasy man to the Culeen lair.

He stayed at least a yard behind the man, giving himself room to maneuver, should he need it. They only walked past about two buildings before the man stopped at a set of steel doors and knocked.

By the time Tony got there, both doors were halfway open, which was a big enough space for four men to walk abreast. Tony stopped just short of the door. He didn't know why, but his gut told him if he walked through those doors, he was dead. He trusted his gut. It was pitch-black inside and Tony couldn't see anyone or anything.

After a second, the greasy man's head and upper torso seemed to float in midair in the darkness of the doorway. "Aren't you coming in? You might as well. In a few more minutes, it will be dark enough for us to come out."

That sent chills down Tony's spine. "Nope, I'm staying right here."

The greasy man opened his mouth, but another voice came out of the darkness.

"Well, then, I will just come to you." It was a throaty, female voice.

Tony knew the Demon Culeen was coming out to meet him, and instinctively, took several steps back. That caused a laugh from the other side of the door. A second later, she appeared out of the darkness. She was exactly as people described: heavily styled and trying to look like the iconic cartoon character.

"Do you like this look? I am becoming so fond of it. It is much easier to attract people when you look like this. Speaking of which… Anthony, wouldn't you like to join me?" She stretched out her hand to him.

He felt her power snaking around him. There was no chanting, just raw power. It felt just like a boa constrictor, coiling around him, squeezing his life away.

"Stop that!" was all he could get out. He was terrified.

She pouted at him. "Stop what? Come; take my hand."

For a second, it felt as if the snake were trying to propel him forward as it squeezed.

"No!" he shouted through clenched teeth. Suddenly leaning forward, instead of taking a step closer to her, he fell onto his knees and started to pant. He was struggling to breathe while resisting her magic.

"How are you fighting me? I said, come!" her voice commanded with harsh authority, combined with a sliver of confusion.

Tony felt the magic around him pulsing stronger and pressing him forward, while still on his hands and knees. His body itched to crawl forward, but he balled his hands into fists while trying to stay put. He dropped his gun with the effort. Sweat dripped off him as he ordered his own body not to move.

"How are you doing that?"

There was a crash of broken glass and several inhuman, high-pitched squeals. The power around Tony suddenly disappeared and he collapsed onto the ground. He looked up to see the Demon Culeen watching something inside the warehouse.

"How did they…?" She turned and looked at Tony. Her eyes narrowed. "You told them, you human scum. I am going to rip your heart out while it still beats, and eat it as I watch you die."

She took two high-heeled steps and lunged for him. Tony's cop instincts kicked in and he rolled out of the way, narrowly dodging claws he hadn't noticed before. As he braced himself to turn and prepare for her next move, his elbow hit his gun. Without any thought, he snatched it up and took a shot at her just as she was about to pounce.

He scrambled when her direction changed and her nails scored his left leg. Ignoring the pain, Tony shot again, aiming directly at the now ragged bodice of her dress. The bullet ripped into her chest. Her head collapsed to the ground, with her arm still out, as if to swipe him again, but she stopped moving. A bloody stream inched toward him. Tony clambered backwards out of her reach, but kept his gun poised, aiming straight at her, just in case.

There was a deafening chorus of high-pitched screeches from inside the warehouse. Seconds later, dozens of black, winged beasts burst from a hole in the roof. They were followed by one very large one, about eight feet tall. Tony had never seen anything like it in his life. He felt a streak of fear, but his ensuing shock squelched it quickly. They were flying straight up, and then east, as if retreating. Tony watched the figures become smaller and harder to see on the horizon.

The Demon Culeen still did not move. If she were human, Tony would have thought she was dead. But in her case, he had no way to verify it. Cheryl came running out of the warehouse in her other form. Several of her feathers were missing and there were long, shallow gashes in her right arm.

"Tony, how are you standing?" She was looking at his leg.

He glanced down and saw it was steadily bleeding, and the lack of pain told him he was in shock. She stood next to him and began chanting over the Demon Culeen. Tony was a little unnerved, but became grateful when he didn't feel anything uncomfortable.

Looking over at him, she stopped chanting. "How did you kill a Demon Culeen, Tony? And how is she not changing back to her regular form?"

Tony held up his gun, and answered, "Magic gun."

She shook her head. "That works on regular Culeen. Not Demon Culeen."

"Damn it, stop changing the rules on me!" After speaking those words, Tony realized his body was rapidly draining of adrenaline and would need medical attention soon. "Look, I'm bleeding, and my gunshots will bring the police here any second; so you better all finish whatever the hell you're cleaning up and get out of here."

Tony could see Cheryl watching him with concern. He also saw flashlights bouncing around in the warehouse. There seemed to be about twenty of them. Apparently, no one could find a light switch.

Tony’s mind reeled as he turned to Cheryl again. "I am calling this in right now. You have maybe ten minutes. But you have to leave me something for when backup arrives." Then he looked down at his leg, which was still bleeding.

Thinking he needed to get off it, Tony moved a few more feet away from the body and pulled out his phone.

When Cheryl saw that, she ran back into the warehouse.

Nine-one-one was his first call. After telling the woman who answered his address and badge number, he said he needed an ambulance. She wanted him to stay on the line, but he refused, insisting that he had to call his captain.

Binns was pretty pissed to learn Tony was alone. He screamed at him until he realized Tony was too quiet. When Tony informed him of his injury, the captain demanded the address and hung up. Tony assumed he intended to head up to Everett himself.

Tony became concerned when he started to feel light-headed. He didn't know how long he watched the Nym carrying things out of the warehouse. He was losing all concept of time in his shock and blood loss. He had never been shot or injured on the job, and previously only suffered a few scrapes and bruises.

A man walked up to him with a cloth. "I am going to staunch the bleeding and say a spell to slow it down even further. I would have been out here much sooner if I’d known you were bleeding out."

Tony nodded. His groggy mind recognized the man. Staring at his face, it finally clicked. "You're that guy I saw with his kid at the grocery store. The one who knew Cheryl."

The other man tightened the cloth around Tony's leg, nodding. He replied before he began chanting. "Gavin. My name is Gavin."

Bells rang in Tony's head and his attention snapped to the man in front of him. "Gavin? You're Chris's husband. I have a few questions for you."

Gavin nodded again and paused in his chant. "Yes, I am sure you do. But right now, you are going to pass out."

Then he tapped Tony's forehead and everything went black.

Chapter 15

Tony wasn't in his bedroom this time, so it took him a second to adjust. He was on a beach, somewhere on Lake Washington. The sky was overcast, but not raining, and small waves lapped at the shore in agitation. It appeared a storm was imminent from a slight wind coming off the water.

As Tony looked around, he saw Chris further down the shore on his left. He didn't think she saw him, so he started moving toward her. Her face was blank and Tony could tell she was lost in thought. The wind lifted her hair over her shoulders and Tony managed to see more of her face. Chris looked remorseful and seemed to be reliving a memory. She had her right hand across her chest, while her left was at the base of her neck, covering her necklace. Her thumb absent-mindedly rubbing the chain.

Tony stopped moving when he was about five feet away. After a moment, he watched Chris straighten up, as if coming out of a dream. That was ironic, considering where they were. She realized someone was standing next to her and slowly turned her head. When she realized who it was, her face revealed her surprise.

"Tony, how did you get here?" She turned her body to face him but didn't move her arms.

Tony couldn't help being overwhelmed with different emotions. Before he knew it, he wrapped his arms around Chris so tightly, if she were still alive, she might have complained. After a few seconds, Chris seemed to melt a little and her arms moved to encircle Tony's neck.

In her initial squeeze, her right hand started moving in a circle on the back of his shoulder as she spoke softly into his ear. "Shh… It's okay, Two-Tone, everything is going to be fine, I promise. I'm not going to let anything happen to you."

Tony gripped her tighter, not realizing he had tears falling down his face. "It's not me, but what I will do to you."

That got her full attention. Her hand stopped moving, and she stiffened, pushing back on his hands in an effort to make him let go. But he couldn't, not yet anyway. This was his friend. She was already tortured. How could he have ever made it worse?

She stopped moving, going very still in his arms. "What exactly do you mean, Tony?"

He heard the words of the older Chris echoing in his head. No, he couldn't tell her. Reluctantly, he released her and took a step back. Chris was looking at him warily.

"You should stop visiting me," he replied.

Chris folded her arms and moved one hip forward, getting defensive. "You're the one visiting me at the moment, Tony. Really, how did you get here? You shouldn't have been able to get here."

Tony knew he had to tread lightly. A defensive Chris made stupid decisions just to defy people.

"It was recently explained to me that by hanging around me, you're making yourself a ghost, instead of going where you're supposed to go. Your help isn't worth screwing yourself over like that."

Tony was surprised when Chris gave a defiant and bitter laugh.

"And who told you that?"

Tony didn't hesitate, seeing a slight shift in her eyes. "A Nym named Porthos."

Chris smiled. "I always wanted to meet her. I've heard she's even more superstitious than I am." She shook her head, and Tony could tell she was about to do what she always did when asked an uncomfortable question: evade. "Tony, that doesn't tell me how you got here. Someone had to show you how."

Tony wasn't about to tell her, or give up on his own point. He sighed, knowing he was in for an argument.

"You need to leave. And go wherever dead people are supposed to go. I don't want to see you until then. If I can keep you here in a dream, then I sure as hell can keep you out too." Tony watched the fire sparking in her eyes. "No, that is not a challenge, so don't take it that way, damn it! You need to get away as fast as possible. You won't be able to handle being around me without trying to help. I know you, and it will drive you crazy." Tony watched as her expression softened.

"I can't just leave, Tony. I... there are just some loose ends I haven't tied up yet, but don't worry. What she told you is an old wives' tale. Why are you saying this, Tony? You were not superstitious before, yet you're so very adamant about this." She was looking at him curiously now.

Tony took a deep breath. He hated discussions where Chris really wanted to know something. She could be irritatingly stubborn. "I can't tell you, Chris."

That only piqued her interest, just like he figured it would.

"The person who informed me pleaded with me not to tell you."

Chris watched him for a moment. "Pleaded? Do I know the person?"

Tony just nodded. She watched him for what seemed like a full minute before looking away.

"Fine." She started to turn away from him, but stopped herself and narrowed her eyes at Tony's. "You're lucky you caught me off guard, or I would so be down your throat right now."

Tony tried, but failed to conceal his smile. "I know."

Chris rolled her eyes at him. "So what do you want, Tony, that would make you put such an effort into tracking me down?"

He felt curiosity tugging at him. "Yeah, where are we anyway?"

Chris's face fell, and she turned to look out at the water. "Someone else's dream."

Her tone made Tony's heart crack. If this were the last time he would see her, he didn't want to see that sad look in her eyes. "Whose dream?"

Chris didn't look at Tony. Her eyes seemed a little bit faraway, but her expression stayed the same. "Gavin, my husband, proposed to me here. This is a beach right outside Kirkland. We were sitting almost in this very spot with my back leaning up against his chest. It was dusk and we were just sitting in comfortable silence when a ring appeared right in front of me. He didn't say anything, but just showed me the ring. He was holding his breath. I know because his chest stopped moving. I reached out to take the ring from him."

She laughed then, "He slapped my hand and told me that only he would put it on or it was staying right where it was." Chris's laugh turned sad, then faded when she looked back at Tony.

"This place is all he dreams about now. I watch him. I know I can't go to him. But I can't stop myself from watching him, just to be with him. Even if he never knows I'm there."

She dropped her gaze then, and Tony's heart ached for her. All he wanted to do was make things better for her. The more he tried, however, the more wrong it seemed.

"Chris... I…"

She waved her hand dismissively, then looked up at him, her face filled with determination.

"Stop it, Tony, I made my choices and I will live with them. But we are definitely changing the subject. What can I do for you?"

Tony could hear Chris reining her emotions in more the longer she spoke. As much as he wanted to comfort her, he knew she wouldn't allow it.

"I need your help with something."

Chris nodded and flopped down to sit in the sand, folding her legs to one side to stop the lingerie she was wearing from riding up. "Good, it's about time that I was useful."

Tony shook his head and sat down beside her. Then, he noticed he was wearing the same flannel pants and Mariners tank top he wore to bed. Neither of them were dressed in anything beach-appropriate.

"Okay, so I have to backtrack first."

When Chris just nodded, Tony told her about the case. He began when Cheryl woke him up; and ended will Gavin tapping his forehead. Chris sat there watching him, listening, and making little sounds here and there, but never interrupting him. When he was finished, she started drawing with her finger in the sand next to her hip.

"I have so many questions but I know that is not what you need from me right now so I will set them aside. We can discuss them another time. There is more at play hear than I realized. I need to poke around a bit before our next meeting. But if you happen to see my husband again please tell him I do not like him risking his life by helping take out Culeen nests."

Chris sighed and took a deep breath, as if clearing her mind. "I wish I could see the notepad so I could tell you what was in it," she replied, sounding frustrated.

Tony perked up at her statement. "I remember some of it. I kept staring at the first couple pages in the hope that it might click, and I would suddenly get it."

Chris gave a small chuckle and moved further away from him. "All right, show me."

Tony concentrated hard to remember the swirls and triangles that comprised the first section of the front page. It took him longer than he would have liked, but he was able to draw most of it.

While he was drawing, Chris scooted around so she could kneel next to him. As he finished, Tony noticed her eyes didn't move from the top line, and her eyebrows were crinkled together.

She pointed to the third symbol. "Could it have looked like this?" She rubbed away the top of the middle line and drew a half circle facing down.

Tony shook his head and redrew the original symbol. "No, it was definitely this."

She furrowed her brows deeper. "But that doesn't make sense. It's like saying, 'the cat in the' and that's it. There is no end to the sentence."

Tony started to doubt his memory. *Could it have been the other symbol?*

Chris let out an exclamation. "Oh, of course." Then she drew an extra hump on the wavy line of the fourth symbol and her brows smoothed out. "Could that have been it?" She asked, looking at Tony expectantly.

He had no idea. "Yeah, maybe. Does that one little squiggle make that much difference?"

Chris gave Tony a look he hadn't seen since high school. It said, Are you an idiot? While also wondering if it were a joke.

"Don't give me that look. It's a valid question."

She rolled her eyes. "Yeah, Two-Tone, the squiggle is important."

Then she returned her attention back to the symbols. She was mouthing as she read, and every once in a while, making sounds Tony never heard before. About halfway through, her eyes went wide and her mouth moved faster, as her reading grew more excited.

When she finished, she grinned at Tony. "I know this one."

Tony was sure his confusion must have shown on his face. "But I only remembered the top half of the page. How could you know the entire thing from that?" Tony looked down at the foreign writing. There were maybe two dozen symbols there, if that.

Chris was still smiling when he looked back at her. "It's a myth. My grandfather taught it to me, though why it was written in Elderspeak, I don't know. Or what it has to do with you. It's a story you tell young kids to teach them life lessons without actually telling them outright. It's the story of twelve men that saved the earth from destroying itself. But this is a strange version. See these letters here?" She pointed to a few symbols in the third row. "This is a... spell, for lack of a better word. Instead of saying the first man put down the dead that evil brought to life, it actually gives the spell that was used to raise the dead in the first place."

Tony's blood ran cold.

She pointed to the next grouping of symbols. "And here, it actually gives the spell that the man used to put down the dead. I've never seen this version before, but then, I've never seen it told in Elderspeak before either."

She was talking with a scholar's fascination and totally oblivious to Tony's reaction. She kept saying how rare it was to see stories written in Elderspeak, but Tony wasn't paying attention. He was too busy staring at the third line, where the key to Chris's damnation was carved in the sand.

Tony's ears pounded with the sound of his own blood running through his veins. His breathing was so fast, he was practically hyperventilating. His body began to shake and he must have knocked into Chris because she peered at him with a worried expression.

"Tony? Tony, what is it? You need to calm down or you'll panic yourself awake. Tony? TONY!"

Chapter 16

He woke drenched in sweat in a dark hospital room. It took Tony several minutes to calm himself down. He needed to destroy that notebook. Searching the room, Tony couldn't find his coat. The panic started to rise but he quenched it. He would find it then destroy the notebook. There was not anything he could do at the moment. The pain in his leg told him he might not be able to walk on it right now anyway. Tony could feel drugs pulling him back to sleep. He went willingly, knowing the sooner he healed the sooner he could destroy that spell.

It wasn't until Tony's second night at the hospital that the doctors let Viggo visit or let Bentley come in and brief him on what happened.

Viggo had not been able to stay long but she informed him they were able to clear Rick of any involvement and that he and Amanda were at home with their daughter, but there would still be an IA investigation. Tony had been overwhelmed by his relief. At least they were okay, knowing that made IA unimportant.

Bentley didn't chastise him for not doing as he promised, but did give him several disapproving looks throughout her visit. She talked about finding Spencer Price and how a blood test had shown a trace amount of something in his system that the lab could not identify. They could tell it was the same compound that was in the other victims. But other than that he was fine. That the techs had called to tell Tony the powder sample he dropped off had gone missing before it could be analyzed.

Bentley told him that when the ambulance arrived he was passed out, presumably from shock and blood loss. He was lying only a few feet from their murder suspect. She had clearly attacked him so there were no immediate questions about her death, but Tony knew there would be an investigation. There was no way around it. The police found about a dozen people heavily drugged in the warehouse, presumably from the same drug the murderer was giving her victims. One of them was Derek Lowman. In a small office off the back room, they found six people drugged and tied up. Among them were Rick and his wife.

By the time Bentley got there, the techs were removing several large bottles filled with an unidentified substance for analysis. She said the warehouse appeared pretty barren. There were pillows and blankets on the floor, and the whole place smelled like unwashed people. She told Tony she was surprised at how stark the place was. She told him the feds were assuming they must have stayed someplace else as well.

Tony knew the truth though. All the Culeen creature comforts had been cleared out, and all that was left were the people they recruited, or whose minds they controlled. Bentley left the hospital after an hour.

Tony had no Nym visitors that could explain what actually happened, or fill in the gaps for him. But he didn't expect them either. It was different now anyway. He knew they existed and where to find them. He could get his own answers in his own time; and he wasn't going to be nice about it. He would not let them wiggle their way out of giving him information either. But for now, he would heal. Then he would concentrate on Chris's case. He planned to find his friend the justice she deserved.

About The Author

Gretchen happily lives in Seattle, Washington where she spends her free time creating new characters and situations to put them in. She also enjoys cheering on her local sports teams, even though sometimes, it seems they are allergic to winning, (except at the Super Bowl!).

She graduated from Central Washington University with a BA in History, and a BA in Philosophy. She loves living in Washington since it provides a wide range of activities, from Shakespeare-in-the-Park to rodeos. At the end of her adventures, she usually unwinds by curling up on the couch, and knitting while catching up on TV shows via Netflix.

If you enjoyed this book, please feel free to leave a review on Amazon, Barnes & Noble, or Good Reads. Reviews are always much appreciated.

You can find Gretchen at:

http://www.gretchensb.com/
https://twitter.com/GretchenSB
https://www.goodreads.com/author/show/7398184.Gretchen_S_B_
https://www.facebook.com/pages/Gretchen-S-B/540293959350712